# A SMALL AND REMARKABLE LIFE
by
Nick DiChario

Introduction by
Mike Resnick

Robert J.
SAWYER
B O O K S

Robert J. Sawyer Books are published by Red Deer Press, A Fitzhenry & Whiteside Company, 1512, 1800–4 Street S.W., Calgary Alberta Canada T2S 2S5.
www. robertjsawyerbooks.com • www.reddeerpress.com

Printed in Canada

**Library and Archives Canada Cataloguing in Publication**
DiChario, Nick
    A small and remarkable life / Nick DiChario.
ISBN 0-88995-336-8 (bound)
ISBN 0-88995-342-2 (pbk.)
    I. Title.
PS3604.I25S63 2006    813'.6    C2006-900358-0

**U.S. Publisher Cataloging-in-Publication Data (Library of Congress Standards)**
DiChario, Nick
  A small and remarkable life / Nick DiChario.
[256] p. : col. ill. ; cm.
Summary: The story of Tink Puddah, an extraterrestrial orphaned on Earth when his
    parents die, is mistaken for a runaway slave. The novel deals with the lives he touches
    and the preacher who tries to save the soul that Tink may or may not possess.
ISBN 0-88995-336-8
ISBN 0-88995-342-2  (pbk.)
1. Science fiction.  I. Title.
813.6 dc22    PS3604.I25S63 2006

Credits:                Edited for the Press by Robert J. Sawyer
                         Cover design by Karen Thomas Petherick
                         Text design by Erin Woodward
                         Cover image courtesy: LifeStockPhotos.com
                         Printed and bound in Canada by Friesens for Red Deer Press

Acknowledgments:    Financial support provided by the Canada Council, the Government of Canada through the Book Publishing Industry Development Program (BPIDP), and the Alberta Foundation for the Arts, a beneficiary of the Lottery Fund of the Government of Alberta.

Canada Council    Conseil des Arts
for the Arts       du Canada

For Nicholas and Josephine DiChario,
the best parents in the known universe,
TO INFINITY AND BEYOND!
With chocolate on top.
No kidding.

# ACKNOWLEDGMENTS

A very special thank you to Mike Resnick, for all of his guidance, support, and career counseling so freely and generously given over the years. The talented writers and teachers who have inspired me so much, including (but by no means limited to) Anne Coon, Nancy Kress, Karen Joy Fowler, Jim Kelly, John Kessel, Octavia Butler, Russell Banks, and Nicholson Baker. The assistance of Marcos Donnelly, Kathryn Larrabee, and Patricia Ryan for helping me improve this book. Miriam Grace Monfredo, for refusing to let me quit during those early years. My writing pals who have kept me engaged in the creative process for so long, including Len Messineo, Norm Davis, and Tim Wright. My long-time pal, Mr. Jimmy (You Can't Always Get What You Want) Goff. The constant good cheer of my dedicated business partner, Dan Plumeau. And finally, Robert J. Sawyer, for giving this book a chance.

# A LARGE AND REMARKABLE TALENT

## Introduction by Mike Resnick

I've been waiting a long time for this book.

Hell, *everyone* has been waiting a long time for this book.

The first time I ever encountered the name of Nicholas A. DiChario was when an unsolicited story arrived in my mailbox for an invitation-only anthology I was editing. I probably should have sent it back without looking at it—and if I had, I might well have robbed the science-fiction field of one of the most remarkable talents ever to come down the pike. Instead I started reading it (just to see how bad a story I hadn't solicited could be, you understand), and by Page 3 I knew that nothing in the world could keep "The Winterberry" off the Hugo ballot. Yes, it was by an unknown, and yes, anthologies had about a quarter the circulation of the major magazines, and yes, there was no traditional science fiction element in it—and there was still no way it could fail to make the ballot.

I wish I could pick horses the way I pick stories. "The Winterberry" was a Hugo nominee, and a World Fantasy Award nominee, and Nick himself was nominated for the Campbell, which is science fiction's Rookie of the Year Award. And we were off and running. From that day forward, it was almost unthinkable for me to edit an anthology that didn't have a DiChario story in it. And since I didn't edit enough anthologies to get my fill of DiChario stories, I started collaborating with him. When we had sold enough collaborations we gathered them and sold them as a book entitled *Magic Feathers: The Mike and Nick Show.*

Not that Nick needed my collaborative or editorial efforts to shine. He made the Hugo ballot again a few years later, and in between produced one of the three or four best novellas of the decade, a strange and wonderful piece called "Unto the Valley of Day-Glo."

In fact, just about *all* of Nick's stories are strange and wonderful. We collaborated on a story for an anthology about kings—and while everyone else was writing about British and French kings, Nick came up with King Kong. It wasn't a funny story, either; that would have been too easy. Instead, it was a sad and sensitive one. For an erotic anthology assignment during the time that *The Joy of Sex* was at the top of the bestseller list, Nick came up with "The Joy of Hats."

We—the reading public, of which I am a small part, and the almost-as-large DiChario fan base, of which I am a small but always-vocal part—kept waiting for Nick to write that first novel and blow us all away. And we waited. And we waited. And we waited.

And while we were waiting, Nick taught some writing courses, and bought a bookstore, and did some other things, none of which we cared much about except that if it made him happy enough or secure enough to finally give us that novel, we were all in favor of it, whatever *it* was.

And then one day came the phone call I'd been waiting for for about a decade. It was Nick. He'd sold his first novel, and would I possibly consider taking a look at *A Small and Remarkable Life*? I explained that if he swore on a stack of Bibles, Torahs and Korans that he would e-mail it to me within twenty-four hours I probably wouldn't come to upstate New York and rip his computer out of his office and take it home with me. A master at the art of self-preservation, he e-mailed it to me that night.

I had no idea what to expect, but I knew what not to expect: there would be no generic space battles, nothing that one could see in the mindless "sci-fi" films that permeate the landscape, nothing that you could look at and say, "Heinlein (or Asimov, or Bradbury) did it better," or even "Heinlein (or whoever) did it earlier."

I'm not going to tell you much about the book you hold in your hands, because you *are* holding it in your hands, and you've either bought it or are preparing to buy it, and Nick will tell you the story of Tink Puddah a lot better than I ever could.

But I *will* note that, as always, it's a story told in a way only Nick could tell it. Where else does a story begin with the rather lengthy funeral of the protagonist? And where else do you feel you know the protagonist better before you're even introduced to him than you know most heroes halfway through a book?

I don't think there's ever been a true villain in a DiChario story. But the one who fills the structural role of a villain here, which is to say, the man who finds himself in opposition to the hero, is guilty of only one "sin": he wants to save the hero's immortal soul. A hero who begins the story dead, and a villain who wants to keep the hero from going to hell. That's the kind of spin my pal Nick puts on the ball.

There are a lot more spins in the pages up ahead, but as always with the best writers in any field, be they the Bradburys and Sturgeons of science fiction, the Chandlers of the mystery story, or the Eric Amblers of the international intrigue novel, the characters are always the most important and memorable things you're going to encounter.

By now you've figured out that I'm glad and proud to know Nick DiChario. After reading this novel, I can truthfully say that I would have been just as glad and just as proud to have known Tink Puddah. There are not a lot of characters I can say that about—but if enough of you encourage Nick to write another novel, I'm sure there will be a few more such characters before long.

# THE BOOK OF
## INJURY

## * * Y E A R 1 8 4 5 * *

Nif Puddah felt dizzy from the pain of his mate's anger. So strong, it was, he could not shut her out of his new human mind.

But Nif knew, for the first time, the warm embrace of the sun, this solar system's perpetual heaving heart, its bulky furnace of hydrogen and helium flaring feverishly to feed the desperate hunger of this planet's insatiable appetite.

And Nif saw, for the first time, the surrounding hills and valleys of the timberland rich with foliage, rising and falling in jagged waves, the pine trees with their stout trunks driven into the dirt and their slim green needles, the oaks and elms and hickories, the endless canopy of blue sky, the spiral flow of white and gray condensed water vapor swirling in atmospheric cells over this alien planet, this vast sprawling rock called Earth.

What a strange and lopsided picture it all painted. So much contrast, so little symmetry. Size, shape, light, color, smell, distance, even life and death molded into disjointed patterns of coexistence—nothing at all like Wetspace.

No, nothing at all like home.

"Assimilation," Nif said. He'd used his voice. Voice, not mind! "We're safe, Ru, we're adapting."

"Safe?" said Nif Puddah's mate. "We are alone! We are . . . we are . . . nothing! Nothing nothing nothing!"

Nif had expected Ru to struggle with the emptiness of her new consciousness, but if he could calm her, help her through the transformation, help her adjust, she would be fine. She *must* be fine. "No, not nothing," Nif said. *Something.* "We are adapting, Ru, look!"

Their metamorphoses had begun—they had each developed two miniature spherical structures of jelly-like eyes with which to see their new world. Bodies shrinking, rounding, bending. Bones to support the exo-matter. Small, bipedal, humanoid creatures they would become. Atoms, molecules, joints, nails, skin, glands, hormones, blood.

Adapt. Assimilate. Survive.

Nif Puddah felt the wind against his newly formed face. Smell! What a wonderful, overpowering sensation, this ability to smell, to bring microscopic particles of physical surroundings into contact with the nerves of one's own nose for the purpose of instantaneous chemical analysis. There were genes in his new body working to produce nothing but these receptors of aroma. Fascinating. Miraculous.

Walking! The walking would be difficult at first, as would other coordination of body and mind, far less comfortable than the curling, rolling, and elongating movements of their liquid otherselves. But to have arms and hands and fingers! To have a face unlike any other! To breathe air—*air* of all things!—such a strange combination of oxygen and carbon dioxide. Atmosphere. Helium, hydrogen, ions, electrons, ozone—

Nothing at all like Wetspace. No. Nothing at all like home.

Ru must find the joy in it. This place was so visceral, so immediate. She *must* find the joy.

"How could you do this to us?" Ru demanded. "Your own son, twelve years in the womb!"

Womb. That was not a Wetspace word. Years. What did that mean? A measurement of time, human time. Ru's mind was adapting without her knowing it. Their son was almost an adult. Soon he would be born.

He would be born a human being, the first Wetspace born human! The first of many, perhaps. A pioneer. Nif's family a family of pioneers.

Pride, hope, longing.

Ru had used the spoken language of mankind, her mouth and tongue functioning, coordinating with her thoughts, *her* thoughts. Individualism. Had she even realized it? Ears, by God, with which to hear these sounds of a world outside of one's own mind. God? Concept, concept, a portion of this people's collective religious subconscious. Nif had picked up the scent of it in his mind.

Assimilate.

Nif felt the hard land beneath his newly formed feet, the depth and density of the earth, the strata—igneous, sedimentary, metamorphic rock, iron oxide, silica, lime, clay, gems, minerals, crystals, the bones of its inhabitants and its long forgotten beasts.

Fungus, mildew, blight, bacteria, pollen.

Adapt.

Assimilate.

Esophagus, pancreas, lungs, kidneys, taste buds, muscle, heart! Heartbeat! Axons leading to spinal cord to thalamus to sensory cortex . . .

Nerve endings.

Nif touched the ground, touched himself, thighs, stomach, chest.

Adapt.

Assimilate.

Ru charged at him in a rage, a newborn animal rage. Already she'd learned how to use her stick-like legs to carry the awkward weight of her human form, how to use her fists as weapons. She beat on Nif's shoulders, on his back, his head. Nif was having trouble with the gravity. "How do you push against it?" he asked Ru.

"You! You! You have done this to us!" she cried.

Nif stood. Ru beat him back down.

Violence: the use of physical force to injure or abuse. Anger, outrage, vehemence. Nif fell against a tree. Trees, plants, flowers, sunlight, photosynthesis. Wind, humidity, solar radiation. Mammals, insects, birds, fish. Water, oceans, fluorine, magnesium, sulfate, sodium, chlorine . . .

"Stop, Ru, please."

"Take us back! Take us back home, Nif, *now!*" She kicked him in the ribs. "Wetspace! Wetspace! Take us home!"

But it was already too late. She must know this. She must.

"Ru, please, it is . . . too . . . late . . ."

Standing at his pulpit, Jacob Piersol looked out at the churchgoers he'd attracted for this day's service. A funeral generally drew a respectable crowd, but he hadn't seen a gathering this strong since Christmas Day, 1852, the year four families of Italian immigrants had passed through just in time for his Christmas homily, on their way to Palmyra, New York.

He cleared his throat and bowed his head in silent thanks. Jacob was no fool. He realized much of Skanoh Valley had come just to see what he would say about the dead man. The foreigner Tink Puddah was no Christian, after all. Oh, he'd proven himself a decent enough member of the community over the years, minded his own business, stayed out of local politics, shied away from village gatherings and festivals and such. He'd pretty much kept to himself up in his small cabin in the hills on the outskirts of Skanoh Valley.

Jacob had always believed Tink Puddah nothing more than a heathenish savage and feared for his misguided soul. And, as any preacher would have done, he harbored a secret resentment for someone who could turn so easily from the Word of the Savior, Lord Jesus Christ, to a belief in . . . well . . . nothing.

Looking out at his congregation, Jacob wondered just how much of that resentment he'd been able to hide over the years, and how much of it had slipped out of the soil and into the crop.

Still, it didn't matter much now. The foreigner was dead—dead and buried—and any preacher worth his salt would take advantage of a full church, regardless of the ill-occasion. Here was an opportunity to show his congregation what a gracious man of God he could be, to teach them a thing or two, a lesson they'd not soon forget: Jacob Piersol was a good, generous man, just like his father, the venerable Nathan Piersol. Jacob had been waiting a long time for them to see that, a damn long time, pardon the expression, and he wasn't about to let it slip away.

And it was spring, by God, *spring,* his favorite time of year, a time of rebirth, a time of hope and new beginnings. Many of these people would rediscover God and prayer and the simple pleasures of hard work—tilling the soil, planting seeds, nurturing their crops—God's good clean labor, the work of the land. This was a time of renewal, and he looked forward to it every year with a thinly veiled eagerness of the soul.

Jacob cleared his throat. "I am glad to see so many people have ventured forth to this special prayer service in honor of our dearly departed friend, Tink Puddah," Jacob said. "It is customary for me on occasions such as this to read Scripture from The New Testament, to offer a guiding light to those who are about to travel the road to the great mystery beyond. But today, my dear friends, in honor of our foreign brother, I am going to diverge from our usual and customary practice."

The multitude looked appropriately surprised. Jacob let them whisper among themselves for a bit before moving on. A weakness, to be sure, his penchant for drama, but he hoped a relatively harmless one in the eyes of God.

Jacob breathed deeply, paying close attention to his measured breath. How often one breathes, he thought, and pays it no heed. Today Jacob could smell the flowering hyacinths. The morning sun shone through the church's mottled glass windows. He remembered the day the glass had arrived at his father's small church, the Vision of Christ Church, back in 1824 or '25. It was enough to stop farm work for near a full day. The parish members had contributed what few pennies they could spare and had ordered the glass special from a new factory in nearby Palmyra. Jacob had been just a boy then.

When his father, Nathan Piersol, had come to this small town years ago, he'd fallen in love with the beautiful valley, the teeming forest, and a girl at the livery with the enchanting name of Wisteria. He'd known immediately that he wanted to stay here forever. The town had no place of worship back then, so he'd organized the building of one. The day the Vision of Christ Church was completed, he opened up his Holy Bible, started preaching, and didn't stop until the day he died. Nathan Piersol was a man who had commanded love and respect, got them both, and gave them both with equal fervor.

Technically, Jacob, like his father, was not an empowered minister or priest of any order. But his congregation wasn't interested in anyone else's institutions or pushy doctrines. They'd built their own church and paid their preacher out of their own pockets. They believed in God. They'd had Nathan Piersol marry and bury them for forty years, and his son do the same when his father wasn't around anymore to do it. They kept God in their hearts and in their minds and on their lips in prayer. That was good enough for them.

Jacob brushed off the memories of his father. This was Jacob's day. Nathan Piersol had enjoyed enough of his own.

Jacob said, "It is no secret to anyone here today that Tink Puddah was a non-believer. It may surprise you to know that such a non-believer does not threaten or insult a preacher in God's service. No, my friends, quite the contrary. It is the non-believers who inspire us, who remind us why we are here: to preach the Word of the Lord. To spread *His* Word. To fight *His* battles."

He paused, taking a moment to feel the Bible in his hands, really feel it, the soft yet firm leather, the thickness of its pages and the weight of its message. His father had carried this same Bible his entire life, or at least for as long as Jacob could remember. It was a beautiful, leather-bound King James edition. His shield, his avenger, Nathan Piersol had called it, clinging to it even at the moment of his painful and sweaty death. Jacob remembered prying his father's rigid fingers from around the spine of the book to wrench it out of his cold hands, as if the old man had been trying to tell Jacob that he was not good enough to carry the message of the Lord Savior, Jesus Christ. Jacob had always resented that: his father's clinging disapproval and stubborn pride, even in death.

"Men like Tink Puddah justify a preacher's existence," Jacob continued. "They validate our missions here on Earth, our service to the Creator. Although I was unable to reach Tink Puddah with God's message, there was a certain beauty and fulfillment in my effort that I might not have experienced had Tink's conversion been a simple matter of introducing him to the Holy Bible."

Jacob pressed the book to his chest and looked out over the crowded room. "I would like to take this opportunity today to thank our foreign brother, in the name of the Lord, for reminding me of my station in life, for keeping me humble, for challenging my commitment to God and his teachings. In honor of the man he was, I will close the Holy Bible from which he succored naught during his all-too-brief lifetime, and I will offer the pulpit to anyone who would like to speak kindly of our friend, Tink Puddah, here under the roof of God."

With that, Jacob Piersol tugged on the edges of his short black frock, stepped down from the pulpit, and sat stiffly in his chair beside the podium. He lowered his head in prayer as his congregation murmured and fidgeted in their seats. He allowed himself a smile, an inner smile, a bit of pride, a bit of vanity, but he was only human after all. He looked forward to earning a great deal of respect this day, something he'd hungered for since his father's death so many years ago.

After a brief silence, old Jed Watkins limped up the center aisle, leaning heavily on his cane. He was wearing a floppy hat and a ragged topcoat. His tobacco-stained beard splayed out over his face and down the front of his chest like a baby's bib. "I'd like to say sump'n, preacher."

Jacob nodded. He couldn't imagine what Jed Watkins could have to say about anything, let alone the foreigner, Tink Puddah. Ever since his logging accident near a dozen years gone, Jed never bothered with church, never came to any of the Skanoh Valley meetings, kept no friends. The man sulked in his small cabin on Pine Hill, fashioning his snake canes. Come to think of it, the preacher frowned upon Jed's canes. For some reason, perhaps because of how snake-like the canes looked, eerie and devilish, Jed's handiwork struck him as blasphemous.

Jed stepped up to the pulpit, looked out over the congregation, and scratched at his scraggly beard. "So this is what it looks like from up here!"

Everyone laughed, even Jacob.

Jed removed his floppy hat and allowed his smile to sag slowly into a frown. "Shoot, I ain't no polic-a-tician, and God knows I ain't no preacher, so I'll just say what I got to say and be done with it. Tink Puddah was as good a man as I ever come across in all my days. Everybody knows the hard times I falled upon when I had me this here loggin' accident." He stuck his leg out so people could see it around the pulpit. It was easy enough to spot the unnatural bend just below Jed's right knee. "I was just a settin' around my cabin feeling sorry for m'self for nigh-on two years, fit for the coffin, you all know it's true. Then one day Tink comes a callin', says he wants to show me sump'n special. He's got this here cane in his hands."

Jed held up the cane for all to see. It was a handcrafted snake cane, a black snake curling around a sturdy post, with a snake's head for a handle. Even the preacher had to admit it was a finely crafted piece of work. He wasn't surprised that it had once belonged to the heathen foreigner, Tink Puddah.

"'Try it out,' Tink tells me. Bein' in my self-pitying way I didn't want to have nothing to do with it, but he kept on me about it. 'Here, just lean on it, give it a try.' So I tried it, just to get rid of the little scrap rat. Right off, there was sump'n about the feel of the cane in my hands, the way it filled my grip, the way it just seemed to lift me up like I done been reconciled with a long lost brother. It kind of woke me up out of a long, dark sleep. To this day I remember taking that cane from Tink's skinny little fingers, and I remember smiling for the first time since my loggin' accident."

Jacob Piersol noticed some nods and whispers pass among his parishioners. He leaned forward with interest. He'd never heard this tale.

"Anyway, soon as I touched this cane it made me want to walk. I had to know where he got it, so I asked him outright. He told me he made it himself. Imagine that! So I asked him, can you teach me to do it? 'Sure can,' he says. And he spends the next couple of weeks at my place, day and night, showin' me how to pick just the right kind of twisted sourwood to make good snake canes; showin' me how to use the chisel, gouge, maul, and drawknife to get the proper cuts in the wood; showin' me how to carve out the curl, score the shaft and rough it out, taper the tail, chisel the scrib of the snake scales, burn the wood black and buff it nice and smooth. Showed me all of it, yes sir, till I had the knack of it and could do it m'self.

"Well, the rest of the story you all pretty much know. Folks up in Saginaw and Palmyra and Buffalo started paying me top dollar for my canes. Folks want them now far away as Pennsylvania and Ohio. Weren't for that foreigner, I most likely would a died a broken man. I make a good cane, mind ya, but to this day I still carry the cane Tink carved. Never been able to match his work. Not even close."

Jed raised the cane up over the podium. "Tink Puddah gave me more than a cane that day. He gave me back my life. So I came here to this service for no other reason than to say goodbye, and to thank him one last time, and to thrash the daylights outta any fool got a bad word to say 'bout him." He glanced over at Jacob then, gave a snort as if to say that includes you, and with that, Jed Watkins returned to his pew.

A few people said, "Amen." Some folks nodded and whispered.

Something bothered the preacher about Jed's story. Why was it he didn't know that the foreigner had taught Jed his snake cane trade, when it seemed most everybody else in Skanoh Valley did? He shook the thought away. No matter. Why should he have known? Jed had turned away from God and the church a long time ago, and Tink was never a churchgoer.

"Thank you, Brother Jed," said Jacob, standing. "It's good to see you in God's house again. Remember, the Lord never turns away from any member of His flock. You are always welcome here."

"Not likely I'll be back!" Jed shouted from his pew.

The congregation laughed, but not too loudly.

Jacob said, "Would anyone else like to speak?"

Young Miss Anna Goodlowe stood up then, made her way out of her pew, and walked up the center aisle. Jacob had no idea what the good Christian girl Miss Anna would have to say about a heathen foreigner the likes of Tink Puddah, unless she wanted to pray for his lost and miserable soul. That would be just like her, though, wouldn't it?

Jacob was happy to see her standing tall and proud and upright at the pulpit. She was a beautiful, healthy young woman. Surely God had smiled upon her. Just to see Anna Goodlowe walk through the church doors every Sunday morning was a blessing. Today she was wearing her best Sunday outfit, a pretty blue frock with a lace shawl and a straw spoon bonnet. She was growing more and more into the beautiful woman her mother had been. Jacob would have to remember to tell her so.

"Good morning, everyone," Miss Anna said.

"Good morning, Miss Anna," they answered.

She smiled and said, "Thank you, Preacher Piersol, for letting me speak today."

He nodded. "Of course, child."

"It's no secret to anybody here that my daddy, Papa Bear Goodlowe, has always had a terrible struggle with the bottle."

That was certainly true. Jacob had tried to counsel him time and again, but he could never get the man to listen. Papa Bear's wife had died on the very day she gave birth to Anna, and he'd harbored both a grudge against God and a romance with the moonshine ever since.

"And I suppose you all know the joy I've shared with my papa lately, him swearing off the bottle for good."

Jacob sat up straight in his chair. Papa Bear had sworn off whiskey? When could this have happened? And why hadn't he known about it? Miss Anna came to church every Sunday. She'd never mentioned it. He'd asked her directly, too, on several occasions. "How's Papa Bear, Miss Anna?" he'd asked. And she'd responded, "Faring well, Preacher Piersol," and nothing more.

"Thanks to Tink Puddah, my papa is a changed man. It all started when Papa Bear was having another one of his rages. He'd sneaked some of my sewing money and bought himself three bottles of mash and when I came home late from the mercantile he'd already drunk through two of them bottles and was heading for the third. He lost his temper with me, kicked over our table and broke one of our chairs and howled like the devil himself. Then he ran out into the woods with his axe, thrashin' at the tree branches, so violent I was scared to chase after him. Finally he collapsed in the woods.

"Lucky for me Tink Puddah happened by then, although I've come to think of it more as providence than chance. Papa had passed out cold, and Mr. Puddah helped me drag him back home. I was crying so hard I couldn't barely breathe. But Tink calmed me down, and when I saw that my papa was all right I couldn't thank Mr. Puddah enough for what he'd done. He helped me change Papa Bear's clothes and clean him up and get him into bed.

"Well, being as upset as I was, I just started talking and crying like a fool. I told Mr. Puddah how much trouble I been havin' with Papa Bear for so many years, how the bottle was killing him and me too because I couldn't take much more of it, of watching my papa hurt himself so bad, and I felt kind of silly telling Mr. Puddah all our personal problems, but he didn't make me feel bad about it at all. He just listened real quiet and patient. Then he told me to lie down and get some sleep, and he would sit by Papa Bear's bed and make sure he was resting warm and comfortable. That's the Tink Puddah we all knew and loved, very generous, always thinking of others."

The Tink Puddah they all knew and loved? Jacob Piersol clenched his fists. Tink Puddah was a heathen, for God's sake. Didn't these people realize that? The worst kind of heathen, Jacob was beginning to see. The foreigner had not only denied the existence of God, but he was a manipulator of innocent souls.

Miss Anna went on: "I was just going to rest for a few minutes, but as it happened I fell fast asleep. It's hard to explain, but I felt real safe with Mr. Puddah there, like everything was going to be all right. When I finally woke up, the morning sun was shining. I glanced over at Mr. Puddah and Papa Bear, and to this day I still can't believe what I saw. There was Tink, sitting in the chair next to my papa just where he was when I fell asleep, but now he was reading to him out of a book. And there was Papa Bear listening, sitting up in bed, sipping on some tea that Mr. Puddah had made for him. I mean, Papa was really listening with all his attention.

"So my Papa says, 'Anna, my child, come and sit with us, you must hear this wonderful story Tink is reading from his book.' I thought maybe I was in a dream, but if that was so, it was the best dream I ever had, so I walked over to Papa Bear and sat on the edge of his bed.

"Mr. Puddah said, 'I'm reading your father a story called *The Old Curiosity Shop*, by Charles Dickens.' Then he smiled and went back to reading the book. At least I think he smiled. As you all know it was sometimes hard to tell, what with the poor man's mouth being so bad-formed and all. But I sat there and watched my papa for a spell. He was really involved in this story by Mr. Dickens. Papa was having the time of his life, sometimes laughing—big, huge belly-laughs the likes I never heard from him in all my days—other times frowning, shaking his head, looking like he might even want to cry.

"Naturally I had chores to tend to so I left the two of them to their story. Come time to prepare supper, I asked Mr. Puddah to our table. He'd earned that and plenty more as far as I was concerned, just by giving my papa a day of peace. But Mr. Puddah said he had to get back to his place and tend to some chores of his own. Well, Papa Bear just about exploded. He said, 'You must stay and continue the story, Mr. Puddah! I never knew people could write stories like this. I thought people only learnt to read and write so they could study the Bible.'"

This drew hearty laughter from the congregation. Miss Anna turned to the preacher, blushed, and said, shyly, "No disrespect intended."

Jacob nodded. "None taken, Miss Anna." But the anger was growing in him, not at the beautiful child Anna Goodlowe, certainly not, but at . . . at . . . what? *Things*. Things kept from him. Secrets.

"Anyway," she said, "Mr. Puddah graciously declined our invitation, but told Papa Bear that he'd come back the next evening and continue the story, under one condition. Papa had to promise not to take another drink all night.

"Well, sure enough, Papa Bear agreed. Mr. Puddah took the last bottle of mash with him and told me I had to watch Papa closely, and that it might be a difficult night for both of us, and I'd have to stay strong. Mr. Puddah sure was right about that. Papa couldn't eat and fell to shaking and sweating, and he paced the floor a hundred times or more, and I think if there had been any more mash left in the house he would have broken his promise and indulged, but as luck would have it, or providence, there was no more.

"When dawn came, Papa Bear hadn't taken a drink for a whole day, and seemed a little sturdier than the night before. Mr. Puddah came back that evening and read some more out of his book, stayed for supper, and read another chapter by lamplight. Then the two struck another bargain.

For as long as Papa Bear refused the bottle, Mr. Puddah would continue to read from *The Old Curiosity Shop*.

"I never would have believed it could work, but Papa Bear stayed off the mash 'til Mr. Puddah finished the book. That's when he told us that Charles Dickens wrote many other wonderful stories, and that if my papa learnt to read he wouldn't need anyone to come over and read to him. He could read any book he wanted whenever he pleased. So they made another deal. Mr. Puddah would teach Papa Bear to read if he promised not to take a drink the whole time he was learning. Well, it wasn't easy for my papa to learn to read. Took Mr. Puddah all through the winter. And the whole time Papa Bear and I had such wonderful times together, talking and laughing, he even told me some stories about my mama. He'd never said a word to me about my mama before, and I never dared ask. Papa Bear put his mind to reading and learnt as best he could, and never took to the bottle once all winter."

The congregation murmured, adding a few nods and sighs along with it.

"Then one evening Mr. Puddah came over with a present for my papa. It was a book called *A Tale of Two Cities* by that same Mr. Charles Dickens. It was a beautiful book with gold trim around the cover. He'd ordered it special from some printing press far away. Mr. Puddah said— and I'll never forget his words—he said, 'Through your own hard work and determination you learnt to read. This book is my gift to you.'

"I started to cry right on the spot, and I think Papa Bear was fighting back a tear himself. He accepted the book, and held it in his hands as if it was a great lost treasure. Then Mr. Puddah pulled something out of the inside pocket of his coat. It was a bottle of mash, the same bottle he'd taken home with him that first night when Papa was in such bad shape. Mr. Puddah set the bottle down hard on the table. Papa looked at it, kind of surprised and uncertain. Then Mr. Puddah said, 'The way I see it, you can have one or the other, the book or the bottle.'

"Papa Bear picked up that bottle and stared at it for a time, then he threw it into the fireplace, and it smashed into a million pieces."

"Amen!" someone shouted.

"Amen!" echoed the congregation.

*Amen,* mouthed Jacob Piersol, amazed.

"That night, after supper . . . " Here Miss Anna's voice faltered, and she swallowed a couple of short breaths, and it was plain as day she was choking back her tears. "That night after supper, Papa Bear and me and Mr. Tink Puddah all sat down at the table, and my papa read to us from Mr. Dickens' book."

"Amen!" shouted the congregation, clapping their hands and stomping their feet.

Miss Anna reached inside her reticule, removed a handkerchief, and dabbed at her eyes. She said, "So I came here to say that there aren't any words that can express the thanks and joy in my heart for the gift given to me and my papa by Mr. Tink Puddah, but I had no choice but to come and say it best I could. Thank you, Mr. Puddah. I know you are sitting right beside God and Jesus and his angels as I speak, even if you didn't believe in God. Thank you so much. I hope one day we'll all meet again and sit down with Jesus and read a book together." She paused, and then said, "Now there is something Papa Bear would like to say."

Papa Bear? A hush fell over the congregation. All heads turned toward the back of the church. The door crept open, and there, standing under the archway, a huge shadow of a man blocked out the sun. The preacher slowly rose from his seat. Papa Bear Goodlowe hadn't set foot in Jacob Piersol's church since the day his wife died of childbed fever fourteen years ago. The preacher remembered that day all too well.

Papa Bear had knelt in the front pew and prayed and prayed to God to save his wife, Ellie, refusing even to look at his newborn daughter or take a meal. Jacob had tried to console him, but the man had wanted to be left alone with God. Later, Jacob and Doc Oberton went to the church to tell Papa Bear his wife had died. The huge man said nothing to them.

He just stood up from his prayers, turned his back on Jacob and the doctor, and walked out of church, never to return. And now Papa Bear stood at the threshold of God's house for the first time since that day.

He strode right down the center aisle, dressed in a fancy suit and tie, his hair all neat and slicked back. He stepped up to the pulpit, lifted his daughter's hand to his lips and kissed it, a gesture so uncommon to the man that it drew a collective gasp from the people in the church.

"I thought I would read something for my dear friend, Mr. Tink Puddah," he said, "something from my daughter's Bible." He lifted the Bible that had been all but hidden in his huge hands. Squinting at the small print, he read:

"*A-hem.* From Matthew, Jesus' mission to His disciples. 'Go not into the way of the Gentiles, and into any city of the Samaritans enter ye not: But go rather to the lost sheep of the house of Israel. Heal the sick, cleanse the lepers, raise the dead, cast out devils: freely ye have received, freely give.'"

Papa Bear closed the Bible and glanced over at Jacob, looking almost apologetic, a look so out of character for the man that Jacob couldn't quite make himself believe it.

"I've always been a God-fearing, God-loving man," said Papa Bear, "even through all these sorry years missing my Ellie. It was Tink Puddah who reminded me there are more important things in life than hurt and anger and self-pity. Maybe he weren't no Christian, but I believe he was a messenger of the good Lord. Freely he did give. I was sick, and he healed me. So I came here to thank Mr. Puddah for what he done."

Papa Bear then extended his arm to Miss Anna. She grasped his elbow, and together they walked down the aisle.

Jacob just stared at them for a moment, not sure what to make of it all.

For the first time in a long time, maybe since his father's death, Jacob Piersol found himself speechless.

* * Y E A R   1 8 4 5 * *

Nif focused his vision on the surrounding trees, the hills and valleys, the expansive blue sky.

Adapt, assimilate, metamorphosis—

Ribs, sternum, femur, spine, vertebrae—

"I want Wetspace!" cried Nif Puddah's mate. She kicked Nif. She struck him.

Why did Ru not see the beauty in this world? Did her gelatinous, globular sight organs not work properly? Did the light not focus as it entered her cornea? Had the signal from the thalamus not arrived at her visual cortex? Or had the cells failed to deal appropriately with her visual fields to interpret color and light, movement and angles?

Nif looked at his hands, his fingers. He covered his head to protect himself from Ru's beating. Head, neck, shoulders, a mind all his own. His own! Nif separate, Nif alone. He ached from it. He ached for it. He trembled in fear. It was wonderful. It was horrible. "Ru, it is happening. We are almost human!"

*"This is all your fault!"*

Her cry hurt less his mind than his ears—sound waves, vibrations of air molecules, piercing down his auditory channel to his highly sensitive eardrums . . .

Barking. Animals barking.

Dogs. Four-legged, carnivorous, domesticated mammals descended from the common wolf.

Two dogs, three dogs, four.

Barking, snarling, biting.

Five dogs, six.

Where had they all come from?

Ru screamed, tried to beat the dogs away.

"Ru!" Nif cried. He reached for her with his mind. She was in agony, so furious a pain that Nif could not think with her. And then he could not find Ru's mind at all.

He had become—no, he *was*—human. Solidification. Separation. Where was Wetspace now? Now that Nif needed the thoughts of his otherselves, the thoughts of his people, where were they? Nif alone, Nif terrified, Nif in pain.

The dogs attacked him. *Beat them back,* Nif told himself with his lonely mind. Beat them as Ru had learned to do. But his arms would not work.

"Down, boys! Down! Down!" came a voice, the voice of a human male. The man was wearing heavy pants to cover his two legs and a garment of woven wool to protect his arms and torso. "What have you got there? Get back, c'mon, boys, get, get, get—"

Nif saw the man yank at the necks and collars of the four-legged mammals. The dogs struggled against the man, but did not attack. Nif could not feel much of anything anymore, not even the great pain. He reached out for Ru with his mind. Nothing, nothing. He could not find her.

Now the man had managed to pull the dogs away, and the animals fell to attacking each other, growling, snapping. The man fought to control the beasts. He beat them with a stick. Finally, he leashed them all and tied them to the trees. So much red blood plasma, serum, red and white corpuscles, no longer circulating through the newly formed arteries or veins, no longer carrying nutrients or oxygen to the cells, no longer clotting, too much damage, dying, dying.

Our son, Nif thought, so long in the womb, and now we have lost him. This thought was his alone to bear, no one to think it with him, no Wetspace to help him mourn, no Ru. Her womb was now ripped open, their son spilled upon the earth, this alien Earth. What had Nif done? What had Nif Puddah done to his family?

"Jesus, God in Holy Heaven," the man said, the Earthman.

Further reference to the collective subconscious of religious belief. What did it mean? Would this God in Holy Heaven fix Nif and his family? If so, how? He could not see its practical use. Nif did not understand.

"Sweet Lord Almighty." The human male was now on his knees, looking into Nif's eyes. The man had hair on his head and face. Nif had no hair yet, none at all. "You don't look like no normal folk. Where you from? Who the hell is ya? My dogs done you pretty bad. I'm sorry. They didn't know what you was, most likely. They was on the trail of a bear. What is ya?"

Speak, answer, voice. Nif, use your voice. What am I? "Man," Nif said. "I am hu-man."

"You don't look much like no man I ever seen, but you talk like one, almost. I'm sorry 'bout what happened. Yer gonna die. There ain't no savin' ya now, 'cept fer yer soul, maybe. Would you like I say a prayer?"

"Taste," Nif said.

"Taste?"

"I have not . . . tasted . . . what it is to be human."

Taste buds. Tongue. Sweet, sour, bitter. How does human taste?

"You ain't makin' no sense, stranger."

"My mate," Nif said, glancing at Ru.

"Mate?"

"Mate . . . companion . . . wife . . . "

The man licked his lips and scratched at his head with his fingers. "Oh, Lord have mercy, that's your wife? I'm sorry, I'm so sorry."

"My son . . . "

The man went over to the small body that had spilled from Ru's womb. "Alive!" he said. "I don't think your boy has been hurt."

My son, Nif thought. In Wetspace, children were born fully developed. Nif sensed that it was not so here on Earth. Had Tink grown enough inside Ru's womb to survive on this foreign planet? "My son," Nif said, "he must survive." *Survive.* He sent this thought out to his new young pearl, reaching, searching, touching. He could feel his son's mind. *Alive!* You are my son, Tink Puddah. Your father was stupid and foolish, but you are alive and you are my son. You must survive.

"How old is he?" asked the Earthman.

How old? Measurement of time. Years. Age. Nif felt the age of his new young planet, just four billion years young. And his son, his son, just born, only— "Twelve. Twelve years age."

"Twelve? Kind of a runt for twelve," the man said. "Look, mister, don't you worry none about your boy. I'll see to it he's took care of. What's his name?"

The dogs barked and growled and whined, causing Nif to shiver.

"Tink Puddah," Nif said.

"Tink Puddah? That's a heck of a name for a boy. Look, here, mister, you're in a real bad way right now. Are you in pain? Do you hurt?"

Does Nif hurt? Yes, Nif hurts very much. "Yes."

"I'm gonna be merciful to you. Do you know what that means? It means you should say a prayer now."

Say a prayer. Would this fix Nif's hurt? He hoped so. He had made so many mistakes. Nif was to blame for all of his and Ru's pain and separation. It was Nif's idea to leave Wetspace. Nif had wanted to explore Earth. If a prayer would fix things, that would be good. But he did not know how to say a prayer. He should ask the man to explain, but he couldn't. He could no longer communicate. He tried to reach out to the man's mind, but there was nothing there.

Prayer, faith, religion, assimilate, theology, intellectual perception, ideational content, adapt, unconquered characteristics of inherited mental life, absorb, phylogenetic development, rejected as non-essential influences. How would prayer help Nif and his family? How?

The man held something in his hands and pointed the tip of it at Nif's head. Is this how people pray? By tube? By pipe? No, this was not an instrument of communication, Nif assimilated. This was a device that ignited a mixture of potassium nitrate, charcoal, and sulfur, and propelled a projectile at high velocity. Why was the man pointing this at the side of Nif's head? There was so much he did not understand. What had this to do with mercy or prayer or making things right?

Nothing, Nif thought. He was dying. Dying. The word echoed in his mind. What a horrible thing it would be to die alone, before one even understood that death was real.

*I'm sorry, Ru. I'm so sorry.*

*Tink Puddah, my son, survive . . . survive . . . survive . . .*

And then the man pulled the trigger, dispatching the projectile from his merciful killing device.

Jacob Piersol watched Papa Bear and young Miss Anna Goodlowe sit down next to one another in a pew at the back of his crowded little Vision of Christ Church. The churchgoers, Jacob knew, were anxious to see how he would react to the story of Tink Puddah saving Papa Bear from his struggle with the devilish whiskey bottle.

Jacob wanted nothing more in the world than to stand confidently at the pulpit and say something perfect and brilliant at this moment, but no words would come. The air had grown still and heavy, it seemed, with the strong odor of sweat and horses and manure. But Jacob could only sit in his chair and watch the reflections of mottled glass play across the heads and shoulders of his congregation as they stared expectantly up at him.

During the pause, Niles Holdstrum stood up and announced, "That was a remarkable tribute to Tink Puddah. The Goodlowes have moved me to speak." He edged out of his pew, headed to the front of the church, and climbed to the pulpit.

Jacob focused with not-very-Christian disdain on the young man now standing tall and straight on the dais. Niles was the only person in the entire church dressed up in a double-breasted frocked coat with a silk cravat. Just recently back from Rutgers University, he still walked around the valley as if he were better than everyone else. The fact that he was young and handsome didn't help. All the young girls swooned over him.

"Mr. Jed Watkins, Miss Anna Goodlowe, Mr. Papa Bear Goodlowe, I would just like to thank you all for sharing with us such words of inspiration, filled with alacrity and poignancy. I am certain I speak for everyone, including Preacher Piersol, when I say that you have moved us deeply."

He'd been doing a lot of that since he'd returned from college, using words people couldn't exactly be sure were complimentary, and speaking for other folks when they hadn't asked to be spoken for. It was an annoying habit.

"I did not know our dearly departed brother, Mr. Tink Puddah, except for seeing him on occasion in the village, to exchange a pleasant word or two of greeting and good cheer. Being deprived of the opportunity to know him more intimately, I feel somewhat a lesser man, and I am envious of those who have been blessed by his kindness and grace."

The preacher felt his heart beating faster. Get to the point, you pompous devil. He was beginning to regret offering the pulpit to anyone who had a mind to speak. He vowed that after today he'd never to do it again.

Niles went on, "And without meaning any disrespect to the preacher, to any of you wonderful people, and certainly not to Doctor Oberton, who is a respected and distinguished physician and cherished member of our fair community, I must pose the obvious question: How do we know that our Mr. Tink Puddah is really dead?"

Niles waited just long enough for what he'd said to sink in, then he repeated it, loudly, dramatically, "HOW DO WE KNOW TINK PUDDAH IS DEAD?" His fist came down hard on the pulpit.

Jacob could not contain his anger any longer. "That's enough, Mr. Holdstrum! I don't know what you're trying to pull, or whom you're trying to impress, but you've gone far enough. You are in my church now, and you will pay proper respect. You may step down."

Niles didn't budge. "My apologies, Preacher Piersol, but I did not realize I was in *your* church. I thought I was in *God's* church, or at the very least *our* church, as your wages are paid by the good people of this town. And as I have spoken about something that concerns the entire congregation—since we obviously all cared deeply about Mr. Tink Puddah, wouldn't you agree?—I should think that I have not gone far enough."

"Don't talk down to me, Mr. Holdstrum."

"Let the boy speak his piece!" hollered Jed Watkins. "He's had a lot of schoolin'. Maybe he knows something you don't, hard as that may be for you to believe."

"Thank you, Mr. Watkins," Niles said. "The fact is I have attended Rutgers University, where I have had the opportunity to study a wide range of disciplines, and of all the things I learned, perhaps the most important thing is to always maintain an open mind."

Jacob searched among the crowded pews for Niles Holdstrum's parents. There they were, trying to slink down in their seats. They were as meek a pair as Jacob had ever seen. He wondered how they'd given birth to such an ungrateful, rotten boy.

Doc Oberton stood up then, fists clenched. "Did I hear you right? Are you saying I don't know a dead body when I see one?"

"What I'm saying is that Tink Puddah was a very unusual foreigner. How do you, Doctor Oberton, or, for that matter, how do any of us know what kind of strange rituals he and his people might practice? We don't even know what land he was from. Look at the Indians right here on our own continent, our neighbors the Iroquois for example. We don't understand a tenth of their practices, how they live their lives, how they die. I've read some fascinating papers about deep transcendental states of consciousness that mirror death in every way—"

"All men die the same way!" Bill Oberton strangled the high-back of the pew in front of him. He was a craggy-faced man who looked older than his years. He'd earned the respect of this community through long, hard days and sleepless nights of nursing people through illnesses and delivering babies and comforting the injured and the dying. Niles Holdstrum wasn't about to win any friends by attacking Bill Oberton. "I know dead when I see dead. He was stone cold."

"Stone cold for how long?" Niles shot back. "Maybe, where Mr. Puddah comes from, people go stone cold routinely for a day or two while their bodies restore themselves. Think about it. Maybe Mr. Puddah's people have control of their body temperatures and their sleep states. I've read papers—"

"You can take your papers and plant 'em in the Garden of Eden for all I care! He stopped breathing!" The doctor's face turned beet red with fury.

"Again, you are speaking in terms of our own biology."

"He was as much a man as he was a foreigner," the doctor said. "Dead is dead."

Jed Watkins stood up. "Heck, I get what the boy is saying, and I'm just a dumb mountain goat." He said this in the direction of the doctor, then he turned and stared at Jacob Piersol. "What's wrong? Can't admit Holdstrum might be onto something? He wants us to dig up the body and be sure, is all. What's wrong with that?"

Niles nodded eagerly. "Correct, Mr. Watkins, a most astute observation. I believe the only way to be sure we are not doing any unintended harm to this wonderful man of unknown origins is to exhume his body and inspect his current state. We'll need to observe the process of his apparent deterioration to make sure he is not, in fact, conscious in some mystical way."

The entire congregation began debating all at once.

"Enough!" Jacob Piersol shouted. "You are bordering on sacrilege, Mr. Holdstrum, and I will not have another word of it spoken in *God's* church."

Jacob didn't really think Niles had intended sacrilege, but he was so furious he didn't care. His position of authority had been usurped right inside the very church his father had built. "This funeral service is officially concluded. Mr. Holdstrum, Doctor Oberton, Mayor

Funkel, I'd like to see you all in my house—privately."

The people, still somewhat shocked by the sudden turn of events, began to slowly rise and walk toward the exit of the church.

"May God be with you all," Jacob Piersol muttered, mostly through his teeth, although he would rather have bitten off Niles Holdstrum's head.

* * * * *

Jacob Piersol often met with members of his congregation in his house, in a small room just off the main porch where he sometimes took his meals, and that was where he led the doctor, the mayor, and that brat of a college boy, Niles Holdstrum. He walked straight out the back door of his Vision of Christ Church, down the mossy cobblestone walkway, and straight through to the back room of the house.

Jacob was so angry he hadn't even waited for his parishioners to file out of church, hadn't smiled or shaken hands with anyone on this day for which he'd had such high hopes, a day so important to him personally as a man of God and to the growth of his Vision of Christ Church. Curse Niles Holdstrum and the obscure knowledge he'd acquired at Rutgers University. The skinny brat had more than a few lessons to learn right here in Skanoh Valley, where his fancy education meant very little to hardworking farmers and builders and homesteaders.

Niles sat at the head of the table, and Mayor Funkel eased his great girth into the chair beside Niles. Doc Oberton paced to the window, looking too furious to sit anywhere. Bill Oberton was a tall, lean, round-shouldered man. For as long as Jacob could remember, Doc Oberton had looked weary. Jacob stood at the end of the table and gripped the back of his chair.

"All right," he said. "Before we get started I would like to hear an apology from Mr. Holdstrum for publicly questioning Doctor Oberton's knowledge and abilities as a physician."

Niles grimaced. "Oh, tsk, for heaven's sake, I'm sorry if I've offended the good doctor."

"You are a young man, Niles," said Jacob. "It may not have occurred to you that the people of this valley not only need Bill Oberton, they need to trust him and have faith in his ability to heal, much like their faith in me."

"I said I was sorry, and before you ask for another apology, I'm sorry if I've offended you or anyone else. It was not my intention to damage anyone's reputation or maim an ego. I don't know why everyone is taking all of this so personally." He fluffed the cravat under his chin. "The point is I have an honest concern that our Mr. Tink Puddah may have been prematurely buried. What could it possibly hurt to dig up the old boy and have a look?"

Jacob Piersol doubted that Niles Holdstrum had an honest concern for anyone or anything other than himself. It occurred to him that the young man might be plying for the mayorship, since his fancy education wasn't going to do the Holdstrum cornfields any good.

"First of all," Jacob said, "digging up the dead is sacrilegious."

Niles smirked. "But Tink Puddah was no Christian. You said so yourself. Did you give him a proper burial?"

Jacob hesitated. That was a tricky question. It depended on what one considered proper. Did Jacob do all of the same things he normally did when one of his people passed away? Well, no, he hadn't given the foreigner his customary Christian blessings, but Tink Puddah was neither a visitor to his church nor a proper Christian, so what was Jacob's obligation?

"I've given Tink Puddah a burial befitting his life and beliefs," he said. "The point is, he's buried now, and he has a right to stay buried. Christians don't condone or participate in foul acts against anyone, living or dead, Christian or otherwise."

"I see."

"I'm not so sure you do." Why did Jacob feel the need to defend himself? Was it because his conduct as a preacher did indeed require some defending? Why hadn't he given Tink Puddah as proper a burial as he would have done for anyone else? Had he harbored such a black spot in his heart for the foreigner that he had actually convinced himself Puddah did not deserve Christian prayers? How had he convinced himself that Puddah did not need God, when he knew in his heart that sinners like Puddah needed God more than anyone?

Niles Holdstrum sighed and shook his head. "We're losing sight of what's important, gentlemen. We're talking about Christian philosophy when you might have buried a man alive. It's like arguing how to save someone who is drowning. Do you offer him a stick, or do you float him a barrel? Either way, the poor fellow must be saved, or the argument kills him."

Doc Oberton continued to stare out the window. From there, Jacob knew, he could see clear across to the back hill where the cemetery lay, where Tink Puddah was buried.

Mayor Funkel took a cigar and a match safe out of his suit jacket, lit it up, and puffed several clouds of thick, gray smoke into the air. He said, "The lad may have a point. What would it hurt to unearth the poor foreigner? No offense intended, of course, to anyone in this room, but now that the question has been raised, well, I'm sure it would put everyone's mind at ease if we were to answer it. If Niles has read papers about Injuns looking dead but being alive, maybe we need to be sure." Sweat streamed down the mayor's sideburns; the man could sweat buckets even on a cool spring day. He had a small tight voice and an oddly constrained delivery, as if he were being strangled. "I have only the community's best interest at heart, mind you. Everyone loved that little fella, no denying that. You saw as much yourself this morning, Jacob."

Doc Oberton turned from the window and marched around the table so that he was standing next to Jacob. He looked as if he wanted to say something, then as if he didn't, then as if he did again.

"Tink Puddah is dead," said the doctor. "He was shot in the head. The reason I didn't want to say anything in church about it, and the reason I haven't said anything to anyone, is because I didn't want to get people all worried and nervous. That's what the marshal in Palmyra told me. I sent the marshal a post the day I discovered Tink's body. He said not to say anything to anyone."

"God have mercy," Jacob whispered. "Tink Puddah was shot in the head?"

"That's right," Doctor Oberton said. "With a shotgun."

"I can't believe it," Niles said. "Murdered?"

The mayor blew a fat circle of cigar smoke into the air. "What's this? Are you saying somebody murdered that foreigner? Right here in our own town? A murder? Why would somebody want to do that?"

The doctor looked down at his hands, the kind of concentrated look that made Jacob want to stare at them, too. There was just the slightest bit of trembling evident in Bill Oberton's fingertips. "The marshal sent word that there has been a gang moving through the area, and it's possible Tink was in the wrong place at the wrong time. But he said not to say anything to anyone, that worrying people was the worst thing to do in the case of a killing like this."

Niles Holdstrum stood up slowly and planted his palms on the table in front of him. "And you and this marshal just took it upon yourselves to keep this whole thing quiet?"

"I told you," Bill said, "there was no sense getting people upset."

"That's right, Niles," said the mayor. "We don't want folks worrying over a foreigner. What's the sense in that?"

Niles shook his head. "This community has a right to know! You have no authority to decide what to tell people around here. This gang or this killer could be a threat to the safety of everyone."

Bill shook his head. "The marshal said the killer, or killers, would be long gone—"

"The marshal said!" Niles snapped. "This marshal of yours must be a very intelligent man. He didn't come to investigate, did he?"

"No, of course not. He said if we had no reason to suspect that somebody from around here killed him, he saw no need to come all the way—"

"He saw no need? Who is he to decide such a thing? The safety of
Skanoh Valley means so little to him, does it?"

"That's enough, Mr. Holdstrum," Jacob said. "You're way out of line."

"*I'm* out of line? I haven't presumed to speak for all of Skanoh Valley."

"Enough!" Jacob said. "You've put your share of words in the mouths
of others."

The doctor picked up his tophat and gripped it tightly. "That's all
right, Jacob. I've listened to just about enough. If you want to tell the whole
world Tink Puddah was shot and killed, so be it. If you want to dig up the
foreigner's body, by all means dig it up. We'll let Mr. Holdstrum, with all
his higher education, decide whether Tink Puddah is dead." The doctor
moved to leave, and with his back to the room he said, "Good day, *gentlemen*," and strode through the house, slamming the door on his way out.

Niles smirked. "Tsk."

The mayor inhaled his cigar smoke. "Doesn't seem much sense in digging him up if he caught buckshot in the brain."

Niles said, "Quite the contrary. Nobody but the doctor has seen that
foreigner's dead body. We owe it to the people of this village to exhume
him and to let them know exactly how he died."

Jacob took a moment to let some of the steam out of his anger; it
would not do to show a lack of control in this situation, certainly no more
than he'd shown already. The morning, somehow, had gone very, very
wrong.

"What do you think, Preacher Piersol?" asked Niles. "Do you agree
with me?" It was not so much a question as it was a challenge.

Jacob didn't like any of this, but he didn't want there to be any question
about the foreigner's death either. And there was something else he might
do. There was, in fact, something he might gain by all of this. Jacob could

deliver a prayer over Tink Puddah's dead body, give the man's remains a proper Christian blessing. He felt as if he owed that to Puddah, and to himself. Maybe this was God's will, after all.

"All right, Mr. Holdstrum," he said at last. "We'll exhume the body."

"Wonderful!"

"But it will be done quietly, in private, do you understand?"

Niles nodded. "Of course."

"I'll talk to Tip Emerson," the mayor said, avoiding the preacher's eyes. Tip was the gravedigger. "Will tomorrow be soon enough for you gentlemen?"

"Perhaps we should make it this afternoon," Niles said.

Mayor Funkel shook his head. "I don't know about that. There's paperwork involved in yanking a body out of the ground, court orders, that sort of thing."

"How long must we wait?" Niles said. "Every moment counts."

"Mayor, maybe this can be done off the record," Jacob suggested. "There's really no sense delaying."

The mayor considered this. "Officially, technically, legally . . . well, I never did much like paperwork."

"Shall we say three o'clock, then?" Niles checked his pocket watch.

The mayor stood. "I'll stop by Doc Oberton's and inform him of the time. We'll want the doctor to be present, of course."

"Of course," Niles agreed.

Fine, Jacob thought, fine, fine, fine. Just leave me alone, all of you. "Let's get this over with and ask the Lord for His forgiveness. I'll meet you at the graveside."

Tink Puddah thought about the day he'd been born and remembered how his father had reached out to him with his mind and then was gone. Gone forever. The dogs had killed his mother and father. He remembered the savage teeth of the dogs, the blood of his parents, the pain of their deaths. He remembered it as if it had happened to him, and in a way it had, for his parents were a part of him now, now and forever.

And here, now, the man—the very same man whose dogs had torn apart his parents—wanted Tink to go with him and the dogs on a bear hunt.

"Don't force him to go," the woman said. "He's too weak."

"Too weak?" said the man. "Too weak ain't half the boy's trouble. Just look at him. He's a little blue-skinned runt with a squished-up face. He wouldn't survive half a day out there on his own. Weren't for our charity he'd be nothing. Nothing 't all. Everybody knows it. You think people don't talk about us? It's time that blue boy started payin' his keep. I got use for him on the bear hunt, and by God he's a goin' with me."

The man and the woman had fed Tink and clothed him and sheltered him from the harsh weather of this planet for two of their human years, here in their log cabin, in the forest among the oak and pine and hickory trees of Pennsylvania. Tink knew he was not from Earth. His parents had told him, not told him in words exactly, but they had a way of letting him know things even through death. He couldn't explain it, but they were a part of him. Sometimes their presence was strong; other times he could feel only a trace of their insubstantial mists. But always there was something there, something that suggested an all-ness he could not quite grasp.

"You know he's not a normal boy," the woman said. She was baking corn bread, and the smell was thick and rich and made his mouth water. "You can't expect normal things out of him."

"Yer dang right he ain't no normal boy. Life is tough for everybody, don't make no never mind if you're normal or if ya ain't. That boy has gotta learn hisself a skill or else he'll never know how to survive when we ain't 'round to shelter him."

"But bear hunting, Darryl, why bear hunting? There's got to be something else he can learn."

"Oh, I don't doubt he can learn anything needs learnin'. He's a smart young coot. You already taught him to read, didn't you? Trouble is I got only one thing to learn him."

"You can teach him to hunt something else, rabbit or squirrel or deer."

"You know it's the bear meat keeps us fed through the winter. Have to shoot me a dozen deer to one bear, and the dogs won't get after a deer the way they get after a bear."

"I could teach him the garden—"

"Look, woman, you already taught him the garden." Often the man called her woman instead of Claudia. "You know I got the gout in m' knees. I can't run the bears so good no more without falling flat out sometimes. The fact is, in another year or two I'll need a boy who knows what's what. He's a smart kid. He'll learn. That's my final word."

This was how most of their discussions ended. The male was dominant on this planet. His word was final. His word was law. Tink liked the woman better. She was soft and kind. But Tink knew he would be going on the bear hunt tomorrow. He could not refuse. The man's dogs had killed his parents, but the man had saved his life. The man had brought

Tink into his home, and it was his word that let him live.

Tink understood the man had done this not for Tink but for his wife, for she had no brood of her own for which to care. Tink understood the man had no liking for one so frail and useless as he. This was a delicate balance, this triangle of need and resentment and fear that held together this house of logs, but none of them could do without it, especially Tink.

He shivered. Even through the warmth of the woman's stove as it baked the corn bread, the fireplace warming the day's water, the thick pine logs of their shelter, his coat made of bearskin . . . Tink trembled.

*   *   *   *   *

The next morning the man, Darryl, woke Tink early. The man had his shotgun strapped over his shoulder. It was a cold, dark morning, late in the fall season. Tink began shivering almost as soon as he left his bed and felt the air on his skin. He could feel the cold even after he dressed; it penetrated the thick fur tunic the woman had sewn especially for him. Tink did not know exactly what kind of being he was, but he knew what he was not. He was not a human being. He was not made for the rigors of this planet. His birth, his solidification, had been cut short by the dogs. He did not understand the why of it, but he knew how to listen to the things inside him that were not words. This planet was not his own. This planet was an enemy lurking, waiting for its opportunity to strike him dead.

Tink smelled the wood beginning to burn for the morning fire. No chatter passed between the man and his wife. The woman kissed Tink on the cheek, ran her fingers through his small tuft of bluish hair, and gave him some corn bread to put in his vest pocket.

Tink's chill deepened when he went outside and the man loosed the dogs from their pens. They yapped and circled and seemed anxious for the hunt. Tink stood frozen, afraid to move. The dogs could tear him to pieces in an instant if they wanted, just as easily as they'd killed his parents. But there was another reason he did not like the dogs: Tink's parents were still frightened of them, and they hid from the dogs even now, hid deeper inside Tink where he could not feel their presence. And when his parents were out of reach, Tink felt cold and lonesome and more vulnerable than ever.

"I know you don't care fer m' dogs," the man said, not as unkindly as Tink had expected. Then he spoke to the dogs, "C'mon, boys, c'mon, steady now, steady." The dogs appeared eager to please. They obeyed the man, wagged their tails and tongues, their paws pattering on the cold, hard dirt. But their muscles were ready to spring, to hunt, to kill. "Come over here, Tink, come over here, now. The dogs won't hurt ya."

The man had a very commanding way with his speech. Tink found himself obeying, just like the dogs.

"That's right," the man said. "Stand right next to me here."

Tink went to him. The dogs fidgeted and trotted around him. They smelled gamey and sniffed at each other's tails. The dogs seemed not to care at all about Tink. They seemed not to remember how they had ripped apart his parents. Sometimes Tink felt as if the man did not remember either. The man had said the dogs had done the killing because Tink's parents had wandered onto the bear's path, and the dogs were in a frenzy and could not help themselves. But wasn't the man responsible, too? The dogs were only dumb animals. What about the man?

"See that?" the man said, delighted with his animals. "The dogs don't care spit about you. It's bear they want. Bear! These here dogs is all mixed blacks and tans, best bear dogs in the world. Alls they care is to get after a bear. They know he's out there. They know it. Look at 'em."

He roughhoused with a couple of the dogs and got them all jumping and yapping again. Then the man reached over his shoulder and took his shotgun in hand. He held it out to Tink. "Today yer gonna carry my gun. I don't expect you to know how to use it right yet. This time out yer just comin' along to watch. But I think you can carry the gun. It'll be good for you."

Tink took the shotgun. It was heavy, very heavy, too heavy. He slung it over his shoulder, trying to imitate the way he'd seen the man carry it many times before, but the strap was not made for such a small person, and he had to hold the strap tightly in his hands to keep the gun from slipping down his shoulder and tripping his legs. There were six dogs. The man leashed them, took three in each hand, and strode toward the woods.

Tink followed, keeping pace as best he could. Tink's feet were tiny, and his ankles often hurt when he walked any great distance without rest. But today he would not think about that. Today he would think only about killing a bear that would feed them through the winter, and about getting home alive.

They did not walk very far before the man stopped and motioned the boy forward. "Look here, boy. This is where the bear has been feeding."

Tink knew that the man had been out scouting for bear all summer long, so he could learn where they lived and where they fed. Bears lived in mostly one place, the man had told him. They might wander as far as twenty miles a day looking for food, but they'd come home, and they'd stay in a certain area as long as the food was plentiful.

"You know how you can tell where a bear has been feeding, boy? Look here the way the bear raked back the brush digging for mast. And you can see signs of acorns. See that? Bear'll eat acorns and mast, hickory nuts, berries, grapes, and worms and insects too. That's it, mostly. Bear ain't much on meat 'les it's starving pretty good. Oh, it'll eat fish and some small critters now and again, but bear don't like to take chances. Don't like being chased, neither. Got to be real careful with a bear. Bear'll kill you if you ain't careful."

Bear. Large mammal, huge hindquarters, coarse fur, humped shoulders, straight muzzle, teeth that grind and tear, non-retractile claws, carnivorous, dangerous when startled or threatened. Of course a bear was dangerous. Of course a bear would kill. Tink had never seen a bear, but he knew them as part of this planet, as things his parents had assimilated. And there was something Tink himself had assimilated: the bear was probably smarter than the man.

"We hunt 'em this time of year because the female's denned for the winter," the man said. "And the male, he'll scrounge for food longer, and he'll be alone so if we trap him he won't be as ferocious. You never want to hunt down a female in the spring, because she'll probably have cubs around, and she'll fight like hell. That's when you get your best dogs injured or killed."

The dogs were itching to run, perhaps already smelling the bear's trail. They circled and yapped and whined. But the man held them tight to their leads. Did the man truly believe Tink would someday be able to do this, to hold the dogs at bay, to command them? The dogs would drag him across the planet's surface until nothing was left of him but dangling bones. What a sight that would be. The man must know this. He must.

"Now, here's what we do, boy. We let Clyde sniff, then we cut him loose first. Clyde's older, got more experience than the other dogs, got a nose can track a scent two days cold. We let Clyde strike the bear's trail and then we let go one dog at a time. We give each dog a few minutes. If we let 'em all go at once they'll sure enough set to scrappin' at each other before they find that bear."

The dogs fought against their leashes, growling, barking. The man let Clyde go, and the lead dog shot howling through the thickets. "Go get him, Clyde! Go get that bear!"

Six dogs, Tink thought. Six vicious dogs to track one bear looking to eat nuts and berries. They would chase the bear for miles, exhausting it, angering it until it had no choice but to turn and fight or run up a tree. Then the man would come along with his shotgun and, from a safe distance, kill it. The man had said he'd once tracked a bear for twenty miles before the dogs finally treed that bear and he was able to kill it with his shotgun, the shotgun Tink now struggled to hold on his shoulder. Tink knew he could not chase a bear twenty miles, or even ten. What was wrong with the man? Why was he making Tink do this?

It did not matter. Tink sat on a rock while the man let the dogs go one at a time. He was beginning to understand about survival. He hoped the dogs found this bear quickly, cornered him against the rocks or forced him up a tree so the man could shoot the bear. If the chase went too long, maybe Tink would not make it back. Is this what the man wanted? Was two years long enough to keep the promise he'd made to Nif Puddah and his dead mate, Ru, to the family his dogs had killed? Did he regret bringing Tink into his home, even for his barren wife?

The man had called Tink a cripple, as if that explained him. But the woman would not allow him that. "He's no cripple, Darryl," she'd said. "Look at him. He's different. Maybe he's a foreigner, I'll give you that, but he's no cripple, and you know it." Not even the woman knew how foreign he truly was. But she'd said this over and over until her husband stopped calling Tink a cripple. Tink did not know why she had insisted on this point, but she had succeeded. It was, perhaps, the only argument she'd ever won.

Normally Tink might have felt good about the woman winning something, but maybe it would have been better if she had allowed the man to think him crippled. Maybe Tink wouldn't be out here today, hunting bear in the woods. Now Tink began to think that this day might not be about hunting at all. There was so much he did not understand.

The man unleashed the last of his dogs. "Ye-ha! Let's go, boy!" He ran into the woods after his dogs.

Tink hefted the cumbersome, double-barreled shotgun to his shoulder and followed as best he could.

When Jacob Piersol climbed the hill out behind his house to the small cemetery nestled in among the poplar and sycamore trees, he found he was the last to arrive at Tink Puddah's grave.

Niles was there, all dressed up in his fancy suit and scarf and shiny shoes, as if he were attending the theater, or some grandiloquent lecture at Rutgers University. Mayor Funkel puffed lazily on a fat cigar, his stomach straining the buttons of his vest. Tip Emerson stood by with his shovel, looking a bit put out and waiting for the okay to get digging. Doc Oberton, much more composed than he had been earlier in the day, stood with his arms crossed in front of him. A couple of others had shown up as well. Jed Watkins, of all troublemakers, leaned on his devilish, black snake cane. And Papa Bear Goodlowe, book in hand, stood tall and straight as a birch tree, at least a head taller than anyone else, with shoulders twice as broad.

The day had turned breezy and a little chill. Jacob had pulled on a frock coat before he'd left his house. He took a moment to button it up, and then he advanced on the group of men.

"I thought we agreed to keep this private," Jacob said, looking straight at Niles Holdstrum.

It was Jed Watkins who answered. "Don't get hives over it, preacher. The boy rightly wanted to tell me and Papa Bear here about the diggin' because he knew how close we was to Puddah. Out of respect he told us."

"I wanted to be here," Papa Bear said. "For my own sense of peace." The preacher glanced at the binding of Papa Bear's book, *The Old Curiosity Shop.*

Niles grinned. He had a way of grinning that made Jacob want to slap his face. No, he thought, stave off the pettiness. This was bad business, digging up the dead, and he wanted to be done with it. He held his Holy Bible to his chest, knelt beside the grave, and bowed his head. He didn't really know what to say in a situation like this. Burying a man was one thing, disturbing his remains quite another. He had thought that he would simply ask the Lord for guidance and forgiveness, but something came over him then, a foul streak of anger, anger at all the men gathered here to perform this loathsome deed, and anger at Tink Puddah, who would not go away even after his death. He decided, then, not to say anything. He'd save his prayers for the blessing he'd planned to deliver over the foreigner's body, and that would be that. Jacob rose to his feet and nodded to Tip Emerson to begin his assault against the earth.

It didn't take long for the gravedigger to hit Tink Puddah's pine box with his shovel. The ground was still loose from the original digging, and Tip had a lazy habit of not forging as deep into the dirt as he probably should. Papa Bear helped Tip lift the casket out of the hole, and then Tip went to work on the lid with a crow bar.

Jacob should have known what was coming. He'd smelled the rot as soon as the casket had been unearthed. Still, it was a shock. The odor was so horrible it far exceeded the normal stench of death and decay. He'd never smelled anything as bad. It was almost poisonous, the way it made his eyes water and his nose burn. Niles Holdstrum had been right about one thing. This was certainly a foreign biology. But Niles was wrong about his other theory—dead wrong. There was no way any part of this shriveled and putrid hunk of rotten flesh was anywhere near alive.

Niles turned his head, looking a tad green. Jed and Papa Bear pursed their lips and *harrumphed,* almost in unison. Only Doc Oberton seemed to come to life with the unveiling. He moved forward and knelt beside the pine box, squinting and inspecting the foreigner's remains. "Well, well, Mr. Holdstrum, take a look at this. From the looks of his body, Mr. Puddah seems to be decomposing quite nicely, wouldn't you agree?" The doctor unlashed his medical bag and fished for a pair of deerskin gloves. He pulled them over his hands and slid the body a bit higher up out of the casket.

Jacob couldn't look for long, but even when he turned away the memory of it was etched upon his mind: Tink Puddah's body, dark and pitted, wet and prune-like, leaking some horrible, thick liquid out of the gaping hole near the top of his skull where the shotgun shell must have split his head wide open, his eyes no more than sunken, shapeless pits. It almost appeared as if the veins in the foreigner's neck had turned outward, warping his throat in what seemed an entanglement of snakes and vines, or the tentacles of some nightmarish beast. Jacob's rational mind told him that Tink shouldn't look so awful after such a short time dead, but he also knew that "rational" and "Tink Puddah" didn't always go together.

Jacob tried to picture the foreigner the way he looked when he was alive. He'd been short and skinny, with an under-developed bone structure, his skin pigmentation soft blue. He'd had a tuft of bluish-black hair at the crown of his head, resembling a patch of sphagnum, his nose and eyes had more the look of a ferret than a man, ears that had somehow managed to develop primarily on the inside of his skull, and a mouth that appeared somehow unfinished and comically askew. Tink Puddah had been the strangest-looking man, foreign or otherwise, that Jacob had ever seen.

Jacob had no idea where Puddah came from, but he'd always suspected there was something more to his odd looks than an unusual heritage—a birth defect, perhaps, or a childhood disease of some sort, maybe even something that had forced him out of his own homeland. Jacob didn't like to think about Tink Puddah in that way: an outcast, lonely and forgotten, the way any other human being might feel.

"Ah, look at this, Mr. Holdstrum." Doc Oberton had opened Tink Puddah's coat, and with a sharp hunting knife had sliced an incision straight down the foreigner's belly. "These organs are blistered to the core. I doubt we'll see any miraculous conversion here. Take a look. What do you think?"

Niles Holdstrum barely had time to turn his head before he retched.

"Is all this necessary, Bill?" Jacob said.

"I just wanted to make sure Mr. Holdstrum saw sufficient evidence of death and decay."

"All right, we've seen enough," Jacob said. "We have disturbed the dead on this day. It's nothing to be proud of. Let us allow Mr. Puddah to rest in peace."

"Agreed," Mayor Funkel said.

Papa Bear Goodlowe stepped forward and placed *The Old Curiosity Shop* in Tink Puddah's casket, then without a word began walking back down the hill.

Jacob Piersol was suddenly glad all these men had come. They had seen it with their own eyes. Tink Puddah was dead—cold, rotten dead. From this day forward, Jacob would never have to deal with the foreigner again.

He felt slightly more generous now. He opened his Bible and knelt beside the casket.

"What do you think yer doin' there, preacher?" Jed Watkins said.

"I'm giving Mr. Puddah a proper Christian blessing."

Jed stepped forward. "Wait a minute. He weren't no believer. What gives you the right to—"

"God gives the right," Jacob snapped. "If you don't want to hear it, then leave." He flipped to 1 Corinthians, Chapter 15, the reading he had prepared before coming out to Tink Puddah's grave, to the gentle, rounded hill that was commonly referred to as Dead Man's Rise, and he began reading.

"'There is one glory of the sun, and another glory of the moon, and another glory of the stars: for one star differeth from another star in glory. So also is the resurrection of the dead. It is sown in corruption; it is raised in incorruption: It is sown in dishonour; it is raised in glory: it is sown in weakness; it is raised in power: It is sown a natural body; it is raised a spiritual body.'"

Jacob did not want to so much as glance at Tink Puddah again, but it was important for him to touch the foreigner's forehead. He wanted to pass a blessing directly from his hand to Tink Puddah's body, just as he would have done for any other member of his congregation.

Puddah's forehead felt oddly soft and slimy beneath his fingers, more like an overripe melon than a human skull. The feel of it alone was enough to curdle his stomach.

"I bless Tink Puddah in the name of the Lord Jesus Christ. Amen."

Jacob stood and turned away from the grave.

Doc Oberton slid Tink's body down inside its casket.

Tip Emerson hammered down the lid, then took his shovel in hand and began digging.

Niles Holdstrum dabbed at his lips with a frilly handkerchief. For once, the young man had nothing to say, much to Jacob's relief.

When a bear is hounded by dogs, the bear runs through the roughest country it can find. It runs through the thickets and laurel and rhododendron, through the dense brush and thick ivy. It runs down slopes and over rocky cliffs and scree. It runs for its life.

A bear, with its massive weight and brute strength, can run where a dog or a man can barely lay a foot. But good men do not quit, and good bear dogs, once they pick up a scent, will sooner drop dead than give up the chase.

But now it was Tink Puddah who was ready to drop dead. The man and his dogs had been tracking the bear for more than two hours, running over the cold, hard terrain. The season's first snow had not yet come, so there would be no tracking the bear by its paw prints; only speed and determination and relentless pursuit would do.

The woodland was dense with sticks and vines. Tink's arms and face were gashed. His legs and ankles ached. His muscles felt as if they were exploding with pain. Tink could barely breathe. He gulped at the cold air. His chest burned from his efforts. He could go no farther. He knew he could not take another step. No more, no more.

But he kept going. He had no idea what pushed him on. Only that stopping might be worse. He might not be able to start again. He might be left behind, lost, abandoned for dead. He knew the man would do that, leave him, given half a chance.

He could hear the dogs now, thrashing in the underbrush. The man yelled, "Hiyeeeeeee! Good dogs! Get after that bear! Get after him!"

Had the dogs finally treed the bear? Or had the bear stopped to fight? Tink did not care. He did not care at all what happened.

"Bring that gun, boy, bring it here. We got us a bear for the winter! A big, fat male!"

Tink went up to the man. He was so tired he could not even lift the gun off his shoulder. The bear was trapped at the bottom of a small embankment, up against the rocks, in among the fallen branches. The dogs had chased it down the slope, and now the bear could not get out. The dogs growled and snapped at the cornered bear. The man really did have good bear dogs. He'd heard the man brag many times about how good his dogs were. Good bear dogs would lunge and snap, retreat and attack a bear, working together. Some dogs didn't have that instinct. Some dogs, when they attacked, would dig their teeth in and hold on. Those dogs did not live very long. If a bear got hold of one of those dogs it would rip the animal apart. Good bear dogs would just keep their quarry at bay until a man could shoot it in the head.

The man grabbed hold of the shotgun, pulling it off Tink's shoulder, and moved to the edge of the embankment.

The bear had already swatted one of the man's dogs so hard it was down and yelping. The bear was furious. A bear trapped and scared was one of the most dangerous of all hunted beasts. Tink could almost smell the fear in this one. Its musky odor rose up the slope, and its deep growl echoed monstrously among the rocks and trees.

Suddenly the man buckled at the knees and fell at the edge of the incline. He dropped his gun and went down hard on his hands.

"*Goddamn!*" he shouted.

Tink had already collapsed. He was sitting on the cold earth, gasping for breath.

"Get over here, boy, hurry up, get on over here!"

Tink could not do it. He could not move another inch. But the man had commanded him to move, so he crawled forward as best he could.

"Damn it all to hell, my knees done gone out. I dropped my gun down the slope, boy. You got to go down there and get it!"

Tink couldn't believe what the man was saying. Go down the embankment and get the gun? The man was crazy. Tink crawled to the edge of the embankment. How was he going to fetch the gun? How, with no strength and no courage, was he to retrieve the man's weapon? No, Tink had done all he was capable of doing. No more, no more.

"Go now!" cried the man. "Go!"

Don't look at the bear, Tink told himself. Whatever you do, don't look at the bear, then maybe . . . no. . . . .Tink decided he was not going to do it.

The man swatted him on the side of the head. "I said go!"

Tink peered down the slope. Don't look at the dogs, he told himself. Looking at the dogs might be worse than looking at the bear. The dogs could kill him just as easily. This was crazy, all of it, the bear, the dogs, the man, the gun. Just find the gun, he told himself. There. There it was. The man's shotgun had slid down the slope, that's all. It was right there in the ivy. No trouble, no trouble at all. Tink could just slide down the incline and pick up the gun and bring it back to the man. The man would shoot the bear, and the hunt would be over. Tink had no idea how he was going to get home afterwards. He was sure he could not make it on his own two legs. The man must know this. Would he carry Tink if he had to? Maybe. Maybe not.

"God-*damn*, hurry up about it, boy. That bear is hurting my dogs!"

Tink slung his legs over the embankment and slid down the slope, slowing himself, edging to the left until the gun was at his feet.

"That's it, good boy," said the man. Tink was not sure whether he was talking to Tink or the dogs.

Tink reached down and grabbed the gun. Suddenly the bear roared. The bear was right on top of him! Tink looked up. No, the bear had just sounded as if it were on top of him. But Tink had told himself not to look at the bear and now he'd gone and looked. The beast was huge. It had to weigh three-hundred-pounds, twice the size of an average black bear. Tink froze. He had the gun in his hand, but he could not turn his back on the bear. If he turned his back, the bear would kill him.

"Get up here with that gun, boy! Get up here now! I got to kill that bear!"

But Tink could not move. Everything hit him all at once. He had been running for hours through the most treacherous woodland in the mountains. How many miles had they covered? His legs were stiff and he could not feel his feet. His lungs could no longer extract breath from the thin air, and the man wanted him to climb a hill with his shotgun. He could not even lift the gun. It was in his hands, but he could not lift it. The bear was only a few steps away. With one surge of its powerful hind legs the bear would pounce on Tink and kill him.

"Damn it, boy, this is no time for you to freeze up." Tink heard the man sliding down the hill. He smelled his foul sweat above him, overpowering even the smell of bear. The man reached down and snatched the shotgun. He slapped Tink out of the way with one angry sweep of his arm. Tink slid farther down the hill, and whatever spell he'd fallen under was broken. He could move again. He could feel his body. He could feel the pain everywhere. He saw everything at once:

The dogs snapped at the bear, kicking up dirt as they dug their paws into the hard, dry earth. Two dogs down, one of them motionless, the other crying and squirming. The huge bear swiped at the dogs, its jaws popping as it growled and bit. The man and his gun lay silhouetted against the embankment like an illusion of shadow and light that belonged in a dream. The oak trees and the pines and the fallen branches that looked so bare and frail hemmed them all in, framing them like a painting, along with the thick rolls of ivy and thatch. The blood of dogs. The drool of bear. The flash of a gun barrel.

"Don't worry, I'm gonna kill that bear for ya." The man was talking to the dogs now, Tink was certain. "Don't you boys worry. I got one of my knees back."

He hopped forward on one leg, dragging the bad leg behind him as if he were a wounded dog himself. He had the shotgun in his hands. He hopped around the oak tree to get a clean shot.

Soon it would be over. One shot and the bear would be dead. The man was a good shot. He'd killed many bears before with just one shot. It was easy to kill a bear with a slug to the head. Their skulls were close to the surface, vulnerable. No more roaring. No more growling dogs. Just the blast of a gun, a killing blast, the tremendous collision of bear and earth, and then the man scolding Tink and beating him for failing. Yes, Tink had failed. Failed magnificently. Perhaps he had performed badly enough so the man would never take him on another bear hunt, but not quite badly enough to be left for dead.

The man, Darryl, hopped around the oak tree, and his knee, his one good knee, buckled again. He cursed and went down hard on his elbows.

Suddenly there came a loud *snap!*—not the pop of the bear's jaws or the dogs nipping at the bear. No, as the man's arms hit the ground, there came the sharp grind of steel hinges and the fierce clap of metal. Tink saw a huge set of steel jaws whip shut over the man's right elbow all the way up to his wrist. Blood spurted. Bones cracked. The man cried out. It was a cry and a moan of anger and hatred and pain and fear all at once. Tink—breathless, exhausted, frozen with fear—could not believe what he'd just witnessed.

"Jesus, God have mercy, I fell in a trap. I fell in a goddamn bear trap, boy."

He was talking to Tink now, not his dogs. His voice sounded panicked and betrayed. The bear reared up on its hindquarters and caught another dog with its ripping claws. The dog yelped once and Tink could hear its bones break against the jagged rocks. There were only three dogs left.

The man was injured. The bear must have sensed this, must have known there was a chance for escape, because now, instead of sitting back and defending itself, it rushed at the nearest dog, its heavy legs cracking branches and drumming the earth. What was happening here? How had things turned so horrible, so quickly?

"Boy, hurry, you got to pick up the gun, you got to kill that bear before it turns on us. Do you understand what I'm saying? My knees are flat out useless, my arm ain't no good. I can't shoot. You got to kill that bear."

Yes, Tink understood perfectly. The dog nearest the bear leaped back. Tink remembered the man saying that the best dogs were always the dogs you lost if you were too slow in killing a bear, because they were stronger and fiercer and not afraid to lunge. That meant that only the man's timid dogs remained, and maybe they would no longer be so eager to attack.

Tink ran forward. He ran to the oak tree, to the man, to the gun, and he lifted the gun to his shoulder the way he'd seen the man do it. It was a Herculean effort. He could barely hold the weapon. It teetered in his arms. There were two triggers on the gun. Which one to pull? It didn't matter. Before the hunt the man would have loaded both barrels. Tink knew that one trigger would empty the right barrel, and the other trigger would empty the left. How could he possibly hold the gun steady, aim and shoot, and then withstand the recoil? But Tink must kill the bear. It was upon him now. It was all upon him. No one else could save them.

"Shoot him in the head, boy. Aim right at its muzzle."

The dogs retreated. They were still growling and barking, but they would not attack. The bear reared up and roared. Tink cocked the dual hammers, aimed the gun, and fired. The blast shocked his ears. The shotgun's kick knocked him off his feet and threw him into the brush at the foot of the embankment. He had missed the bear completely. He knew it as soon as he'd pulled the trigger. He had fired too high, so high he must have shot clear out of the embankment.

The sound of the blast spooked the bear into leaping forward. The animal closed the distance between them in a heartbeat, jumped right on top of the man, tore and slashed at him, then ran up the slope, pounding through the trees, disappearing into the forest.

Just like that it was over. The bear was gone. The man was down and bleeding. The gun lay smoking in the dirt.

Tink's ears rang like church bells in his head. He got dizzy trying to stand, so he sat back down. He couldn't move his shoulder. The kick of the gun must have injured him. He struggled to his knees. He made his way on his hands and knees over to the man. The man was bleeding everywhere. The bear had slashed open his chest and neck. Most of the blood was spilling from his neck. The trap had snapped clean through the man's elbow and wrist and was causing his fingers to twitch.

So this is what it was to hunt bear. This is what it was to have meat for the winter. The man's body shook, and he gurgled when he breathed. He looked at Tink. He just looked at him. There was much to read in that look. The man was dying. He knew it. Tink knew it. The man hated Tink and he hated dying. Tink wondered if the man could have ever imagined things turning out this way. He wondered if the man had taken Tink out into the woods to kill him, or had taken him on the hunt simply because he didn't think Tink would survive, and now it was the man who would not survive, and he wondered if, beyond all reason, the man had really done it for Tink's own good, as he had told the woman, Claudia, back at the cabin.

How had this happened? All the man had to do was shoot the bear when it was trapped and helpless, and the two of them along with the dogs might have been on their way home to the woman. And now look. Look at this mess. Look at the steam rising from the man's wounds. And what was that stink? Had the man let go of his bowels?

"Are you in pain?" Tink asked.

The man nodded. It might have taken all of his strength to nod.

"You're not going to live. There is no way to save you." The man nodded again. It was not so much a nod as a subtle movement of his forehead and eyes. "Do you want me to end your misery?" Tink whispered, perhaps not wanting the man to hear him. But the man heard, all right. *Yes*, the man said with his eyes. *Yes.*

Tink picked up the gun. It felt a bit lighter this time, maybe because the fear in him was not so heavy. Tink's shoulder stung a little, but it was not as badly injured as he had first thought. The man followed Tink with his eyes. Nothing else moved now, not even his twitching fingers or trembling body, just the eyes. Tink knew why the gun felt lighter. Things were over. Everything was done. He rested the stock of the gun on the ground, the barrel against the man's head. He did not want to pull the trigger, but the man might live a long time in pain before he died. Tink must be merciful. This was the way to do things here on Planet Earth. Mercy.

"You should say a prayer," Tink told the man, not sure exactly where he'd learned to say such a thing.

This time when he pulled the trigger he got down on the ground and braced his shoulder to receive the kick of the shotgun. He was ready for it. This time it did not hurt so much.

It was up to Jacob Piersol to clear out Tink Puddah's cabin, to pack things that might be of use to the community, and to ready the premises for a young couple, newly wed, who had asked him if they might take over the small cabin and work the foreigner's remarkable garden.

The young people who wanted to move into Mr. Puddah's cabin were still living on the boy's father's farm, the Roberts' farm, but the boy had gotten his father's blessing to strike out on his own. The young girl was already with child, and the preacher thought that Tink Puddah would have approved of them moving into his comfortable little home.

Officially, technically, legally, Tink Puddah had died intestate, without a will in the state of New York, and the government probably had a claim to his land. But that wasn't the way things worked around here—never had and never would as long as Jacob Piersol had a say in it.

Of course he could have delegated the task of disassembling Tink's belongings to another member of his church, Miss Anna and Papa Bear Goodlowe, for example. She and her father would have gladly volunteered. But this was something Jacob wanted to do himself. At least that was what he'd thought. Now, walking up the dirt trail toward Tink Puddah's cabin, he was no longer quite so sure. Why was Puddah still troubling him?

All week long Jacob had gone to sleep at night with Tink Puddah on his mind, dreamed of the foreigner, and had woken the next morning tired and frustrated. During the day Jacob could get lost in his work and his responsibilities and put the foreigner out of his mind, but whenever there was a lull, those thoughts returned. It was almost as if something remained undone between the preacher and the strange little man who'd lived up here on the hill.

Sometimes Jacob would remember the dead Tink Puddah that Tip Emerson had dug out of the grave, the ghastly smell, and the gaping shotgun hole in his head. Other times he would remember the stories Jed and Papa Bear Goodlowe had told at the funeral service. Most often he would think of the first day he'd met the foreigner, the day he'd walked this very path with his father's Holy Bible in his hands and thought to bring Tink Puddah the Word of God, and the foreigner had told him there was no such thing as God. He frowned at the memory. He had failed Tink Puddah, failed to save his soul. He wondered if God was going to hold that against him on his day of reckoning.

Black flies buzzed around Jacob's head as he reached Puddah's stone walk. A bit of morning dew had dappled the tall, green weeds. A squirrel foraged near the roots of an elm tree. The foreigner's old plow mule was tied to a post. Papa Bear and Miss Anna had been feeding and caring for the animal since Puddah's death, and unless there was a greater need for the mule among his congregation, he would give it to the young Roberts family.

He went over to the cistern, pumped himself a handful of fresh water, and brought it to his lips. It was good, sweet, clean water, no traces of sulfur, best well in the area. Most people had a pipe running into their cabins for pumped-in water, but Tink Puddah apparently saw no need for that.

The foreigner had a knack for living simply and making the most of nature. He sure knew his way around a garden. He planted just enough tomatoes and corn and lettuce and cabbage every year to keep himself fed. Everyone in Skanoh Valley grew corn to feed their animals and to make corn meal and corn bread and hominy, but no one grew it as rich and sweet as Tink Puddah.

He also grew things like sweet potatoes and beets that were not so easily won. Beets were hard to tend. You had to keep the weeds off them every day or they wouldn't grow, and they would likely die in a hot spell no matter how much you cared for them, a heap of trouble for a harvest that might not pan out. Sweet potatoes were tricky, too. You had to plant them in a good rich bed and cover them for a long spell to keep them dry. They had a tendency to rot, which meant a lot of work for nothing if you didn't have a little bit of luck.

So Tink worked extra hard on his beets and sweets and grew plenty more than he needed so he could sell and trade them off for tools and clothes and other goods and supplies. Got to be so nobody else bothered planting them because they knew they could count on Tink. The foreigner was smart that way. He knew what he could grow and what people needed and wanted. And he knew what they didn't.

Out back the preacher found some tools in a small shed. He would leave those for the young Roberts, too. Not all that much, really. Some shovels, hoes, spades, rakes, mattocks, a scythe. Tink had made himself a wooden-tooth drag harrow that the preacher figured he might as well leave to go along with the mule. Hanging on a peg there was a hand-tied trammel, probably made for snaring grouse.

Jacob walked up to the foreigner's cabin and hesitated. The air smelled fresh and new, with the tang of forest pine. It was good air, clean and crisp, the kind of air that inspired him to do God's work, and that's what this was, after all, God's good work.

He pushed his way in, ducking just a bit as he went through the door. It was a tiny cabin for a tiny occupant, reminding Jacob of a doll's house. The Roberts would likely need to add on before long. But it was a functional home. It had a good size fireplace, a small bed, a sawbuck table with two chairs in the kitchen. There, in the corner, a large soapstone. An oil lamp on a stand in the main room. A grindstone. A tin tub that would have been too small for a normal adult, in which the foreigner must have bathed. There was the smell of mildew about the place, along with firewood and ashes, mountain air and stone.

A mahogany trunk was positioned at the foot of the bed. Jacob looked inside and found some woolen socks, a couple of homespun shirts, a pair of leather shoes, galluses, and a collection of candles. And something else. What was this? A Bible? Jacob pulled the book out of the trunk. The Bible was fire-damaged, badly blackened. It was the Bible he had given Mr. Puddah when the foreigner first built his cabin up on this hill. The preacher had ordered it special from the printing press in Palmyra. He shook his head. What cause could a man have to burn the Holy Bible? If Jacob Piersol had any doubts that Tink Puddah was a heathen, this surely settled it once and for all.

He walked over to the hearthstone, picked up a poker, and stabbed at the logs and frilly ashes. Beside the fireplace and on the wall there were blood stains. Tink Puddah's blood. Jacob tried to imagine someone holding a gun to the tiny man and pulling the trigger. How could anyone do something like that? True, Tink was a foreigner, but frankly the man wouldn't hurt a fly, probably wasn't strong enough to beat one arm-wrestling.

Perhaps whoever had done the killing had been frightened by the looks of him—the bluish skin, the dwarfish stature and malformed mouth, the oddly inverted, cowlicked ears—Jacob could at least understand that. He shook his head and said a prayer over Tink Puddah's blood, as if that would somehow wash away the sins that had occurred here, whatever they might be.

A killing in peaceful Skanoh Valley. He hoped that Niles Holdstrum would keep his mouth shut about it, but somehow he doubted the man could keep his mouth shut about anything, even if he wanted to.

The only fancy thing in the foreigner's cabin was a Boston rocker. Jacob wondered how he'd gotten hold of it. It was a dark, cherry wood, spindle-backed chair with curved arms that looked like smooth, roiling waves. He sat in the chair and rocked for a while, trying to get a feel for the place. What would it have been like to be a godless heathen? What would it have been like to be Tink Puddah, small and frail, all alone in the world? He thought about his own father. What would you have done, Nathan Piersol, with this stubborn little man? Would you have somehow found a way to save his soul?

Jacob heard footsteps approaching the cabin. The door swept slowly open and light flooded the room, followed by a tall shadow.

"Jacob?" It was Bill Oberton.

"Yes."

The doctor stepped halfway in and took off his hat. "I knew you were coming up here today. I thought I'd see if you needed any help. I've got my wagon just down the hill, in case some things need carting away."

Jacob smiled. "You mean you wanted to make sure I was all right."

"I've been a little worried about you. I know Tink Puddah's death has got you troubled, especially since you learned he was killed."

"Come on in, Bill. The concern of a friend is always welcome."

Bill Oberton stepped inside the cabin, his boots landing heavily on the floor. There was a clean, grassy smell to the doctor that made Jacob appreciate him all the more. He twirled a chair around, straddled it, and sat down face to face with Jacob. "The way I figure it, a preacher always tends to everybody else's needs. I reckon he never gets much of a chance to work on his own."

"I'm afraid you're right about that."

Bill fiddled with his hat for a minute. "Talk to me, Jacob. We've been friends too long for you to have to suffer alone."

"There's not much to tell." The preacher rocked back and forth in Tink Puddah's Boston rocker, thinking about it. Actually there was a lot to tell; it was finding the words that proved difficult. "As I sat and listened to Jed Watkins and Anna and Papa Bear Goodlowe talk at the funeral, something started gnawing at me."

"I figured as much," the doctor said.

"Why was it that everyone in the valley except me seemed to know the story of Jed's snake canes? Why was it that Miss Anna had been able to tell her problems to Tink Puddah, a godless foreigner, when she had never been able to sit down and talk them out with me? Why is there such a chasm between me and the people I serve? My father never had that problem, never would have allowed it to happen. When did I let them slip away from me, Bill? Has the breach always been there, and if so, why have I been blind to it for so long?"

Bill reached inside his jacket and pulled out a shiny tin flask. He unscrewed the small, black cap and took a swallow. "Care for some spirits?"

"I might be persuaded."

Bill handed Jacob the flask. When he and Bill were younger they'd spent a number of evenings talking about religion and doctoring, passing a flask back and forth. In those days, they'd always seemed to raise more questions than answers. The questions seemed somehow more important then. Jacob wasn't so sure that was true anymore. "This must sound terribly mundane to you, Bill, all this dwelling on my failure, but to a man of God—"

"No, no, not mundane at all. I know exactly what you mean. Being a doctor isn't all that different sometimes. People look to both of us for help, help with things that more often than not they don't understand, and half the time *we* don't understand."

Jacob took a sip of whiskey and winced at it. "Home brew," he said, and leaned forward to hand the flask back to Bill. "Maybe what bothers me most was the way Tink Puddah reached out to them, and I couldn't. Why was he able to touch their lives? I have to wonder about my own efforts. Take Jed Watkins, for example. Here was a man after his logging accident as sorry and depressed as I'd ever seen a man in all my years as a preacher. He was angry at what had happened to him. When I went to console him, he lashed out at me, blamed God for his problems. And what did I do? I took offense, as if I had a right to be offended in the service of the Lord. Jed shunned God, so I shunned Jed. Near the same way I handled the problem with Papa Bear Goodlowe. Papa Bear swore off the church, so I swore off Papa Bear. Is that any way for a preacher to act?"

"You're being too hard on yourself, Jacob."

"Tell me, if a patient of yours broke a leg and refused to let you set it, would you turn your back on him and let the leg rot?"

"We both treat people in need, but doctoring up physical ailments isn't the same as trying to patch up the human soul. There's no equivalent in religion to setting a bone. You tried to reach both those men. You kept on Papa Bear for a long time."

"But in the end I gave up. No, if something's broken, you try to fix it. If somebody's sick, got the shivers and the fever, even if you don't know how to fix things, you reach in your bag and try calomel, jalup, or cinchona. For the good of the patient, you don't give up trying."

Bill made a movement with his shoulders that came close to a shrug. "In medicine there comes a time when you can't help a patient no matter what you do, and there are times, even, when what you do makes matters worse. I would imagine the same holds true in religion, except it's not quite so easy to tell exactly when you've botched things up." He took a swig from the flask and handed it back to Jacob.

Jacob held the flask steady for a moment, admiring its clean, silvery surface. He could almost see himself in it. "A preacher is supposed to know things like where to draw the line or when he needs to intervene, or else he's a lousy preacher. For a doctor, that decision is most likely made for you by the injury or the sickness you're treating." He took a sip, and then another, before giving up the flask.

"All right," said Bill cheerfully, clearly warming to the challenge of their conversation. "But think about this. Almost every doctor there ever was knows that when he fails a patient, more likely than not there's another doctor out there who might have succeeded. What I'm saying is, sometimes you do what you do, maybe it isn't enough, maybe somebody else could have done better, but you tried your best. Do you see what I mean? Feeling sorry for yourself won't fix a damn thing. You've got to learn from your mistakes, and hope you get another chance to make up for them next time around."

The doctor smiled as if he'd made the point to end all points. Perhaps he had. He took another swallow of booze and offered the flask to Jacob, but Jacob held up his hand in surrender. Everything his old friend had said made perfect sense, but none of it made him feel a stitch of thread better.

"Homebrew never used to bother you," muttered the doctor.

"What do you think happened here, Bill? Why would somebody kill Tink Puddah?"

The doctor frowned. "Doesn't make much sense, does it? All I can figure is, maybe, like the marshal said, some gang came by looking for food or horses, thought they were going to surprise some old coot in his cabin, and when they found a blue-skinned foreigner, maybe they took a fright and killed him."

"How did the place look when you found it? Any evidence of a struggle? Did Miss Anna tell you anything?"

"Miss Anna came to fetch me. She said Tink had planned to stop by their cabin and hadn't shown, which wasn't like him. She really didn't think there was anything seriously wrong. When I got here, I found him stretched out dead with half his head shot off." The doctor motioned to the bloodstains. "Not long dead. There was no sign of a struggle, but then what kind of a struggle could little Tink Puddah put up? If there was anything of value in the cabin, I imagine the killer, or killers, took whatever they wanted."

Jacob rocked in the chair and was surprised at how loudly the wood groaned. Or perhaps it was the floor that groaned. He hoped it wasn't his bones, the way they'd felt lately, stiff as boards. "You should have told me," he said.

"I know, Jacob. I know. But the marshal said not to breathe a word of it to anybody. He said it would be weeks before he could get here and I might cause a panic if I was to make people afraid. I guess I was hoping his death would pass over without much notice."

"Hmm, I guess I was, too."

"Might have if it hadn't been for that loud-mouth Holdstrum." Bill slipped the flask back inside his coat pocket. "I might as well tell you this flat out. I know you're not going to like it."

"That sounds ominous," Jacob said.

"Niles Holdstrum . . . well . . . Niles is stirring up more trouble."

"Good Lord, what could that Rutgers brat possibly be up to now? The horrible sight of Mr. Puddah's body wasn't enough for him?"

"He was giving a speech at the village square before I came out here. He started out fine, proposed that the community set up a scholarship fund in Tink Puddah's name for anybody in Skanoh Valley with a mind to go on to university study."

"Nice sentiment, although I can't say as I knew Mr. Puddah to be an especially learned man, nor do I see a real need for a scholarship in the valley. Nobody around here is interested in college."

"Nobody but Niles Holdstrum," Bill said. "But he didn't stop there. He started getting folks all riled up about Tink Puddah being shot to death right here in our community, right inside his own cabin. He's saying that if the killer isn't hunted down and brought to justice, nobody around here is going to be safe. He's saying it's going to get so thieves and killers think this valley is an easy mark, and anytime they want to rob or murder somebody, they'll know they can do it here in Skanoh Valley."

"This cabin isn't even in the valley."

"Which is probably why Tink Puddah is dead."

It was Jacob's turn to frown. "Niles is vying for the mayorship."

"I know that, and you know it, but the mayor doesn't have a clue. He's supporting Niles."

"What do they aim to do?"

"They aim to demand the marshal get down here from Palmyra to investigate," Bill said.

"What's the likelihood of that happening?"

"Pretty good if Niles really wants to make a stink about it."

Jacob sighed. "Well, maybe it's for the best. An investigation might make everybody feel better."

The doctor shrugged. "I doubt it. I know enough about these things to tell you they never improve anybody's humor."

Jacob ran his hands along the smooth, polished wood of the rocker's curved arms. "Bill, did you believe Tink Puddah was a foreigner? I mean, did you really think he came from another country?"

Bill considered this. "It never mattered. Nobody around here thought much about it one way or the other. He was different, that was all. Besides, what else could he be other than a foreigner?"

"I'm not sure," Jacob said. "His dead body, it was horrible. Is that normal for a decomposing body? *Any* body?"

"Not exactly, but men weren't meant to know all the answers. If a doctor and a preacher haven't learned that much, they haven't learned a damn thing."

Jacob rocked for a moment, listening to a flock of sparrows rise out of a tree just outside, all at once, as if spooked. "I sometimes wondered if maybe he wasn't so foreign, if maybe he was even born around here somewhere, an abomination at birth, and his parents hid him until he was old enough to care for himself, then kicked him out on his own."

"It's a thought," Bill said. "Sure couldn't rule out the possibility. Can't see where it matters much now, though. What's the point of speculating?"

"What did you tell the marshal about Tink Puddah? Did you tell him what he looked like?"

"No, I couldn't. How do you explain Tink Puddah? It's different if you've seen him. Sometimes if you stared at him long enough he almost looked halfway normal. But how would you explain him to somebody else? You'd sound like a damn fool."

Jacob rocked to his feet. "We've got a cart to fill," he said.

"There's not much here, Jacob. It's kind of sad."

"I don't know. There was an efficiency about the way Tink Puddah lived. No more and no less than what he needed, than what nature afforded him. He lived very much like a preacher would want to live. I think I could have learned from him, Bill, if I'd given him half a chance."

"I think you should take the chair," Bill said.

"What?"

"The rocker. Take it. Keep it. Maybe if you have something of Tink Puddah's around your house . . . I don't know, maybe it will help you remember that he was just a man like the rest of us—well, maybe not exactly like us—but flesh and blood, and he lived his own life and made his own decisions, and there was nothing you could have done to change that."

Jacob smiled. "That's an awful lot of responsibility to afford a rocking chair."

The doctor laughed. He stood and walked over to the trunk near Tink's bed. "Come on, I'll give you a hand with this. And remember what I said. You can't change the past, Jacob, you can only learn from it. You'll do better next time around. You'll see."

Jacob noticed the strong texture of the doctor's hands. A reflection of the man, he thought, of his internal strength, the hands of experience and loss and a lifetime of wisdom. A lot of power to afford a pair of hands, he thought, but it made perfect sense in that moment, and it all added up to one irrefutable fact: Bill Oberton was stronger than Jacob Piersol could ever hope to be.

"Maybe you're right, Bill, but how many chances does a man get to save a soul?"

The man was dead. His three best bear dogs were dead. The other three dogs had wandered off. Tink sat in the frigid air, watching the setting sun. His lungs burned. He was alone, completely lost in the woods. He thought that if he could follow his trail back to where he and the man had started the hunt, from there he could probably find his way home, but what were the chances of that, and how long would that take? Soon it would be dark. Tink was so exhausted his body scolded him for even thinking about such a journey. If you are fool enough, his body seemed to say, go on without me.

Besides, by tomorrow someone would surely be looking for him and the man, Darryl. Wouldn't they? The woman would fetch someone to come look for them. She was a worrier, that one, and she knew they were supposed to return home before dark. She would know something had gone wrong, although she probably had no idea how terribly wrong. And what about the man who had set the steel bear trap? At any moment he might return to check his trap. Tink might get help from that man when he came. It would be safer for Tink to stay, to wait, to hope for the best for a while before venturing out.

But could he really count on getting anyone's help? No, he could not count on anything on this planet. The man coming for the trap might just as easily kill him. Tink did not relish the thought of explaining his odd looks to strangers. The woman and the people who lived in the cabins around them knew Tink, knew what he looked like, knew he was different. Would someone else—anyone else—understand?

Regardless, Tink would have to prepare himself for spending the night alone here in the cold, dark forest. He would have to find a way to keep warm. He would freeze to death in his little fur-lined shirt and pants and his bearskin tunic, and his shoes made of hedgehog hide.

He cleared out an area and then built it back up with branches and vines and twigs, the same way he'd seen the woman build up the wood for her boiling pot. He found some flint and char cloth the man had been carrying and struck them together until he drew a spark. It took him awhile, many sparks, but finally he got the fire smoking. His fingers and toes were stiff from the cold. He would have to watch the fire carefully, fan it, feed it, keep it interested in staying lit.

Once the fire looked strong enough to burn on its own, Tink decided to try and take care of the dead man. He was afraid the smell of the body or the man's blood might attract wolves. He wished that he had something to wrap the body in, a cloth or a blanket, but he didn't. He took the huge hunting knife off the man's belt and began cutting long strips of curling ivy. The ivy was thick with green leaves, and had a strong scent. He pushed the ivy under Darryl's body, and then he rolled the man over and over until Darryl was wrapped in it. Tink then took the dead dogs and pushed them under the man.

The temperature had already dropped below freezing. Light snowflakes began to fall. The air felt brittle. The cold would help keep all of this death from smelling. So the cold would be good for him and bad for him; the cold might save him or kill him, like everything else on this planet, a planet of remarkable contradictions.

Tink thought about this as he tended the fire. If he could keep the fire going, it would save his life, but a fire out of control could easily kill a man, or a man's home, or a man's animals. Bear meat was good for you.

If you could kill a bear, the bear might keep you fed for an entire winter, but it was bad for you if the bear killed you first. The right berries were sweet and healthy, the wrong berries could swell your throat and strangle you to death. Without the seasons, there would be no rebirth on this planet, but birth of a kind meant death of another kind. Always the things that sustained you, things like muscles and knees and guns, could turn against you. Tink did not know where his parents had come from, but he knew—he sensed—that wherever it was, their home was nothing like this, nothing at all like this, and he longed for that place right now.

When the sun began to fall below the horizon, it painted a beautiful picture of dazzling ruby with brushstrokes of dusty gray across the sky, but it also grew unbearably cold down in the embankment, even beside the fire. Tink shivered so badly he wanted to throw himself on top of the flames and be done with it. Something he could not understand prevented him from doing this. Although he was not fully human, he knew he was at least partially human, and somewhere along the way, Tink realized unhappily, he'd developed an instinct for survival.

Tink suddenly felt hungry. He dug into his vest pockets and pulled out the corn bread the woman had given him. During the day it had been reduced to crumbs. Tink licked at the crumbs, but his hands shook so badly from the cold that he dropped most of them onto the ground.

It was dark, and he could not risk leaving the fire to search for berries. He went over to the man, rolled him over, took one of the dead dogs by its legs, and dragged it to the side of the fire. He took up the hunting knife and slashed the dog open. The dog was Clyde, Tink noticed, the man's lead bear dog. An awful stench poured out of the beast, along with a clot of steam. He reached inside with the knife and tried to cut away Clyde's guts and liver and heart and entrails. He did so clumsily. He tried not to get blood all over himself, but there was no avoiding getting blood on his hands and arms. Because of the cold it was slow blood, not as messy as it might have been.

He went over to the patch of ivy and cleaned himself as best he could then gathered more sticks for the fire. He sharpened two short, slim sticks with his knife and stuck the heart and liver of the dog on the ends of the sticks and perched the raw meat over the fire. Before he had been worried about the smell of death, and here he was cooking meat on an open fire. He didn't care. He was starving. Tink thought he had once heard the man say that predators would avoid a fire. He hoped so. Or maybe he didn't hope so. What difference did it make?

Tink tried to avoid thinking about how the meat tasted and smelled. He had never liked the smell or taste of meat. He needed to eat to survive, so he ate. When he sat down next to the fire again, he decided not to waste Clyde's carcass. He leaned over and stuck his hands and feet inside the dog's body. More blood, more stink, but the dog and the fire warmed him.

Clyde had swallowed his tongue, and Tink was surprised at what a horrible sight this was to him, how it made him want to vomit, or reach down inside the dog's throat and clear its airway, as if the dog might somehow breathe again, gutted husk that it was, if Tink could just help it along.

Tink closed his eyes and thought he might sleep for a while, but he couldn't do it. He was too afraid the fire would go out and he would freeze to death, or the predators would come, or rescuers would pass by just a few steps away and he would miss them. Why was he fighting so hard to stay alive? Why? He did not even belong on this planet. Why had his parents come here? He searched inside himself for the answers. Sometimes if he looked inward, he could find answers and strength from his parents, even if he wasn't sure about the answers and couldn't say exactly where the strength came from. But this night there were no answers, and little strength.

At some point, Tink fell asleep. He dreamed. He dreamed of a different world where all the space was wet. He dreamed of his parents and their moving cells, their inner choanoderms projecting slowly outward, their thick mesohyls and smooth, soft layers of wet flesh caressing him. Around him swirled a liquid world that washed his pearly central cavity.

Tink's dreams were more like memories. He always remembered them perfectly, and felt that somewhere at the core of his existence they were true, and he had actually been there, and had seen not just passing images in his mind but living memories complete with sensations. He felt himself rolling, elongating, rolling, elongating, the Wetspace moving through his chambers, inhalant surface to exhalant surface, through intercommunicating nerves.

Wetspace, yes, that was the word, although he did not know exactly how it had formed in his mind. Suddenly he'd seen it. He was part Wetspace, where all became one, and Wetspace was part of Tink, where one became all.

$$* \quad * \quad * \quad * \quad *$$

When Tink woke, the sun had risen, and his campfire had died. He was so cold and stiff he could not move for some time. He pounded his hands and feet against the ground just to see if he could feel them. Finally his fingers and toes tingled back to life. At least he had survived the night. What promise did the new day hold? He was faced with the same questions he'd faced the night before.

Should he try to find his way back home? Should he wait for help? Should he wait for the man who had laid the trap? He hated to wait. There was danger in not doing anything, the danger of a strange man finding him, the danger that he might not be discovered at all and would have to spend another night like the one he'd just spent. Could he survive two nights out here in the wilderness, in this frozen forest? But there was danger in moving, too, perhaps more danger. He might go the wrong way, and help would reach him too late or not at all. Where would he be then? Hopelessly lost.

Finally he decided that he must at least try to find his way back home to the Earth woman, Claudia, try to help himself before he gave up completely.

Tink rolled the man's body next to a large oak tree near the edge of the embankment. He tried not to look at the man, or the man's frozen face, almost as blue as Tink's skin. He pulled apart some of the ivy and searched the man for anything he thought might be useful. He found two more shotgun shells in the man's pocket. He loaded the gun and hefted it over his shoulder. He took the man's belt, too. He did not know why, but he thought he might be able to use it for something. He grabbed the man's huge hunting knife. He took the flint and char cloth with him just in case he needed to start another fire.

After that, he placed some sticks and branches over the body and piled on some rocks. Tink then decided to think clearly, to pretend that he knew what he was doing, that he was in absolute control of himself and his destiny and had every intention of surviving. He found, preposterous as it seemed even to himself, that this helped, and that he was suitably weak and stupid enough to believe it.

He climbed out of the gully and tried to figure out which way to go. This would not be so easy. There were no footprints or paw prints to follow because of the rocks and brush, and because of the snow that had canvassed the ground overnight. He would have to look for other signs— broken branches, crushed thatches, dog hair, perhaps, or traces of the man's chewing tobacco. An experienced woodsman might have had no difficulty finding the correct trail, but already Tink was in trouble. There were no signs anywhere. Which way should he go?

Tink tried to remember. Which way had he and the man come down into the embankment? Which way had the bear run? He did not want to follow the bear deeper into the woods. It was all a blur. Maybe he should wait, after all. No, no, he would just pick one way. What was the difference? He didn't care anymore. If the man had wanted him to die, if the man had taken him on the hunt because he was hoping Tink would not have the strength to survive, he would probably get his wish.

Tink chose a path and began walking through the woods. He moved swiftly enough to keep warm, but no faster. His legs and ankles and feet and all of his muscles still ached not only from the cold weather and great exertion of the previous day, but from his lack of rest. He had slept a little bit, but it had not been a restful sleep.

The temperature grew slightly warmer as the day grew old. Tink ate some red berries and tree bark. He found that the bark tasted the best to him and seemed to revive him. His stomach hurt, though. He excreted an unusually large amount of waste, wet and burning. The dog meat, he suspected, had made him ill. His hips and knees ached. He rested for a time and listened to the wind rattling the brittle, bony branches of winter dead trees, their fallen leaves rustling, the sound of sticks and stones playing in the forest.

Then he walked again.

He thought, with some dread, about finding Claudia and telling her how sorry he was that her husband had died and how the bear had killed him. Tink had put the bullet in Darryl's head, but the bear had done the killing. How would he tell her this? He hoped that she would hug him, and they would hold each other for a long time. She would be thankful Tink was alive and proud of him for surviving and showing her husband mercy. He hoped for the best. He missed her. Claudia. Maybe he could begin thinking of her as his mother from now on. He would try. Claudia. Claudia. *Claudia, I'm coming home.*

It seemed as if he had been walking a long time, forever to be exact, before the sun began to creep below the tree line. This time there were no pretty pictures painted on the horizon, only a cool, bleak, colorless canopy that gave Tink the impression of sitting at the bottom of a swamp, looking up through murky water at an endless, unreachable sky.

Tink walked along the edge of a sloping gully rimmed with shale. None of his surroundings looked familiar. He had probably traveled in the wrong direction. But he remembered the man saying once that there were more rocks and mountains in Pennsylvania than in New York. If he was walking toward Pennsylvania he was going the right way. Regardless, it looked as if he would have to survive another night alone in the wilderness. No one had come for him. There had been no sign of anyone all day.

He searched for the mouth of a cave, or perhaps an overhang or a fissure in the stone, anything to protect him from the cold. Finally he noticed a split in the gully wall. The split did not go very deep into the stone, but it was just right for him to sit up in, or even stretch out flat on the ground. At the mouth of it he built a fire. He warmed his fingers and his toes. After a while he thought he might even be able to sleep, or at least get some rest. He felt safer here than sleeping out in the open.

That was when Tink heard the dogs. Dogs barking, coming toward him.

Had Claudia's friends come searching? Perhaps they had found the dead man down in the embankment, and now they had come to save him. That must be it. Please, let that be it! But Tink was afraid, too. The sound of dogs terrified him. He would wait behind his fire. What choice did he have? It made no more sense to greet the dogs out in the open than it did to run from them. He would be safe here, where the dogs could not get too close. He would be safe until the men came to save his life.

And they came.

Tink could see them coming down into the gully. The dogs out in front, but the men not far behind. He could hear their voices now. "Good dogs! Good boys! 'At-a-boy!"

The dogs raced down the gully and came barking and growling up to his hole. Tink was surprised to find that he had at some point picked up the shotgun, and he was aiming it out at the dogs. He didn't know why he'd picked up the gun. He had no intention of shooting a dog. The dogs tried to get past the fire he'd built. Tink fended them off with the gun barrel as they danced around the flames. His heart pounded. What was taking the men so long? Why were they allowing their dogs to do this? If he hadn't found this shelter the dogs would have ripped him apart by now.

The men came, finally, shouting at their dogs, pulling them back, lashing them, leashing them. Two big men looked at Tink huddled in his tiny den behind the fire. "It's got Darryl's gun," one of them said, leveling a revolver at Tink's head.

"Don't shoot," said the other one. "We got to bring it back alive."

"C'mon out of there," the man with the revolver said, kicking dirt over the fire, stamping it until he snuffed out the flames. "There ain't no way for you to escape. Put the gun down and come out or else we'll cut the dogs loose on you."

Why would they want to loose their dogs on him? Tink would be glad to come out. He just wanted to go home to Claudia. His Claudia. He pushed the shotgun out of the den and crawled out. Before he could even stand up they grabbed him by the arms. One man hit him in the face. The blow exploded behind his eyes. Tink saw black stars. The pain stung his nose and pinched his eyes shut. They hit him again and again.

There was a lot of cursing going on. "Dirty scum," one of the men said. "Sonofabitch killed Darryl," another said. "Bastard blue boy—"

*No!* he wanted to scream. He hadn't killed anyone. It was just mercy. The bear had killed! You don't understand! But they had slugged his mouth so hard that now Tink couldn't speak.

The men got a rope and tied him up. They tied his wrists behind his back and they tied his ankles. Then they kicked him around some more. They swore and spat on him. Tink hurt so much that he became numb all over.

"Easy, now, easy," said one of the men. "Come on, fellas, take it easy. That's enough. We don't want to kill it."

"Why the hell not?" another said.

"Yeah, why not?"

"C'mon, Jordan, let's do it now. We take this bastard home and maybe Claudia decides she wants to keep it."

"Easy, boys," said the man defending Tink. "This ain't about Darryl anymore. Darryl is dead. This is about his wife. Claudia deserves the right to confront her husband's killer. She's got that right. How would you feel, Lester? Think about it. If somebody killed one of yours, you'd want to stand up to him face to face, wouldn't you? He'd be yours to kill, wouldn't he?"

"Or yours to let go," Lester said.

"Maybe so," said the first man, Jordan. "But he'd be yours. Besides, we'll fix it so she won't say no, you'll see, we'll fix it."

This seemed to settle the men down. They left Tink on the ground while they gathered their guns and dogs and the body of Darryl, which they had carried along with them.

Tink decided that he would never get home. These men would kill him, or they would let the dogs after him, all because of a misunderstanding. He would die just as his parents had died, by the fangs of dogs. This made no sense to him. This planet made no sense. Chaos, chaos.

Then, suddenly, inexplicably, Tink decided he was going to be all right. Yes. It was not so hard to think this way. The men were bringing him home to Claudia. She would hold him and take care of him. If the men didn't get drunk and decide to kill the bastard blue boy first, or decide to let him have an accident with the dogs, Tink might be home safely by tomorrow. Home where he could eat some corn bread and feel the warmth of the fireplace.

Calm down, forget about the cold and pain, Tink told himself. If you can survive a few more hours, you will have survived the entire ordeal. It would be nothing more than a matter of time. Time moved in fits and starts here on this planet, great chunks of tragedy and joy, agony and survival, hope and fear irreversibly linked, a linear progression of cause and effect. This was not necessarily so where Tink's parents had come from. Tink thought life and death and time were very different there. But here, now, he still had a chance.

One of the men lifted Tink and threw him over his shoulder. The man's body was warm, and his coat smelled of hay and chicken feed, farm animals and sweat, a sweat ages old that had worked its way into the deer-skin cloth of his coat, sweat that belonged not only to the man, but the man's father and grandfather, too.

Tink closed his eyes, concentrating on the warmth, nothing else. Ignore the dogs. Ignore the angry men who wanted to kill him. Don't say a word, Tink Puddah. Maybe they will forget you killed, although it had been nothing but a mercy killing. They didn't understand that yet, but they would. Now was not the time to explain. They would not listen. Tink would only make matters worse if he tried to speak.

The man carried him on his shoulder for a long time. Then another man carried him, a man who smelled of mule dung and pigs. Darkness came, and Tink was certain they must be very near the woman's house, for the men did not stop to rest, and they seemed to be walking faster. They lit torches, and very shortly after that, one of the men said, "We're home, boys." Tink could not tell whether the man was talking to the other men or to the crazy, barking dogs.

Tink smiled at the sight of the woman's house. How could he smile when he was so hurt and cold and his jaw felt like a brick? He was bruised all over. The blood from his nose had frozen to his lip. But he smiled anyway. It was over. He had survived. Now all he would have to do was explain things to the woman, Claudia, and everything would be all right. In the end, people would thank him for being merciful to the man.

The bear hunt was over. The man had died. There was no bear meat for the winter. But Tink didn't care about any of that. He longed for the woman's arms. Everything was going to be fine. The men had taught him a great lesson, even Darryl had taught him something valuable, although the man had probably meant to kill him. Tink had learned that making people understand was the key to survival. He only needed to make people see things as he had seen them. He only needed a chance to make them see. That would not be so difficult, would it?

The Skanoh Valley Vision of Christ Church doubled as a meeting hall, and on this spring evening it was crammed full of villagers, even more people than had come to Tink Puddah's funeral service. Strange, Jacob thought, that this gathering, too, was for Tink Puddah. A vote would be held tonight to decide on whether the marshal should be called in to investigate the foreigner's murder.

"I don't think there is any question," Niles Holdstrum hollered from the front of the church, "that we must *demand* an investigation and send word to the marshal *immediately!*" He pounded his fist on the podium.

Doctor Bill Oberton leaned over and whispered in the preacher's ear, "I don't know why he's getting so riled up. Nobody has disagreed with him yet."

"Yet?" Jacob said.

Bill answered with one swift nod and added, "I aim to have my say."

Jacob felt uncomfortable sitting in a pew. This was his church after all, and he belonged at the pulpit, but when meetings were held here he was just another villager. Niles railed on for a bit, talking about securing a safe and peaceful home if not for us then at least for "our little people, our children, our future."

The crowd was behind him—that was plain to see—they were nodding and clapping and some even stomping their feet. When he finished he sat down and Mayor Funkel moved to the podium, shifting his great weight forward, and asked if there was anyone else in the hall who would like to speak before he asked for a show of hands.

Bill Oberton stood and waited for people to quiet themselves before speaking. "I don't need to hide behind a podium. I'll give it to you straight from right here. I was the one who found Tink Puddah dead. He'd been shot in the head, the work of a ruthless killer, or a band of killers who then took whatever they might have found valuable and high-tailed it out of here into the hills. I corresponded with the marshal myself. Marshal Braddock was his name, from Palmyra, and he said that whoever was responsible for the murder would be long gone. The marshal was already working on tracking them down. He said there was no sense in him coming all this way to follow a cold trail."

He had the attention of most everybody now, except for Niles Holdstrum, who made a show of yawning.

Bill went on, "What I'm trying to tell all you folks is, it would be more of a help if we left well enough alone. We'll only slow the marshal down if we make a big stink and he has to come down here. If we leave it be, he'll be able to track the killers that much quicker. What we're doing here, in my opinion, is we're over-reacting to the situation, thanks to Mr. Holdstrum. It was a horrible thing what happened to Tink Puddah, I agree, it was a frightening thing, and we'll all miss him, but if we really want to help bring his killers to justice, leave the law to the law."

A murmuring set about the place. At least there were some folks who'd listened to the doctor's reasoning. He'd made a lot of sense, but it had been Jacob's experience not to lay a heap of stock in common sense, especially when emotions ran high.

Holdstrum rose out of his chair and said, "That was a very nice speech, Doctor Oberton, and you've raised some interesting points." He swaggered up to the podium again. Niles sure did enjoy being the center of attention. "I'm sure that it's true the marshal is a very busy man, and he's probably chasing gangs and killers all around the state, and far be it from we people, we simple, honest, trusting, hard-working, law-abiding folks, to bother such an important government official."

A few people in the audience chuckled. Niles played the interlude for all it was worth. "But let's think about this for a moment, shall we? The longer Tink Puddah's killer remains at large, the more he's going to begin to think he's gotten away with murder in Skanoh Valley. Maybe he meets a few of his friends and brags about it. Maybe he and his friends decide to hang around in the hills, watching, waiting to see if the people of this community care enough about one of their fellow citizens to contact the marshal in Palmyra. If they see we don't, maybe they decide to come back and try their luck again, steal some horses, who knows, if the mood strikes them, maybe take another life or two, only this time it might be yours!"

He paused again, glaring out at the crowd. Jacob wondered if the brat had studied drama at Rutgers University. Niles pointed directly at the doctor. "Or yours! Or yours!" He poked the air. "You see, for us, the *victims* of this horrible crime, and mark my words we are all victims until justice is served, I assure you, there is more at stake than the marshal's busy itinerary."

This brought a roar of approval from the crowd. Niles was quite the formidable little speechmaker. He would make a fine mayor someday.

Bill whispered into Jacob's ear, "Now that Tink Puddah is dead he's a fine, upstanding citizen of Skanoh Valley. When he was alive he lived so far out in the hills you couldn't even see his place from the tallest tree in town. Niles couldn't have found Tink's cabin with a compass and a map—"

"And furthermore!" Niles pounded the podium again, calling for quiet and getting it. "Furthermore, who are we to say that Tink Puddah's killing was the work of a drifter or a gang? How do we know that it wasn't someone in our own community? How do we know that it wasn't someone sitting right here in this hall? What were you trying to hide, Doctor Oberton, by covering up Tink Puddah's brutal slaying?"

"That's enough!" Jacob shot out of his seat. He had a full, deep, sonorous voice, and when he wanted to use it he could demand plenty of attention himself: "Quiet, everyone! This has gone far enough. There will be no finger-pointing in this church!"

Jacob looked squarely at Niles Holdstrum. "Mr. Holdstrum, you have made your case, so you can stop campaigning now. We have come here to vote on calling in the marshal, not on a new mayor. Come election time you can play the fiddle all you like, but these are hard-working people, and you've already taken up too much of their valuable time. Mayor Funkel, I think we can proceed with a show of hands, don't you agree?"

The mayor suddenly looked a bit pale. The flesh around his eyes rose slightly in dismay. He gathered himself, moved to the podium, and nudged Niles Holdstrum out of the way. "Yes, yes," he said, "I think we've heard quite enough from our clever Mr. Holdstrum. Everyone in favor of requesting the marshal to come to Skanoh Valley and investigate Tink Puddah's murder, raise your hands and say, 'aye.'"

"*Aye!*" came the response, nearly unanimous.

"Those opposed, raise your hands and say, 'nay.'"

There were a few nays, Bill and Jacob among them, but it was clear who had carried the day.

"It's decided then," the mayor said. "Tomorrow, *I*, the elected Mayor of Skanoh Valley, shall personally send word to the marshal in Palmyra that the people of this community are demanding justice be served. I promise you that *I* will get results. Thank you all for coming. This meeting is adjourned." He struck his gavel on the podium.

The people started talking all at once as they rose from their pews. Doc Oberton said to Jacob, "Thanks for taking control of the meeting. That little college brat was just looking for trouble."

Jacob patted his old friend's arm. "Did you see the look on Mayor

Funkel's face when he finally realized what the kid was up to?"

The doctor laughed. "You'd have sworn he'd seen a ghost."

"Ha! I don't think old Funk will give Niles Holdstrum quite so much room to talk from now until next election."

They walked out into the night air. A warm breeze moved through the center of the village. Jacob stopped for a moment to enjoy it. The marshal from Palmyra, he thought, will be summoned to Skanoh Valley. Would Tink Puddah never give him any peace? Didn't these people realize it was sometimes better to leave the dead be? Jacob shook his head. No, these thoughts were foolishness on his part. Everything would work out for the best if he left it in the hands of the Lord. When you came right down to it, that was all that anyone could ever do. Trust in the Savior. Trust and ye shall be free.

$$* \quad * \quad * \quad * \quad *$$

*That night, Mary Magdalene came running up the steps of the Vision of Christ Church while Jacob read by candlelight from his father's Holy Bible. Mary barged through the front door, and Jacob looked up from the Scriptures. Mary was out of breath, trembling.*

*"What's wrong, Mary?" Jacob asked.*

*"They have taken the Lord out of the sepulchre, and we know not where they have laid him!" She fell to her knees and cried.*

*Jacob stood. His Bible fell to the ground and landed with a clap of thunder. "They've taken the Lord's body? Who? Why?"*

*But Mary could not answer through her sobbing.*

*Jacob ran out of the church. He ran to his house, lit an oil lamp, and headed up the hill toward Skanoh Valley's small cemetery. He slipped on patches of muddy sod and wet leaves. Tree branches clawed and stabbed at him through the darkness of the surrounding wood. Jacob felt the damp night wind wrap around him like a cloak.*

*When he came to Tink Puddah's grave he saw that it had been dug up.*

*He fell to his knees and searched the dark grave with his hands, but found nothing there except a shallow hole and its dank soil.*

*The soft glow of the oil lamp flickered at his side, and he heard something howl in the night, a coyote or a wolf. Everything outside the circle of light was cloaked in the raven-black wings of night. The smell of damp earth chilled him. Then Jacob began to weep, out of frustration, out of helplessness, for he knew not what to do.*

*Out of the moonless night, two angels dressed in snow white robes approached him. They seemed to float over the graves in the cemetery. One of them went to the head of Tink Puddah's resting place, and the other went to the foot.*

*Jacob knelt before them and prayed: "If you have borne my master away, please tell me where you've laid him. Please."*

*And then one of the angels came forward and grasped Jacob's shoulder, shaking him, shaking him . . .*

"Jacob! Jacob!"

*Through the haze of Jacob's lantern, the two angels came slowly into focus.*

"Jacob!"

It was Bill Oberton, and standing next to him the gravedigger, Tip Emerson. They both stared down at Jacob, looking concerned.

"Jacob, are you all right?" Bill asked. "Tip saw you running up the cemetery hill with your lamp. What is it? Why are you out here digging at Tink Puddah's grave?"

Jacob glanced down at the ground beneath his knees. He was, in fact, at Tink Puddah's grave, but it was not exactly dug up, except for what little bit of dirt he'd clawed off with his own hands.

"A dream," he whispered, more to himself than to Bill or Tip. How long had he been out here clawing at the earth?

Tip scratched his scalp, like a dog itching at fleas. "What kinda dream coulda sent you runnin' out here?"

Don't ask, Jacob thought. He didn't want to so much as think about it, let alone discuss it. He was wearing his nightclothes and his long, cotton robe. His heart pounded, and sweat streamed down the sides of his face. He looked at his hands covered with dirt; they were trembling the way Mary Magdalene had been trembling in his nightmare. No, he didn't want to discuss it. "A very bad dream, Mr. Emerson. A very bad dream indeed."

"C'mon," Bill said, helping Jacob up off his knees. "We're going to walk you back down to your cabin and make sure you get into bed and stay there."

"Thank you," Jacob said. And he meant it.

The men threw Tink Puddah on the ground and went into the house to talk to the woman, Claudia. Tink hoped this would not take long. He could not survive much more of the cold, the untended cuts and bruises, the pain in his bones. He was sure the skin on his wrists and ankles where he'd been tied with the rope had worn clean through to his tendons. He shivered fiercely.

Finally a man came out for him and yanked him to his feet. Tink understood he was probably expected to hop along beside the man, but he was too weak, and he let the man drag him all the way into the house. He could not help himself. He had no more strength. They would be sorry later, all of these men, for their cruel treatment of him. They would be sorry when they learned the truth, and Claudia scolded them.

The man brought Tink in the cabin and dumped him on the floor. Tink could hear the shuffling of feet. He could smell tobacco smoke and logs burning. It was dark except for the fire, which warmed him instantly. Tink was amazed at how hard the warmth hit him. It actually hurt. The cold had numbed most of his pain, but now, even the suggestion of heat bit deeply beneath the core of his worn body. This, too, would pass. Maybe not for a while, maybe not for the first few days or even weeks, but eventually his body, if not Tink himself, would forget all about the punishment he had endured, or he would not be able to go on.

No one had yet said a word to him. They had dropped him on the floor and left him there. Why weren't they untying the ropes from around his wrists and ankles? The ropes were killing him. Where was Claudia? Tink rolled over so that he was on his side. The men were standing silently. Now he could hear sobbing. A woman was crying. Claudia? Tink knew it must be her, although he could not see her.

*There!* There she was at last, walking toward him, a man beside her helping her walk, the man named Jordan. She was weeping. This hurt Tink. He was surprised at how attached to her he'd become. He hadn't meant for this to happen, this feeling of attachment. Perhaps it had not happened at all until he had gone on the bear hunt with the man. It was then that he realized how much he missed her and needed her and wanted to be with her. Maybe the man's death would be good for them both. They could be happier together than ever before. The woman had never been happy with her man, Darryl. Tink knew this. He could tell. Maybe that was why the man hated Tink so much.

When the woman approached Tink, two men came over and jerked him off the floor. Tink winced. The woman looked him directly in the eyes. Tears streamed down her cheeks.

"My Darryl is dead," she said. "They tell me you killed him. They tell me you shot him in the head with his own gun." Her body shook when she spoke these words. "Do you know what it is for a woman to be widowed? Do you know?"

Tink felt so sorry for her, to have to feel such unbearable grief. Tink's body had shaken, too, when he almost froze to death, a different kind of shaking, but just as terrifying. All of this was the man's fault—Tink's pain, the woman's anguish. Things had been fine until he'd decided it was time for Tink to hunt bear. Darryl should have known better.

"Did you kill him?" the woman said through her tears.

"I shot him," Tink said. He hadn't spoken in so long that his throat stung, and his voice sounded dry and scratchy. "But it was the bear that took his life. He was hurt, dying. I gave him mercy."

"How could you?" she asked, sobbing.

What did she mean, how could he? "He was dying. He was in pain. I—"

"You killed him! You just up and killed him after he saved your life and took you in and fed you and gave you a home! You just up and killed my husband, my Darryl, up and shot my man . . . killed him . . . shot him . . . do you know what you've done? Do you know what you've done to me?"

"No," Tink said. He did not know. Why wasn't she listening? "Your husband was clawed by the bear. Ask the men. They must have seen what the bear did."

"There weren't nothing wrong with Darryl," said one of the men, "'cept for a shotgun shell through his head."

"They say they found you running away with his gun and his belongings," Claudia said.

"I was trying to find my way back home. I—"

"You killed him!" she screamed. She almost fell to her knees, but the man beside her gave her an arm and a shoulder to catch. "Do you know what it is for a woman to be alone? I've lost my husband, my husband," she said, weeping.

"C'mon, now, let's sit you down and get you some tea, okay?" said the man. "Don't you worry, we'll take care of this here boy. We'll give him justice come morning."

"No, wait!" Tink said.

Someone slapped him so hard across the face that his neck twisted around like a loose rope. He saw black stars again, and a horrible dizziness broke like waves against the side of his head. How could these men say they hadn't seen what the bear had done to the man? The bear had cleaved the man wide open. *Look at the body!* Tink wanted to scream to the woman. Please, just look, then you will know the truth, then everything will be right between us. *Look at the body!* But his mouth was swollen, and he had no strength to gather air in his lungs, and the woman was already gone, and the men hauled him outside, outside into the cold night, some of them laughing, some of them whooping.

"You're gonna git lynched t'morrow, blue boy, we're gonna hang you high from a tree!"

What was wrong with these men? Why did they want to kill him for no reason? Tink had only shown their friend named Darryl mercy. That was the way of this planet. That was the way. Mercy.

They threw Tink into the hay barn.

"You can sleep like an animal tonight," said one of the men. "Even that's too good for the likes of you. You won't never put 'nother gun to a white man's head after tomorrow."

They slammed the barn door, but they were no longer laughing. Tink listened to them walk all the way to the house, the woman's warm house. Claudia.

What had happened here? What had gone wrong? The men were going to hang him, a lynching, they said. Tomorrow they would tie a rope around his neck and swing him from a tree, and he'd done nothing, nothing but show the man named Darryl mercy when he'd probably wanted Tink dead. Why? Why did they hate Tink Puddah, who had never harmed anyone?

"Look at the body." The words, the words, Tink had finally gotten them out. "Please, look at the body." But there was no one left to hear.

Tink began to cry. He had never cried before. He thought he might be incapable of it. Now he knew otherwise. He cried for a long time and couldn't stop. Tomorrow he would die. He said this over and over to himself. Tomorrow Tink Puddah dies. Tomorrow, die, tomorrow, die, tomorrow, die.

It was the thought of death, finally, that brought an end to his tears, the same thought that had started them flowing in the first place. Tink did not belong here on this planet. He was not human. People hated him for no reason. People lied and wanted him dead. He decided that in death he might come to know who and what he was supposed to be, in death he might become one with his parents. He felt them inside him now, now more than ever, calming him, reassuring him. Death was not the same thing for Tink as it was for the men and women of Earth. He knew that now. Death would be better. How could it not be?

Tink crawled deeper into the hay and curled up to keep warm. After tomorrow he would no longer be tormented by the cold. He would not have to live in fear of dogs. His fight for survival on this planet would be over. It was too bad that he'd learned so much about survival only to die the next day, but that's all that was too bad about it. He would welcome the dying itself. He would miss the smell of hay, and the woman's corn bread that was the best thing he'd ever tasted, and he would miss the woman's warm arms. But there would be a different kind of warmth awaiting him.

Tink heard a sound at the barn door, someone fumbling with the latch. Perhaps the men couldn't wait until morning. Perhaps they'd decided to get it over with in case the woman changed her mind. Sure, why not get rid of Tink Puddah so they could get home to their families, to their warm beds? Have some whiskey and lynch the blue boy, the helpless little blue boy bastard. Good. Fine. All the better.

But it was not the smell of whiskey, or the laughter, or the anger of men that entered the hay barn; it was a strong, musky animal scent along with an inhuman silence; whatever it was did not belong here; it was something wild, something afraid.

Tink did not know whether to burrow deeper into the hay, or to roll out where he could see what it was. What sense was there in hiding? Tomorrow he was going to die. It was foolish for him to fear anything at this point. He crawled out of the hay on his elbows and looked out toward the open barn door.

There, illuminated by the light of the moon, was a huge black bear.

Tink, in spite of his newly discovered courage, gasped in fear. This was not just any bear. This was the giant bear he'd faced in the gully. This was the bear that had killed the man named Darryl. He knew it. He would never forget that bear as long as he lived, even if it were just one more night.

A dream. This must be a dream. He had fallen asleep in the hay and soon the men would come and shake him, pick him up, string a rope around his neck, accuse him of murder, and then take him out of his misery. Another mercy killing. First this dream, and then eternal peace.

But in the meantime this was a very real dream. The bear snorted and moved forward. Tink decided not to be afraid. He would be curious instead. What did the bear want? The gigantic beast strode right up to Tink and lowered his nose. Tink did not shrink away. He realized, looking into the round black eyes of the mammoth beast, that he'd never been afraid of the bear, not really. He'd been afraid of the man and his dogs, but not the bear. He'd been afraid of the hunters, not the hunted. This made a great deal of sense, suddenly. There was a certain rightness about it. Even Tink's parents thought so; he could feel it.

The bear bit at the tangled rope tied around Tink's ankles; it only took a moment for the bear to bite clean through the rope, freeing Tink's numb feet. Tink felt nothing, not even the earth beneath them. He thought that this must be a blessing. He couldn't imagine the pain he would feel when his feet finally awakened. The bear then began biting at the ropes knotted around Tink's wrists.

Tink did not understand any of this. Did the bear follow the men all the way back here? How did he know Tink was in trouble? Why did he want to free him? If he thought about it long enough, Tink would have to admit that he was either dreaming or crazy, so he decided not to think about anything. Better to pretend the bear was actually here, biting at his ropes, setting him free.

Tink rubbed at his torn and swollen wrists. He tried to stand, fell, tried again, fell. The bear offered his furry shoulder for Tink to grab hold of. Tink took it and pulled himself to his feet, and together they managed a few awkward steps toward the barn door. The night air was cold, so very cold, but the bear seemed to be made of heat.

The barn door creaked in the wind. The moon was high and bright. Tink and the bear walked toward freedom. What a ridiculous thought, freedom. There would be no surviving in the wild, no surviving on his own. Tink was as good as dead. What was he doing? Why not let the men kill him tomorrow? That would be best. Get it over with. Why was he struggling to survive? He didn't want to live, yet something inside kept pushing him, pushing.

*Survive, survive.*

Tink turned his head away from the moon that seemed to be promising impossible hope. He saw something on the ground beside a bale of hay. Maybe it was something trying to call him out of this dream and return him to reality. Ah, yes, there on the ground lay the body of the dead man, Darryl. It was a cold, hard, ice-blue body. It did not have much of a shape, but its head was oddly caved in. Here in the darkness, one might have thought that it really was the shotgun shell that had killed the man, not the bear at all. Well, they had done it together, really, Tink and the bear. And here they were, the two murderers together again.

This was so impossible that Tink thought maybe he had in fact died. Maybe the cold had taken him after all, and he was now playing out some bizarre theater of the dead, walking through an afterlife not with his parents, as he had always imagined, but with this bear, this giant heroic beast that might have also died for all Tink knew. If that were the case, things might not be so bad after all. He would have died before the men could satisfy their sick pleasure in hanging him.

There was a burlap sack lying beside the man. Tink let go of the bear and looked inside it. It was Darryl's shotgun and hunting knife. Someone must have thrown the sack down beside him and forgotten about it. Tink pulled the gun out of the sack and held it in his hands. He was surprised at the anger that filled his heart. With the gun in his hands, he wanted to kill. He wanted to walk up to the house and destroy the men who had treated him with such cruelty. He wanted to teach them a lesson, every last one of them, and show them something of their own injustice. He lifted the knife. If he couldn't kill them all with the gun, he would finish them off with the man's hunting knife.

But the bear was waiting for him, sniffing the air, glancing back over his shoulder. *Come,* the bear seemed to be saying, *Come with me.* And Tink knew that he could never kill anyone again, no matter what, not even in the name of mercy.

He put the shotgun and knife back in the burlap sack and slung it over his shoulder. He would take the weapons with him. He needed them more than this dead man, Darryl, needed them. Staggering under the weight of the sack, under the weight of his injuries, he followed the bear outside. The bear leaned over, as if offering Tink a ride. Tink grabbed hold of the thick black fur at the bear's nape and climbed onto its back.

"Let's go," he said to the bear.

Let's go far away. Let's walk off the edge of the world, you and I, and find a place where there are no hunters or hunted, where there are no men to define life and death and mercy to suit their needs. Let's go where no one will bother us again.

But even as these thoughts entered Tink's mind, he knew there was no such place here on this planet, on this bitter, alien land called Earth.

# THE BOOK OF PARDON

Jacob Piersol had invited Doctor Bill Oberton, Mayor Funkel, and Marshal Braddock over to dinner. He'd asked Betty Louise to cook something special and stay a little later than usual to help out. She was always agreeable when Jacob entertained guests, had a real liking for serving up big meals and watching men eat. She felt in her own way, Jacob knew, that she was serving the Lord, and in her own way she was. He couldn't help but enjoy the fruits of her labors.

She'd cooked up a tasty rabbit stew for a main course, fried squash and beans, mashed potatoes drowned in one of her special gravies. She'd whipped up some corn biscuits and a pigeon pie, and Jacob and his guests had filled their bellies shamelessly.

"You got yourself a real fine cook there, Minister," said Marshal Braddock.

"Don't I know it." Jacob didn't much like being called a minister—his father had been called a preacher, and Jacob preferred that designation as well—but to be polite he didn't bother to correct his guest. He went over to his desk and rolled back the chiseled hood, where he kept a stash of his finest cigars. "I don't suppose I could interest any of you gentlemen in a cigar?"

"I've never been known to refuse a good cigar," Mayor Funkel said.

"Oh, now, that would be downright sinful," said Doc Oberton, laughing.

"In that case," the marshal said, "I'll take two." And sure enough when Jacob offered him the box, the marshal reached inside and picked out two cigars.

Anyone from town could have told you that Marshal Braddock wasn't from around Skanoh Valley. Muttonchops and the handlebar mustache were popular in the larger townships, and you didn't see very many fancy frock coats in this little farming community. He had a way about him, too, a certain curtness that bordered on rude. Jacob wondered if it was partly an act. Certainly the man was rough around the edges, as Jacob would have expected of any man who was used to dealing with killers and thieves, of any man who spent a lot of time tracking and thinking like them, maybe even living like them. Perhaps the marshal had plenty of reason to take two cigars out of Jacob's box and feel just fine about it.

The men lit up, puffed on their cigars, and sat quietly in the main room. Betty Louise opened the door to let some cool, fresh air into the room.

"Have you heard the latest news about Kansas?" Marshal Braddock asked.

"I think the Senate will vote Kansas into the union," Mayor Funkel said. "But the question remains, does Kansas want into the Union?"

"They'll vote against slavery," Jacob said. "The entire country needs to open their hearts to these Negro people."

Braddock exhaled a cloud of smoke. "Maybe so, Minister, but I see the North and South moving farther apart."

Doc Oberton frowned. "I hope you're wrong."

"Me, too," Jacob said. "I'd hate to see this country go to war against itself."

The men were quiet for a long time. Jacob was so enjoying the silence, the taste and harsh smell of good strong tobacco, and the crispness of the evening spring air that he was reluctant to speak. But he was curious about the marshal's investigation into Tink Puddah's death, and finally asked Braddock how he was faring with it.

"To be honest, there just ain't much I can do at this point," said the marshal. "You've got a killing near a month old. No murder weapon. No evidence or witnesses. The victim's home has been cleaned up and cleared out of most of its belongings, which pretty much inhibits any examination of evidence."

Jacob sighed. "That's my fault, I'm afraid. It's common practice around here not to allow waste. We had some needs to fill in the community, and a young couple was planning to move into Mr. Puddah's cabin. I didn't think it was important to leave the place be."

"No need to apologize, Minister. You had good reason to do what you did. But as it stands, we can only guess at what happened, and my best guess, like I was telling the mayor here earlier today, is that your friend, Mr., eh . . . "

"Mr. Puddah," Doc Oberton said.

The marshal nodded. "Right, Puddah. Your friend was either killed by a drifter or a gang, and in either case the guilty party is long gone. It's a tragedy, to be sure, but most times we'll catch up with the culprit sooner or later when he tries it again. Maybe he'll rob or kill somebody else and he won't get so lucky. He'll leave behind a witness, or somebody will take a shot at him and maybe wound him or even kill him. Most often a reward does the trick. Eventually we'll get him. We get him alive, he might or might not confess to the murder of your friend, Mr. Tink Puddah, but if he does, I'll be sure to let you know."

"That's exactly what we tried to tell Mr. Holdstrum," the mayor said. "We told him that fella wouldn't be long for these parts. I apologize for having to drag you all this way for nothing."

Jacob glanced at Bill Oberton and the two men shared a private smirk at the mayor's sudden change of heart.

"Oh, don't be sorry, Mayor Funkel. If it gives your folks here in Skanoh Valley peace of mind knowing the law is here when you call for it, then it wasn't a waste of time at all." He turned the cigar casually between his fingers. "There was something I thought a little odd, though."

Bill edged forward in his chair. "Oh? What might that be?"

The marshal seemed reluctant to let that go. "I wonder if the preacher has any whiskey in the house."

Right on cue, Betty Louise entered the main room with a tray of glasses.

"Will Kentucky bourbon do?" Jacob asked.

"Ah, more than acceptable. Your hospitality is to be commended." The marshal took a glass, gulped it down, and before Betty could turn away he waved his glass at her, indicating he'd like another. "What I found odd was the way some people seemed to refer to the victim as 'the blue boy.' Why is that, I wonder?"

The mayor cleared his throat. "Oh, yes, well, you see, our Mr. Puddah looked a little different, that is, he didn't exactly have a normal look."

"What kind of a look did he have . . . exactly?"

"I think he was just different right from birth," the mayor went on. "He was very small, small in the way that one might consider deformed if one were pushed to it, dwarfish, really, and Mr. Puddah had a face that was kind of squashed in, and his skin, well, his coloring . . . "

"He was blue," Bill Oberton said.

"Oh, I see. *That* kind of different," Braddock said.

Jacob carefully set his cigar down on the edge of a malformed, clay ashtray, a particular favorite of his made by Betty Louise's young daughter at the day school. "He was from a foreign land, Marshal Braddok. Nobody knew where. The fact is he was kind of secretive about it. But when people say he was blue they mean it. He wasn't black. He wasn't a Negro, if that's what you're thinking."

The marshal nodded, taking in the information without much expression or, thought Jacob, much interest. He seemed more fascinated by his second drink of bourbon, which Betty Louise had left on the end table next to his chair.

"The truth of the matter is," Jacob said, "we accepted the foreigner—Mr. Puddah—for who and what he was. It didn't matter the color of his skin or what he looked like. The people around here respected him, which is why we are so concerned about justice being served, you understand."

Jacob was suddenly sorry he'd asked about the murder at all. Did he really want to know how the investigation was faring, considering that there was no investigation to speak of? The marshal's presence here was simply a matter of propriety, a formality at best. Jacob wished it were over and done with. It had been the talk of the valley for a month, and for that month he couldn't get the little foreigner out of his mind. Although he hadn't suffered any more bouts of sleepwalking, his dreams had persisted, nonsense dreams all mixed in and mixed up with Christian symbolism.

In one dream Jacob was out fishing beside Lake Galilee, and Tink Puddah walked up to him and said, "How's the fishing?" Jacob answered, "Not so well, today. All my nets are empty." Then Puddah said, "Come with me, and I will teach you to catch men."

In another dream Jacob was a tiny sheep, the one white sheep among hundreds of blue sheep, and all of a sudden Jacob looked up and found himself alone, lost, and frightened. Then he saw Tink Puddah striding toward him, staff in hand. From over the hill he heard the other sheep crying, and Jacob ran toward Puddah, thankful to be found. He felt so relieved that he nearly leaped into the foreigner's arms. Puddah said to him, "Let us return to the herd now, my little friend, and I will sing a song for you and dance for joy, for I am far happier over saving one lost sheep than over the hundreds who were never lost."

Just last night the preacher woke in a sweat when he'd dreamed he was a Canaanite dwarf working near the city of Sidon, along the Mediterranean Sea, and Tink Puddah came walking along the docks. Jacob threw himself at Puddah's feet and said, "Son of David, I beg you, save me for I am afflicted with a terrible disease. I'm a dwarf. And Look at my white skin!" And Puddah answered, "I have not been sent to save your pitiful white souls. It is not right to take the children's food and throw it to the dogs." And Jacob responded, "But even the dogs eat the leftovers that fall from their masters' tables." Tink Puddah thought about this for a moment and said, "You are a white dwarf Canaanite of great faith. What you ask will be granted." And Tink Puddah reached out and transformed Jacob into a blue-skinned man, and healed him of his dwarfism.

Jacob Piersol's dreams troubled him. Why was he dreaming of Tink Puddah as Jesus the Savior? What were his dreams trying to tell him about Tink Puddah? What were they trying to tell him about Jacob Piersol? None of it made sense to him.

His father would have known, would have known immediately with the confidence of John the Baptist. *"It's like this, Jacob!"* his father would have scolded. *"Can't you see it? You're missing the meaning."* Then his father would have shaken the Bible at Jacob and said, *"Look beyond the words in front of your nose, son. It's not just text, it's sacred text. It is speaking to you. What is it saying?"*

Oh, it was true, Jacob had read the words of The King James Bible over and over again, and through practice he'd developed the craft of explaining those words, but the meaning, that was another matter entirely. He was not the natural-born preacher his father had been. His father had a way of turning a parable to fit every need. As a boy, Jacob often missed the point of a parable even after his father explained it to him. Jacob Piersol's father had tutored him to be a man of God. He'd learned by watching his father, by deep concentration to lesson after lesson, by blood and sweat, as his father used to say. *"Stop trying so hard, Jacob. Feel the Lord in your heart. Be one with Him. Then the lessons will be easier."*

But this was not to be. At least not for Jacob. The harder he tried, the more frustrated he became. If he tried not to try so hard he inevitably lost his way. Jacob's course had been an arduous one. Did this mean he could not serve the Lord? No. He had become a most devoted servant. He was a crusader, perhaps all the more inflamed for his lack of natural affinity, for his desperation to feel the Holy Spirit in his soul. God could not have asked for a stronger soldier than Jacob Piersol. He'd always thought that someday he might win oneness with the Holy Spirit by sheer conviction, the same oneness that seemed to fill the heart of his father so effortlessly. If not . . . well . . . if not, then he would die in the attempt. Surely God would smile upon him in the afterlife. He must, or else there was no justice in the world, none at all, not even in death.

Before Jacob was aware of how much time had passed, his bourbon was gone, and he and his guests had smoked an entire box of cigars.

He walked the mayor and the marshal and Bill Oberton outside into the darkness, into the night air, to the sound of cicadas and grass rustling softly in the breeze. Mayor Funkel and Marshal Braddock said their good evenings, thanked the preacher for his hospitality, hopped up into the mayor's buggy, and headed back toward the center of town.

Doc Oberton went to his horse and hoisted himself into the saddle. "Are you all right, Jacob? You got awfully quiet after dinner."

"I'm fine, Bill."

"You haven't had any more sleepwalking spells, have you?"

"No, I haven't. There's nothing to worry about."

"I think Puddah's death has got you more upset than you're willing to admit."

Jacob smiled. "All right. It's got me upset. I'm admitting it. Now go home and get some sleep."

The doctor nodded. "You'd better do the same. You're looking tired these days." He reined his horse around and headed for home.

Jacob stepped onto his porch and looked out into the night. Sleep. He wasn't exactly hungering for it. He knew the foreigner would probably be waiting for him in his dreams. A cool air tickled the hair on his arms. He breathed in the smell of grass and maple trees and grandfather oaks. He listened to the black birds singing crazily in the darkness. Spring. His favorite time of year. A time of rebirth and renewal.

Unfortunately this spring had blossomed into a time of frustration and restless slumber, a time of murder and unresolved conflicts. He was glad Marshal Braddock would be returning to Palmyra on the next coach. Tink's death was not the new beginning he had hoped for. It was a distraction, a curse, a blight. Maybe with the marshal gone, things would return to normal.

*   *   *   *   *

Jacob was exhausted, but he couldn't sleep, so eventually he crawled out of bed and sat on his porch in the rocker, Tink Puddah's Boston rocker. He still thought of the chair as belonging to the blue boy who once lived up on the hill overlooking Skanoh Valley, and he probably always would. Strange how the chair fit him so well. Wouldn't Puddah have found a smaller chair much more comfortable?

Jacob's eyes wanted to close, but he fought against it. "What are you trying to tell me, Tink Puddah?" he spoke into the darkness.

Perhaps his problem was not so much Tink, but what Tink stood for, his heathenish denial of God and how Jacob could not penetrate it, as he could not penetrate so many things. It was the gift Jacob lacked, the gift to reach out and touch people with the Word of the Lord, the gift to answer their needs, the ability to heal. The problem was not just Tink Puddah, Jacob realized. The problem lay within his own unworthy soul.

Why could he still not feel the Lord in his heart after all these years? Why could he still not be one with Him after a lifetime of prayer and devotion? Where had he failed? Was it a lack of faith? No, no, impossible. His faith was the only thing that saved him. What was the Lord's purpose?

There was no easy answer, and he doubted there ever would be. Let it go, he told himself. Time. Time was the answer. Someday, Jacob Piersol, you will know the reason for your struggles, for Tink Puddah's life and death, someday it will come to you, God willing. If Jacob had only been able to hone the same patience and constancy as the venerable Nathan Piersol . . . Ah, well . . . time.

Jacob rocked for a while. He was about to return to bed when he noticed a small circle of light dancing through the trees. It bobbed softly on the air. A firebug? No, it was too large for a firebug and too solid for a cluster of them. As the light drew closer, Jacob saw that it was spinning. He saw bright sparks pass from its core. The light continued to dance toward him. He stood up and leaned against the railing, peering at the oddity.

As it drew near, the light grew so radiant that Jacob had to blink to keep his eyes trained on it. It came closer, closer, and finally swirled right up onto his porch. Jacob backed away, giving it space, squinting and shielding his eyes.

This must be a dream, he thought. There was no other explanation. He must have fallen asleep on the foreigner's rocker and—

The ball of light spun faster. It smelled faintly of vanilla, of Betty Louise's sweetcakes cooling on the windowsill—what a strange way to think of a Holy Light—for surely if this was not a dream it must be a Holy Light of the Heavenly Father, a beacon come to guide him during this most difficult time, to give him strength and courage, a Holy Light sent, perhaps, to heal him.

Faster, faster, sparks caromed off the spinning core and floated around him. Jacob's eyes adjusted to the radiance. He reached out and cupped a spark as it fell flickering into his palm, and the spark cooled his hand, a coolness like the spring air itself, like the water of a mountain stream.

The Holy Light brightened and expanded. Jacob squinted and tried to look closer. He did not want to look away. The oddity seemed to be reaching out to him, calling him.

A white, oval blaze formed into a solid, glimmering pillar of light, and then the pillar pulled itself in at the middle and pushed out at the top and bottom into . . . into . . . the beginnings of a body, two arms and two legs and a warped head.

Jacob's eyes stung, yet he refused to look away. If this was not a dream, God in Heaven if not a dream, then a revelation! It was written that God revealed Himself to men in the form of pure light. Could it be?

The Holy Light slowly transformed into the body of a man, no, wait . . . the body was too small, too thin, too bent . . .

The foreigner. The foreigner, Tink Puddah!

There was no mistaking it. That was without a doubt the foreigner's tiny body, his misshapen head and skinny arms and legs. The bright white light turned blue, the delicate blue color of Tink Puddah's skin, and then his features, his face—the button black eyes, the squished nose and lips, the inverted ears—it was Tink Puddah himself who now stood on Jacob Piersol's porch, Tink Puddah with the bright white Holy Light dancing all around him.

Fear gripped Jacob's heart. This made no sense. He thought of the Tink Puddah they had dug out of his shallow grave a month ago, stinking of rot, leaking slime. Had the foreigner come back to punish Jacob for the desecration of his body? No. Please, no, not that. Jacob was not to blame. His conscience was clear.

But the foreigner didn't seem interested in exacting any sort of vengeance. Puddah stood before Jacob, a perfect Tink Puddah, not rotting or decayed, perfect except for the wound to his skull, the shotgun wound that must have killed him. The top of Puddah's head was missing, and he bled from it.

Tink Puddah smiled at Jacob and said, "Hello, Jacob Piersol." A thin line of blood trickled down the side of his face.

Jacob could not speak.

"Come to me, Jacob Piersol," the apparition said. "Do you not recognize me?"

Jacob was certain that he would not be able to move. But to his surprise, at the foreigner's command, he stepped forward.

"Touch me," Tink said.

Jacob's terror gave way to fascination. He was repulsed by the specter in front of him, but attracted to it also. Was this a dream or a revelation? He wanted to run away—no, he wanted to burrow deep inside the foreigner's Holy Light and hide there forever. A part of him wanted to love Puddah while another part of him wanted to hate him. But the strongest part of Jacob Piersol wanted to know why. *Why* was Tink Puddah here, now, asking to be touched?

Jacob reached out and touched gently, with his fingertips, the foreigner's hand. It was not the touch of death. Puddah's hand was warm. The hand was *alive*. Is this what Tink Puddah had wanted to tell him? That he was alive? No, of course not. Puddah's head had been shot off. He could not be alive. He could *not* be. Jacob had seen the dead body with his own eyes, had smelled the rot. This was not Tink Puddah at all. A dream. More real, more disturbing than his other dreams, perhaps, but still a dream.

Unless . . .

Tink Puddah looked at him with his black eyes, but the look was somehow soft, not cold or dark. "Feel my injury," he said.

Jacob shook his head. "No."

"You have touched me, yet you doubt that it is me. Feel the wound, see if I am real."

"No," Jacob said again. In spite of himself he reached for the foreigner's head. "I will not, I will not . . . " but he could not stop himself.

Jacob touched the wound. It was supple and wet, like clay. Blood came away on his fingertips. Blood.

The Blood of Christ?

No, what was he thinking? This could not be. But . . . but . . . was it not Christ who had appeared to his disciples after he'd risen from the dead? Was it not Christ who had said to Thomas, *"Reach hither thy finger, and behold my hands; and reach hither thy hand, and thrust it into my side: and be not faithless, but believing."* Yes, Jacob knew those words well. John, Chapter 20, Verse 27. Is this what Tink Puddah had been trying to tell the preacher for so long? Tink Puddah, this little blue man, was the Son of God?

No. Impossible. You are insane, Jacob Piersol.

Unless . . .

Unless . . .

Yes, he should have seen it a long time ago. How could he have been so ignorant? It was written that the Savior would open the minds of his disciples so they might understand the Scriptures. It was written that the Messiah must suffer, and that he must rise from death. Jacob had been blind to it, as so many had been blind to the first coming of Jesus Christ. But now he had seen—he had been shown—*shown*. God had chosen him, Jacob Piersol. He fell to his knees in front of the Savior, bowed his head, and kissed Tink Puddah's feet.

How could Jacob have been such a fool? He was not worthy. "Forgive me, my Lord, please, please."

Tink Puddah put his hand upon Jacob's head. "It is written that in the Messiah's name the message of repentance and forgiveness must be preached. It is also written that the power from above would come down upon the disciples. I forgive you, Jacob Piersol. I give you the power of God to preach the Word of the Lord. Go to Palmyra, and bring my message of peace and love to the poor, the needy, the hard-working people who have lost their way. I make you my disciple."

Jacob wept. He could not help himself. He, Jacob Piersol, who had tried so hard, for so long to feel the Holy Spirit within him, to feel the touch of Christ's hand, had finally been chosen, had been chosen to spread the Word of the second coming of the Messiah, Tink Puddah. He'd received a mission. How? Why? He did not know. It did not matter. One did not question the wisdom of God.

Tink Puddah drew his finger across Jacob's forehead. "I bless you in the name of the Father and the Foreign Son and the Holy Gun."

The Foreign Son? It would be difficult to get used to that, but Jacob must accept the truth. The Holy Gun? What was that? Jacob did not understand. Why was he so stupid? *I will accept this!* he scolded himself. I have been chosen.

Then the Holy Light began to swirl around Tink Puddah. It whipped into a frenzy, sparks flew, taking Tink Puddah into its bright white grasp, turning the Savior into a spinning ball of radiant yarn, the Holy Light of God spun from the loom of Heaven.

The cool spring air skirled through the preacher's hair and the wind howled and settled, howled and settled. The foreigner retreated into the sky, into the stars, and returned to the Kingdom of Heaven. It was written that after Jesus blessed his disciples, he was taken into Heaven.

And then all was calm. Black birds sang and bullfrogs croaked. Jacob could hear a dog barking out on the road. Crickets, cicadas everywhere. Jacob was still on his knees. Tears of joy cascaded down his cheeks. He had been forgiven his sins and his stupidity. He had been offered a second chance to preach the Word. Glory be to God. Jacob had been touched . . . touched . . . touched . . . by the Lord Savior, Jesus Christ. Jacob had been chosen by the Messiah, Tink Puddah. His father had never been chosen. No, but Jacob Piersol had. Glory be to God.

Tink Puddah spent that winter with the bear in its den, curled up next to it, feeding from its warmth and strength and animal life force.

Once in a while the huge black bear would leave the den to forage for food, return with some bark or nuts or winterberries for Tink, or a fish he'd plucked from a stream through the broken ice. But mostly Tink slept and did not feel especially hungry.

It was during this time that Tink dreamed he was not only part human, but part bear as well, and part everything that made up this strange and terrifying Planet Earth. It was during this time that he dreamed of Wetspace.

In his dreams, Wetspace swirled around Tink Puddah, undulated, bubbled, gurgled to equilibrium concentration, flowed and flooded the internal and external compartments of his being. Tink Puddah swam in the buoyancy of eternal liquids, gathering chemical compounds, dissolving, distributing, consuming and being consumed by the detritus and antibiotics and squalamines of the microorganisms of life, feeding from the mutualistic symbiosis of the strange, dreamy circumstances of his otherselves, his origin of life.

Tink became the nutriment and conscious/subconscious matter of Wetspace. Tink was mind and liquid, formless and form. All was diluted and dispersed by the inner currents of the one benign aquatic environment of their pearly organisms.

In his dream world, Tink had found the silent sea that spoke with the mind of all elements, of all organic and inorganic chemicals, of all circular memories, past, present, future, past, present, future, past . . .

In his dreams, he tried to question his parents about their incomplete transformations to Planet Earth, and they seemed to reassure him in that way in which Tink had become accustomed—no words, no direct communication, but a fluid, comforting presence, a soothing, mellifluous internal affirmation of their undying faith in him.

Tink could almost grasp the *how* of it. Their imperfect solidifications seemed to involve an absorption of all matter, all life, internal and external. Not being fully solidified had left his parents and Tink not only incomplete humans, but incomplete everythings. So Tink was a bear, a moth, a fish, a bird, even a bit of the dogs that terrified him so.

He was part otherworld, too, part of the Wetspace he'd dreamed about. But his other world was very far away. He would never know his other self the way his parents knew themselves, or the way they knew Tink, for that matter, but without it he could not have become the little bits and pieces of everything he had become.

This understanding, Tink knew, was the beginning of his healing. This understanding was the beginning of his life.

*   *   *   *   *

In early spring, Tink and the bear ventured from the den and parted company. The long winter's rest had changed Tink in ways he could already feel. Finally, he had an identity. There was a place for him here in this harsh world. He would no longer have to think of himself as an outsider, as someone who did not belong. He was the earth and the sky and the water. He was plant and animal. He was no longer filled with anger or grief or confusion. Tink belonged. This was the place of his birth.

And more.

More.

As Tink traveled through the woodland, he began to see that this world would protect him and provide for him. When he was thirsty, he would find a stream. When he was hungry, he would discover a bush or a patch of mushrooms or berries to feed from. He could make a fire whenever he wanted, sometimes by doing nothing more than gently rubbing two branches together. The wolves would watch him from afar with a different sort of look in their eyes, not a hungry look, but a look that was curious and respectful. When he was tired, he could fall into a deep and restful slumber without fear.

It was during one of these deep slumbers that Tink was wakened by an explosion—such a fierce explosion it bounced him into the air and dropped him down hard on his hip. The ground and the trees shuddered, and the explosion numbed his ears.

Through the numbness broke the scream of a man. It came from over the hill, in the direction of the rising sun. Tink slung his sack over his shoulder, got to his feet, and scrambled up the slope. At the top of the rise he looked down into the rocks below. A man lay moaning in the weeds beneath him.

Tink scrambled down through the pine trees, slipping in the dirt and on the stones. Across the field, thick gray smoke poured out of a gaping hole in the earth.

Tink knelt beside the man, startling him for a moment. "Are you all right?"

"M' leg, m'leg is busted up dang sho to hell busted."

The man writhed in agony. He was a young black man. He clinched his eyes shut, groped uselessly below his knee. Tink placed his fingers delicately over the spot where the bone seemed to be poking out of the man's overalls.

Instantly Tink felt the injury, the deep core of the wound where the bone had cleanly snapped. He wanted to pull his hand away, but couldn't.

He was fascinated by what he felt there, by the subtle stirring he sensed beneath the surface of the skin as his fingers explored the damaged bone. And then Tink felt something else, something he could not describe, a certain measure of relief, of pardon. He felt the injury, and he felt its healing, and they both came together like the cupping of hands, like day becoming night, not two, but one. Suddenly, one.

All of this took but a moment, a few short breaths.

The man had stopped trembling. He was calm now. His leg bone had come together beneath Tink's touch. There was no more pain twisting his face. He sat up straight, the black man did, as if he'd been smacked out of a restful sleep. "What happen to m' leg?" he said. "It ain't no more broke. All a sudden it ain't broke."

"I don't think there was anything wrong with it," Tink said, not at all sure of what had happened. "I think you were just scared."

The man shook his head, reached down and touched his leg. "No, no, it was broke bad f' sho. I knows it was."

"The explosion," Tink said. "What happened?"

"The explosion! Jimmy! Jimmy's down there!" The man jumped up awkwardly, as if he wasn't sure his leg would support him, but as soon as he saw it would, off he ran, across the gravel toward the thick gray smoke.

Tink followed. He saw that mounds of dirt and gravel and railroad ties had been piled across the landscape, and far off in the distance, felled trees and pitched tents. The ground felt hot from the explosion. Tink coughed from the dust that hung loosely in the air.

"Jimmy! Jimmy!" the black man hollered. "Oh, God, oh, God, oh, God," he said, kneeling beside an older man whose clothes had been blasted to shreds. "Jimmy's dead f' sho, dead dead dead."

Tink looked over the black man's shoulder. The man named Jimmy had a scraggly beard and a pockmarked face. Some of his teeth were yellow, the others rotted out. His skin was shaved like a carrot stick, ripped and torn all up and down his body, and he oozed blood from a thousand different wounds. But he was alive. Tink could feel it. A presence, a core, a spark of life remained.

"His heart is still beating," Tink said.

The black man leaned over and put his ear to the man's chest. "Lord have mercy you right, you right, stranger, but there ain't hardly a bref left in him. Oh, God." The black man started to cry. "He gonna die f' sho, ol' Jimmy."

"Calm down," Tink said.

The man lifted his head and there was blood on the side of his face, ol' Jimmy's blood. His lips trembled. "They'll blame me. They'll say it was my fauwt. They always blame me for everything, but it weren't my fauwt. I didn't do nothin' but drill the hole. It was Jimmy's fauwt. He must a poured the powder too soon. He always in a rush, Jimmy is, oh Lord—"

"What were you doing?" Tink said.

"Cuttin' through stone. We was strikin' fo the railroad."

"Where are the other men?"

"Rest a the crew 'bout a mile back. They're comin', and I'm in big trouble. Oh, Jesus, Lord, you gotta hep me. You gotta fix up Jimmy like you done fixed m' leg."

"I didn't fix your leg," Tink said. "There was nothing wrong with your leg."

The man clutched Tink's shoulder. "Please!"

"I want you to run back and get help," Tink said. "Can you do that?"

The black man nodded. "Will you stay wit' Jimmy? Will you help Jimmy?"

"Yes." Tink would stay with Jimmy, but he didn't know if he could help him. He didn't know how he'd healed the black man's leg, if in fact that was what he'd done. Maybe he hadn't. Maybe there really had been nothing wrong with it. Tink didn't understand. "I'll try."

"Lord, you a angel, ain't ya? You a angel a mercy. You don't look like no man. You talk like a man and you walk like a man, but you a angel a mercy. I never knowned angels was blue, but now I know. God watches over all mens. He sent you down to save me and ol' Jimmy."

Tink shook his head. "No, nobody sent me. Is there a doctor on your crew?"

"Yessir, mista angel, sir."

"Can you go get him?"

"Yessir, mista angel, sir. You stay here wit ol' Jimmy and fix 'im up good now. You fix 'im up good!" He scrabbled to his feet and ran off.

Fix him up good. Tink was afraid to touch Jimmy for fear the man would unravel under his fingertips. He was shredded from head to toe. And his spark of life was almost gone. Jimmy would not survive. There was no way he could live long enough for the doctor to get here, and even if he did, what could a doctor do for him? Jimmy was as good as dead. So why was Tink afraid to touch him?

Tink reached down and placed his fingers lightly on the man's chest. He searched for the spark, the core, the hint of life he thought might still be in the man—what did the humans call it?—maybe they had no word—the soul, perhaps. Was it still there? Yes. Although the heartbeat was gone now.

Tink let his fingertips explore this insubstantial mist. He found that he could touch it, roll it between his fingers. He found that he could keep it still even as it tried to slip away. He pulled it back up into the man's body. He felt the man's heartbeat, a heartbeat from nowhere. It came once, twice, again and again. Tink kept his fingers pressed to the man's chest, and then he felt something else, something very strange. He felt the railroad:

This man's life was the railroad, drilling through solid rock to pack the dynamite, leveling the roadbeds, laying the locust-wood cross ties. The man had helped build trestles and he'd worked a bridge crew. He'd worked a hoist mount for raising lumber onto a flat car. He'd shoveled coal. When he was a boy, he'd slept in the boiler room of a locomotive where his father worked in the dead of winter with only the coals burning in the firebox to keep them and the engine warm. This was so strange, Tink thought, this man's life force tied into his life's work.

But Tink needed to concentrate on the pardoning now. With his other hand he touched the man's bare leg, where his overalls had been ripped apart. Almost as soon as he touched the skin he felt it closing and tightening under his fingers. Tink touched other parts of the man's body. Each area he touched, he pardoned. The man's heart now had a strong beat. Tink touched more skin—fusing, healing, fixin' ol' Jimmy up good.

Jimmy's heartbeat strengthened. His eyes flashed open. "What the Christ happened?"

Tink blinked, shook his head. The man had snapped Tink out of a trance, although he hadn't thought of it as a trance while he'd been in it. "You were shaken by the explosion," he said.

"What explosion? Wait a minute. The blast? The powder blast? Jesus, I'm all right. I can't believe it." He looked down at his ruined overalls. "What the heck happened to my clothes? Who are you? What's wrong with you? You don't look so good, stranger. Your skin supposed to be that color blue, or you got some kind a disease?"

"No disease. I'm fine. I should be going, though, if you are all right."

"I'm breathin', ain't I?"

"Yes," Tink said, wiping some of the man's sticky blood off his hands. "You are breathing."

Jimmy reached up and felt his head. "Must a been knocked out for a spell. Alls I remember is the blast. Wait a minute. Where's the boy? He okay?"

"Your friend is fine. He went to get the crew doctor."

"Crew doctor? Gadsakes! He'd likely kill me afore I woke up."

Tink helped the man to his feet. He could hear the far-off voices of approaching men. "It's time for me to go."

"Where you headed?"

Tink thought about this. Where indeed? He didn't know. "Really, I must go."

"Well, sure, whatever you say," Jimmy said. "Thanks for your help. Why don't you stick around for some grub? Least I can do is offer you a meal for your trouble."

"Thank you, but I'm not hungry."

Tink grabbed his sack and headed off into the woodland.

*   *   *   *   *

The railroad men tried to follow him, Tink knew. He could feel their pursuit. But if Tink did not want to be found, the trees and the rocks and the earth would hide him.

The men did not search for long. They had a railroad to build. How could they explain to their bosses that they'd wasted an entire day traipsing through the woods on the trail of a little blue-skinned angel? This thought amused Tink, the thought of the men telling their bosses how they'd looked all over for the blue angel of mercy who had healed the black man's broken leg and saved ol' Jimmy's life, the bosses all dressed up in their fine coats and hats, fingering their waxed mustaches, wondering if they should fire everyone on the spot for drinking whiskey on the job.

But where was Tink headed? A place, a destination. Was there somewhere he belonged?

Tink thought about Jimmy's life force tied to his vocation. These people, these human beings, were defined by their purposes in life, their places, their work. Tink was a part of this planet now. He belonged here. But where here did he belong? What was his proper place and purpose? He decided to concentrate on this, and only this, so he would not have to concentrate on how he had healed the black man and Jimmy of their injuries. His newfound ability to pardon was more frightening to Tink than anything else, because he did not know where it came from. He knew it was a powerful thing, and power meant trouble on this planet. This world did not appreciate power.

Tink could feel the Earth's distaste for things that surpassed its own jealous forces. The land contrived against power; the sun and the moon and the wind contrived against power; the great waters contrived against power; even animals and men contrived against it. Although everything that contrived against it also seemed to hunger for it. Still, Tink feared that his power to pardon had transcended the natural laws here.

Had Tink always had this ability? He thought of the man, Darryl. Could he have healed the man instead of shooting him in the head? No, he remembered touching the man and he'd felt no sense of healing. The power must have awakened during the long winter with the bear, when he'd healed himself and made peace with this harsh planet. But he did not want to think about any of it.

He concentrated instead on a place to go, a place to be. He searched inward. He searched his own mist. Now that he had touched the mist of other men, he knew where to look. Now it was easier for him to search inside himself, to find that place that held secrets and answers, the place that held his own spark and the spark of his parents.

Tink decided he would go to a town. That was his answer. Be near people. Learn about vocations. It did not matter what vocation. The first thing he came across would be fine. Tink would live more like a man than an animal. This made sense. He was almost a human being. He was closer to man than he was to any other living thing. He would roam for a while. He would learn about the land. He would explore this troubling power of his that allowed him to pardon injuries. But then he would find a place. He would go to a town and learn something of this life force of vocations that defined the people here on Earth.

Tink Puddah finally had a purpose.

Outside the small town of Crawford Hills, Tink Puddah discovered the cropped pasture where the boys met each Saturday morning to play their game of base ball.

Tink had wandered past the field one day as he'd been traveling through the woods. Drawn by the boys' excited voices and laughter, he'd tracked through the pines and hardwoods, the patches of skunk weed and sprawling ivy, to find out what all the commotion was about. He sat among the thickets on the outskirts of the field, hidden, but fascinated.

It was a curious game, he thought. The boys had split up into two teams, and each boy took his turn swinging a long, flattened paddle, hitting a small, hard ball about the size of an apple, while the other team fielded their hits. The fielders would attempt to put the paddler out of the game by either catching the ball in the air or on one bounce, or, failing that, by throwing the ball and striking the paddler with it before he reached a safe base.

The game, Tink could tell, involved expending an enormous amount of energy—running, paddling, throwing, clapping, hollering—and even after players were put out of the game they were allowed to return. A great deal of vitality was required just to compete. There seemed no end to the boys' enthusiasm or to their contest.

The boys were having so much fun that Tink felt a strange sort of vibration rise up from the field, a force that very nearly contained a life of its own. Riveted by their game, he watched the boys play base ball for the entire day. It was sunny and cool, birds fluttered in the treetops, black and red and gray-haired squirrels scurried through the underbrush, and insects investigated Tink's blue skin. But he ignored them all while he watched the competition.

Tink found that it was a struggle for him to sit still while the boys played. Their delight was infectious. He wanted to participate. He was disappointed when dusk came, and the boys ran off to their homes for supper.

Tink decided to remain in the woods of Crawford Hills to see if the boys intended to come back and play again. He did not expect them to return on Sunday, for Sunday was a sacred day for many men and their families, a day for practicing their religious rituals. During the week, he knew, there would be school and chores. But he hoped that on Saturday the boys would return.

They did. They came running out onto their field with paddle and ball even before the sun had cleared the ridge. It was a clear, bright morning, and the scent of pine wood and tall, thick grasses filled the air. Tink felt the same joy and energy coming from the boys that he'd felt during their previous outing. He watched them play all day long as they laughed and ran and perspired under the hot sun.

They took a break to drink water from a cistern and to eat apples and bread for lunch. Then the boys kept playing until it was almost dark. Although a score was tallied and a winning team declared, their presence seemed to linger in the field long after they'd left the game behind. In a strange sort of way, it seemed as if their game of base ball had never really ended at all.

The next Saturday it rained. Tink thought about moving on then, or perhaps venturing into the town of Crawford Hills to pursue a vocation, but he decided to wait another week for the boys. There was something pure and simple and happy in these young ones that Tink had never seen or felt in the adults. It was worth exploring. It was worth trying to capture for himself.

The next Saturday the boys returned to the field. The sun shone, and a cool, fresh breeze cut across the cropped pasture. The trees seemed drowsy, the light soft and purified. It was not yet summer, so the days were comfortable with the promise of a deeper heat. Tink decided to take a chance with the boys. He walked down toward their playing field from his hiding place, just as they began to divide into teams.

The boys were so intent upon making their teams that Tink actually made it almost all the way up to them before they noticed him. He was glad for that. This way, everybody could see him all at once. He didn't want to give them a chance to think too much, or to fear him.

"Hey, look at that!" cried the first boy who saw him.

"Hello," Tink said. "I would like to play, if that's all right."

"What the heck is that kid?" one of the boys muttered, pointing at him.

"He's a nigra," said a chubby boy, the largest and perhaps the oldest of the bunch, stepping to the fore. "And he ain't playin' with us."

Tink had not expected this to be a simple task, convincing the boys to let him play. But if he persuaded the big one—he seemed to be the boy the others listened to most—he might have a chance.

The chubby boy held the paddle tightly in his hands. "Get lost, nigra."

"He's not black," another boy said, another of the older boys and the tallest of the lot. "What's wrong, Chet, are you color blind all of a sudden? That boy's blue as the sky."

"He's a nigra, Richard," answered the fat one. "And this is a white man's game. My daddy says so."

"Look here, maybe we all don't feel the same," said the boy named Richard.

Tink decided not to interfere. He did not feel in danger. The boys wanted to play their game of base ball more than they wanted to argue.

They were anxious and excited. Tink wanted to play, too. This would be worth the risk, he thought, if they allowed him to play.

"I ain't playin' with no nigra and neither is anybody on my team!" The fat boy, Chet, stamped the head of the paddle into the rough grass.

"Fine," Richard said. "You don't have to play with him. You got twelve. We only got eleven. We'll take him. That'll even up the teams."

Chet's face turned pink with fury. "He don't belong on no ball field at all. That's the way it is."

Richard smiled. "What's the matter? Afraid you're going to get beat by us?"

"I ain't afeared of nothin', 'specially no nigra."

The other boys waited impatiently, dressed in their torn old shirts and breeches held up by their frayed galluses. It seemed that they were used to these two boys making decisions for them.

They all stared at Tink, perhaps trying to decide whether he was in fact a "nigra." Tink did not understand what difference that should make. New York, he knew, was a free state, not a slave state. He did not understand why there were such things as slaves at all, why one man's color of skin would make him less a man with fewer rights of life. Regardless, here in New York there should not be a problem with it.

The chubby boy was very upset, though. Tink could feel his growing rage. He did not want to spoil the boys' game. He might have to leave before things became too tense.

"If you're not afraid," Richard said, "then you'll let the blue boy play on our team."

"C'mon, we wanna play, Chet," said a very young blond lad, swatting at a honeybee that buzzed around his head. His silky bangs were chopped unevenly over his ears.

"I don't like it," Chet said.

A few other boys said, "C'mon, who cares? C'mon, let's just play, will ya?" Most of the boys wanted to play the game.

Chet finally gave in. "All right, but if it don't work out and I decide he goes, then he goes, simple as that."

Chet lifted the paddle and spat on the flat of it. The paddle was about a yard in length, with a short broom handle cross-tied to it in order for the boys to get a good grip. "Wet or dry?"

"Dry," Richard said.

Chet tossed the paddle spinning into the air. When it landed on the ground he said, "Wet! We're up first."

"Let's go," Richard said to Tink. "We're in the field. My name is Richard."

"Thank you for standing up for me. My name is Tink Puddah."

"That's a weird name. Are you from another country? You must be. I've never seen blue skin like that. What country are you from?"

Tink jogged along beside Richard out into the field. "I come from a place very far away."

"What's it called?"

"It's called Wetspace," Tink said.

"Wetspace? That's a very unusual name. Where do you live now?"

"I came from over the hill."

"Ah. Fayette? That's a pretty far walk. Do you know how to play base ball?"

"I've seen the game played, but I've never played it myself."

"Oh, well," Richard said without sounding disappointed. "You can play in the outfield next to me. The whole point when you're in the field is if somebody hits the ball to you, you got to catch the ball in the air or on the first bounce, or you got to peg the runner out. Whatever you do, don't let the ball get past you or it'll be a score for sure. Once we get three outs on them, we get to bat. It's a long throw from the outfield and you're a pretty small kid, so if the ball comes to you, just toss it over to me, and I'll throw it in. Okay?"

"Okay."

"Put some distance between you and me. You need to cover that area over there. I'm going to cover the center."

Tink went to the right, where Richard had pointed. Way up field somebody picked up the paddle, and all of the boys began hollering, just as they had on the previous Saturdays. Already, it seemed, they had forgotten about Chet's argument with Richard.

*"C'mon, Jeb, throw it over!"*

*"Hit it, Andy, hit it!"*

*"Three-out the side, Jeb! Pitch it in!"*

*"Get a hit, Andy!"*

*"Let's go, boys! Three and out! Let's go!"*

Tink Puddah felt the swell of excitement building in him. He didn't scream any words—he was self-conscious about saying the wrong thing at the wrong time. He wanted to fit in with the other boys without anyone noticing. Fitting in would be a remarkable experience for Tink Puddah in itself. He placed his hands on his knees and bent slightly forward, glancing at Richard to make sure his posture looked identical. His heartbeat quickened. Here he was, playing the game of base ball. Could this be possible?

The boy, Jeb, lobbed the ball toward Andy, and Andy smacked it with the paddle. The ball rolled to one of the boys in the infield who picked it up and hurled it at Andy, but Andy ducked and lunged toward a bush to the right side of the field. All the boys on Chet's team shouted, "Safe! Safe!" They clapped their hands and whistled.

Tink had learned a lot by watching the boys play. The bush was first base. Andy was allowed to stay safely upon the base because the boy on Tink's team had failed to peg him with the ball. Andy would be allowed to stay there until he was pegged off base, or until he scored a run coming all the way around the infield, or until his team was put out three times.

Now another boy picked up the paddle and waited for Jeb to lob the ball. This boy also hit it hard, harder than Andy, but a player on Richard's team caught the ball after one bounce. "Out!" they all cried. "Out!"

"All right, good catch!" yelled Richard. "That's one out," he said to Tink. "Two more and we go to bat."

Tink nodded. He placed his hands on his knees again, mimicking Richard, hoping for the opportunity to catch the ball.

Two more boys came up to bat and paddled safely, but Andy, while trying to score a run, was pegged out by one of the infielders. "Out! Out!" yelled the boys on Richard's team. Chet argued. He said that Andy had scored before he was pegged, but it was obvious Andy was hit well short of the proper scoring area. The argument was settled when Andy ruled himself out. No score.

Then, with two outs, with a runner standing at the rock that was second base and another runner standing at the huge tree stump that was third, Chet picked up the paddle and walked up to hit.

"One more out!" shouted Richard. "C'mon boys!"

Tink could hear the thrill in Richard's voice and feel his tension. Richard wanted very much to put Chet out. Jeb lobbed the ball to Chet, but Chet didn't swing. He let a couple of pitches pass before he finally swung, and when he did he smacked the ball so hard it lined straight through the infield, directly toward Richard. Richard ran in on the ball to play the first bounce, but when it hit the ground it must have struck a rock or a root in the field, and the ball caromed high over Richard's head.

Tink instinctively ran for it. He didn't think there was any chance he could make the catch, but he ran as fast as he could. He ran diagonally, back, back, and it almost seemed as if the ball floated upon the air, sailed in the breeze over Richard's head, suspended, waiting for Tink to run under it.

Tink suddenly realized he might have a chance to make the catch after all. He ran all the harder. But the ball seemed to fall suddenly, faster than it should have, as if finally recognizing gravity. Tink leaped with all the strength in his thin legs, stretched full out with his arms and hands extended, and the ball smacked into the palm of his hand at the same moment his body struck the rough earth.

Tink caught a face full of dirt and grass, but he also caught the ball.

"Out! Chet's out!" Richard cried, his sharp voice peeling back the air around Tink's ears.

Tink looked up at the ball gripped solidly in his right hand. It felt coarse and firm, almost like mule skin. Out. Chet was out. Tink spat the dirt from his mouth and grinned.

Richard ran up to him and jerked him to his feet. "What a great catch, Tink! I've never seen a catch like that!" All the other boys on his team came running over to him, hooting and hollering. "Great catch! No score! C'mon, we're up to bat! They didn't score!"

Richard brushed the dirt off Tink's shirt and patted his head. "We never once put Chet's side out before a score. I can't believe it."

Neither could Tink. What fun! What incredible fun to be a boy and to have a game like this to play—the game of base ball. But there was something more to it than the sheer joy of competition. The game exposed a purity of spirit in these young ones that Tink had never seen before. It was as sweet and warm as syrup from a maple tree, yet at the same time cool, fresh, and clean, like snow melting into a mountain stream.

Tink could not wait to get his hands on the paddle. He wanted more than anything to swing the bat and strike that little ball with all his strength. He wanted to know how it felt to run around the bases and score a run. Tink allowed himself to imagine, just for a moment, the freedom that might yield. But Richard decided Tink would paddle last on the team because he'd never done it before, and although Richard's team scored eight times, the last boy was pegged out before Tink got his chance.

Tink ran out into the field again with Richard. This time Richard gave him more space to cover.

"How do you like playing so far?" Richard asked.

"This is the most fun I have ever had in my life."

Richard laughed. "Wait 'til you hit."

In the field, things did not go so well for Richard's team this time around. The boys on Chet's team performed much better at bat and dodged a lot of throws and scored twelve runs before the last out. Tink touched the ball only once, when it rolled through the infield.

This time the boys on Richard's team were not so cheerful running off the field, but their moods quickly heightened as they reached the paddling area.

"All right, boys, let's come back!"

"Let's get some hits, now!"

"We can score, too!"

"Hit and run, boys, hit and run!"

They seemed very much like little men, intense and concentrated, but without the cloudy confusion of adult minds.

"Tink," Richard said. "You're batting first this time."

Tink felt his heart race. He ran over and picked up the paddle. It was heavy, but Tink thought he would be able to swing it without too much difficulty.

Richard came up to him and put his arm around his shoulder. "The whole point is you've got to hit the ball and run. You've got to touch all the bases before you score, and if you get pegged, you're out. But the most important thing is, you've got to hit the ball first, then worry about getting around the bases. Let me show you how to hold the bat."

Richard put Tink's hands around the grip, one hand above the other on the broom handle. "Make sure you keep the face of the bat flat out when you swing, like this, or you'll miss the ball entirely. Have you ever paddled a canoe?"

"No," Tink said.

Richard shrugged and scratched at his sweaty forehead. Tink, apparently, had rendered his comparison useless. "Well, it's like paddling a canoe. If you don't flatten the paddle you won't get any water, but if you've never paddled a canoe, don't worry about it. Just keep your eye on the ball, and don't turn the flat of the bat over when you swing."

"I understand," Tink said.

"Go ahead, then. Don't be nervous. If you can hit half as well as you can catch, you'll be topnotch."

Tink stepped up to the den—that's what the boys called it, the den, a large patch of grass they'd turned over so that it was all dirt. Tink took a practice swing with the paddle before he stepped up to bat. He'd seen the other boys do this. He took another swing. The paddle whisked through the air. His swings felt awkward, but he could do it. Tink was very nervous now, even though Richard had told him not to be. He squeezed the handle of the paddle and stood sideways in the den, his left shoulder facing the pitcher.

The boy on Chet's team who was pitching, a very young boy, lobbed the ball toward Tink. Tink stepped forward and swung the paddle with all his strength. He missed. At the last moment, trying to swing harder, he'd rotated his wrists and the paddle's edge had turned down. Tink's momentum spun him around in a circle and he fell to his knees.

Chet, playing out in center outfield, laughed uproariously. He laughed so hard he fell over on the ground, making a show of it. "What a stupid nigra!" he hollered. He didn't even get up. He stayed on the ground, laughing.

Tink felt himself getting angry. He'd done just what Richard had warned him against. He'd turned the paddle sideways.

"That's all right, Tink," Richard called out to him. "Everybody misses. Even big-mouth Chet."

Tink returned to the den. He had learned the first rule of hitting the ball, or not hitting the ball. It didn't matter how hard you swung. Tink did not have to try to be stronger than he was. Hitting was all about stepping forward and making contact with the flat of the paddle.

Tink took another practice swing. He got himself set in the den once more. The boy lobbed the pitch. Tink swung the paddle and smacked the ball, smooth and clean. He cast the paddle aside and ran for the first base bush. The ball bounced twice and hopped through the infield, out toward Chet in center.

Richard jumped up and shouted, "Keep running, Tink, keep running!"

Tink touched the bush and ran for the stone that was second-base. Chet finally got up and ran for the ball. He picked it up and Tink could see Chet grinning, his arm cocked, ready to hurl the ball at him. Chet had been baiting Tink to run for second. At that moment Tink wanted more than anything in the world to safely reach the second base stone before he was pegged out.

But Chet was close; he threw the ball at Tink with all his might; the ball shot toward Tink on a fast, straight line, as if it had a mind of its own and was zeroing in on him. Tink had no time to think. He twisted sideways. Tink had the advantage of being a slim target. When he turned, there was almost nothing of him to hit. The ball whisked by, barely missing his ribs.

Joy and relief washed over him all at once. He stepped on the second-base stone and ran toward the stump that was third. The stump was much farther away than the distance from first to second, and the boys were still trying to retrieve the ball Chet had hurled past him.

As Tink neared the stump, he looked to see where the ball was, to see if he could possibly make it all the way to the den. He couldn't see the ball but he spotted Richard jumping up and down, shouting, "Run, Tink, run it in!"

Tink ran for the den. A boy finally snatched the ball. He threw it desperately at Tink, but the throw was nowhere near as fast as Chet's throw, and Tink dodged it easily and ran across the den.

"Score!" his team shouted. "Tink scored!" They all ran out to him and hugged him. "You've done it, Tink!" cried Richard. "Your first time at bat and you scored a run!" Tink felt so ecstatic he could barely breathe; it was a combination of excitement and exhaustion. It was the most exhilarating feeling Tink had ever experienced.

"I scored!" Tink cried. "I scored!"

Tink had to sit down to catch his breath. He sat down the whole time the other boys paddled. They scored enough runs to tie the game before Tink had to jog back to the outfield.

Tink got two more hits later, although he did not score again. Chet's team won, but the game was close, closer than it had ever been, according to Richard.

"Tink, come back next week, will you?" Richard said. "Can you come back?"

"Yes, I will try my best to return," Tink said.

"Good, maybe you can talk your folks into letting you stay at my house for supper. You would be welcome."

"Or mine," said another boy walking by. "Any of us."

"Yes," Richard said.

Tink smiled. "Thank you. Thank you all very much."

The boys walked away into the dusky evening.

Tink returned to his place in the woods and built a small fire near some trees felled by a storm, in among their cracked and splintered trunks and roots. It was a very comfortable spot. Tink had made it his home for the past several weeks. He had built up a roof of thick leaves and moss to shield him from the rain and to insulate him.

Tink collapsed there, his every muscle aching. His feet and ankles hurt almost as much as the day he'd gone on the bear hunt with the man named Darryl. But this was a different kind of pain altogether, a revitalizing pain. How very strange that Tink felt so good, so sated. He decided not to try and pardon his own pain. He did not know if he could, but it didn't matter. Tink wanted to feel this hurt. It reminded him of the game, of the diving catch he'd made in the field, the balls he'd hit, the run he'd scored. It reminded him of the boys cheering him and hugging him. He had been one of the boys, and they had accepted him.

Base ball.

Tink could hardly wait for next Saturday. Maybe the pain would be gone by then. Maybe not. He didn't care. Tink would play anyway. Nothing could keep him away.

✶　✶　✶　✶　✶

By Saturday a hot spell hovered over Crawford Hills. It was humid, and Tink struggled under the weight of the air. He was sweating as he walked down toward the cropped field where the boys were all excitedly discussing something. They had not yet begun to separate into teams.

Richard saw Tink coming and waved to him. "Tink, come look at what Chet brought!"

Tink approached the mob of boys and could see, in Richard's large hands, a long, smooth, rounded, wooden bat.

"It's a *real* base ball bat," Richard said, his eyes alight. "Chet's father bought it in Albany. And a real base ball, too! Who's got the ball?"

Tink saw some boys tossing a new, white ball back and forth. Richard held the bat out to Tink.

A real bat? Tink smiled up at Richard. He did not know the paddle was not the proper implement to use in the game of base ball. It made no difference to Tink, but the boys were obviously very happy about it. Tink reached for the bat.

But it was Chet who grabbed it. "Oh, no you don't. No nigra is touching *my* bat. It's my bat and I say who uses it."

"C'mon, Chet," Richard said. "No reason to be selfish."

"Yeah," said some of the other boys. "We're all here to play. Let's not argue again."

But Chet shook his head and stared at Tink with clear and precise hatred. Sweat spotted the boy's chubby face as he strangled the handle of his new, slick, polished wooden base ball bat.

Tink decided, suddenly, that he would try to pardon Chet's hatred. He thought he might be able to do it quickly, with a slight touch, an unraveling of the mist that must be causing this violent inner pain, a hidden wound in the young boy. Tink could at least try. He might be able to help Chet without the boy even realizing it. Tink reached out and touched Chet's forearm—

"Yah!" Chet yelled and swung the bat at Tink.

The bat slammed into Tink's shoulder and dropped him to the ground. He fought against the searing pain, against a rapidly encroaching, speckled blackness. He gripped his upper arm and pulled at the pain with all his inner strength, pulled the pain up and out of his body. *Out! Out!* He pulled and pulled. Tears flooded his eyes.

Chet cocked the bat again. "Stupid nigra! Did you see that? He was trying to fight me!"

Richard jumped between them. "Chet, what's wrong with you? You've hurt him!"

"He was trying to fight me!" Chet yelled.

"No, he was not!" Richard put his hand on the thick of the bat and stopped Chet from swinging again.

"Stupid nigra," Chet said. "You all seen what he done."

The pain was so fierce that Tink did not know if a bone had been broken. He massaged his shoulder, pulling out the pain, soothing the bone, pardoning, pardoning. He could feel the injury receding under his desperate grip. Had Tink done it? Had he pardoned his own injury? It seemed not to hurt as much. He felt better. Yes. He could do it if he had to. Now he knew for sure. If he remained conscious, if he fought off the speckled blackness, if he stayed in control of himself, he could pardon his own injuries.

"Tink, are you all right?" Richard helped Tink sit up.

"I can't believe you did that," one of the other boys said to Chet.

"Yeah," said another. "You just hauled off and hit him for no reason."

"What's wrong with you!" Chet shouted. "Are you siding with that stupid nigra?"

"Hey, that's enough of that kind of talk," Richard said, probing Tink's shoulder with his fingers.

"I saw it, Chet," another boy said. "You was right. The nigra made a move for ya and you took a swipe at him, fair and square."

"That's right," Chet said.

Richard stood up. "Fair and square? How can you say that? You beat him with your base ball bat. How can you call that fair? You're three times his size. You're very lucky Tink is all right."

"Lucky, is it? I'll show you lucky—" Chet raised the bat and glared at Richard.

Richard moved forward. Chet was rounder and heavier than Richard, but Richard was taller and stronger, his chest full and wide, his arms thick and taut. The other boys cleared aside, giving them room to brawl.

"No!" Tink said, struggling to his feet. He was still in pain, all the hurt was not yet gone, but Tink could stand, so he stood and came between the two boys. "Please, no, Richard, I'm all right. This is foolish. There is no need for anyone else to become injured. Please. I'm fine."

"You're lucky," Chet said to Richard. "That nigra saved you from a beating." He turned around and snatched his new, white base ball from one of the boys. "I'll bring back the bat and ball when you get rid of the nigra. C'mon, boys, who's with me?"

Some of the other boys followed Chet as he marched off the field.

"I'm sorry about this, Tink," Richard said. "It's not your fault."

"No, I am the one who is sorry. I've broken up your game."

"No you haven't," another boy said, the very young one with the silky blond hair. "We still got the paddle and the old ball. We don't need no new stuff to play with. Never did."

"That's right," Richard said, "and we've got enough players for seven on each team."

"Thank you," Tink said, "but I'd better be heading home. Chet hit me very hard. I'm sore. I don't think I could play for long. I should probably start home before it really hurts a lot."

Richard frowned. "Maybe I should have Doctor James take a look at you."

Tink shook his head. "No, really, I'll be fine, but I should be going."

"You'll come back next week, won't you?" some of the other boys asked. "Don't let Chet scare you off."

"Yes, of course I'll come back," he answered them, lying.

Before Tink walked away, Richard came up to him and said, "Tink, wait." He looked at Tink with a sadness beyond his years. "I wish I could have gotten a chance to know you. I think you are a very special person. I'm sorry it had to turn out like this."

Tink nodded. Richard understood, Tink knew, that they would never see each other again. "You are a wise young man."

They shook hands, something Tink had never done before, although he'd seen others do it often. He liked the handshake. It was firm, friendly, honest, and in this case, sadly, it was final. Somewhere inside him there was hurt, a kind of hurt that was different from the physical pain of being beaten by a bat. Some injuries, he realized, could not be so easily identified, or so easily pardoned. The human part of Tink was a complicated mixture of strength and weakness, struggle and endurance, and the overwhelming forces of hope and fear.

They turned away from each other then, Richard toward the boys he must now lead, and Tink toward Fayette, toward the town Richard had mentioned that was a far walk from Crawford Hills.

There, perhaps, Tink would discover his vocation among people he did not know, people he would probably never understand.

## ✶ ✶ Y E A R　1 8 6 0 ✶ ✶

Jacob Piersol watched his old friend Bill Oberton rein up in front of him, his horses kicking dust into the morning breeze.

"Ho! Jacob!" shouted the doctor. "Where are you headed?"

"I'm going out of town for a while." Jacob had hitched up his mule and buckboard and had thrown a sack of his belongings onto the flatbed. He was just about to hop up to the seat when Bill came riding down the road.

"Betty Louise came to see me," Bill said, dismounting, a cloud of dust rising behind him. "She said you told her not to come back—I mean—told her you wouldn't be needing her cooking and cleaning for a while. She said you were acting a little dazed."

"Dazed?" Jacob chuckled. It was nice to know that the hand of the Lord, the touch of Christ, had dazed him. That was the least it had done. "I have some important work to do for the church, Brother Oberton. It can't wait."

The doctor fussed with his reins. "What kind of work could be more important than tending to the spiritual needs of your community? That's your calling as a preacher, isn't it? Take something mighty important, I would imagine, to leave behind your responsibilities here, just like that, without making arrangements."

Jacob smiled. Apparently his old friend had been paying attention to their conversations all these years, enough to toss his words back at him.

"My mission elsewhere is very important, too. I have to go to Palmyra. I need to go where the people are open-minded about religious reform. They need to hear the word I carry, almost as much as I need to carry it to them. If I tried to explain it to you, Brother Oberton, you would think I was crazy."

"I already think you're crazy, Jacob. You let Betty Louise go, you pack up your belongings and tell me you're headed off to preach in Palmyra—and what's this Brother Oberton nonsense? It's me, Bill, remember me? We've known each other for forty years."

"I haven't packed all of my belongings. Just some clothes and a few personal items. I expect to return. In the meantime, the Lord will provide." Lightness, weightlessness of body and mind was important to Jacob. The memory of that feathery touch of the Holy Light in the palm of his hand remained with him, a message of scarcity and temperance, Jacob was certain.

"How long will you be gone?"

Jacob shrugged. "Don't know. As long as it takes, I imagine."

"You can't just up and leave like this. Whatever you're going through, Jacob, give it a few days. Let it settle. Then we'll talk it over, you and I, and—"

"I've already given it longer than I should. I've wasted near my whole life—no, no, that's not right—I shouldn't say that. Things have gone according to the Lord's plan, and I couldn't have done things any differently, but the Lord's plan has changed for me now, Bill."

There was serenity for Jacob in this thought. He looked out across the landscape at the early wheat and corn and hay that had comforted him for so many years of his life. The sun seemed to spread over it like butter, melting between the crevices. Jacob was no longer an early crop. He was full and rich and in his prime—well, actually, past his prime—but if it hadn't been for all his failings, a lifetime of failings, he would not have been worthy of the Lord Tink Puddah's forgiveness and grace. He would not have been chosen. Now the time had come to move on, out past the hills and valleys of this lonely little town he'd called home for so many years.

Still, the doctor was a life-long friend; he deserved an explanation, or as near to one as Jacob could offer. "Did you ever hear of Shakerism, Brother Oberton?"

"I've heard of the Shakers," Bill said.

"Do you know what they believe in? They believe that their leader, a woman by the name of Ann Lee, is the embodiment of the Second Coming, the feminine spirit of a bisexual God. They believe in mystic healing. And there are people in Palmyra following this woman."

"That's always the way it is, isn't it? If there's one person to speak, there's two people to follow."

Jacob nodded. He hoped so. "There's an amazing cross-section of beliefs in Palmyra. The Catholics, Presbyterians, Baptists, Protestants and Unitarians, even the Mormons—"

"So what, Jacob? So there are a lot of people there who believe in a lot of things. What has that got to do with you and the people of the valley?"

Jacob rested his hand on the rear wheel of his buckboard. How could he make Bill understand? "This little church of my father's has served our community well. It's all these people have needed, all they've wanted over the years. But there comes a time when people must move on. What do the Presbyterians believe in, Bill? Do you know? Or the Methodists or Universalists, or for that matter the Jews? Let's face it, these people in Skanoh Valley wouldn't have a clue as to what others believed if their very lives depended on it. They have no spiritual curiosity. In a way, it's fitting. It's almost as if our church, our little Vision of Christ Church, was waiting for a man to emerge from it with a special calling."

"You're losing me, Jacob. That sounds to me like reason to stay. If your people need guidance—"

"No. What I'm trying to say is that Skanoh Valley isn't ready for what I have to offer. I think my father did what was best for him and what he thought was best for the community, but he hasn't prepared anyone for the day of reckoning. I need to test my message first on those who are more open-minded. Besides, I'm not my father. What was right for him isn't necessarily right for me. I am a much different man from Nathan Piersol. I have a different calling."

"That's nonsense, Jacob."

"Bill." Jacob hadn't wanted to tell Bill everything, at least not everything about his vision. It wasn't that Jacob doubted his revelation; what he doubted was his old friend's ability to believe and understand. But did it matter? The truth was the truth. Those who were willing to accept it would be saved, and those who were not willing . . .

"He came to me, Bill. The Savior, the Messiah came to me. Tink Puddah has risen from the dead."

"Tink Puddah? Risen from the dead? What in God's creation are you talking about, Jacob?"

"Tink Puddah gave me a mission to preach the Word of God in Palmyra, and there is nothing you or anybody can do to stop me. I would die first. I would gladly die before ignoring the Lord's instructions. Do you see that? I want you to grasp the *veracity* of it, Brother Oberton."

Bill took a step back, probably without even realizing it. "Yes, I can see it. That's what scares me. I've never seen you like this."

"Of course you haven't. I've never been touched by Christ before. Does that mean anything to you? It does to me. It means I'm alive. For the first time in years, I'm *alive*."

Bill shook his head. "Don't you hear what you're saying? Tink Puddah didn't even believe in God, and you're telling me he rose from the dead and asked you to preach the Word of the Lord? Don't you see what's happening to you? Puddah's death has been eating at you for months. You've been sleepwalking. You've been dreaming about him. So you've had another dream. Maybe it looked and felt like a vision, but it's all coming from your own mind, Jacob, believe me. It's nothing to throw your life and your life's work away for. You must know that. We need you here. We all do."

Jacob smiled sadly. "You're a kind man. I wish it were so, old friend, but it's not. No one really needs me here. They have each other. They have their faith. They have the land and their simple lives. I'm tolerated as a mere shadow of my father, which is about all I can say for my years of service in Skanoh Valley. The truth is, they will replace me and not even notice."

"No, you're not seeing all the good you've done." Bill's horse shifted uneasily at his side, twitched its ears and shook its mane at a pesky black fly. "Of course you're not your father, we all know that, but that doesn't mean—"

"Bill, Bill, please, it doesn't matter. I've seen Tink Puddah rise from the dead. I've touched him with the tips of my very own fingers. It was no dream. It was Tink Puddah." He opened his palms to cup the air, God's precious air. "I have touched the Lord. And the Lord has touched me and challenged me."

Bill Oberton looked away. Jacob couldn't remember a time when his friend could not look him in the eye. It was not easy to stare down the barrel of strength and justice and truth. Especially truth. This was something Jacob was going to have to get used to, this weakness in the face of the Lord. He must learn to stand before it with determination and purpose.

"Do you know the disciple who was closest to Jesus after His resurrection?" Jacob asked. "It might surprise you to know it was Thomas, doubting Thomas. Jesus had such incredible patience with him. Thomas had a hard time believing in the resurrection, believing his own eyes even as the risen Christ stood before him. So Jesus told Thomas to come and touch His wounds. He was not angry, as He had every right to be. No, no, He recognized something in Thomas. He knew how much Thomas wanted to believe. After that they had a special bond. I have a special bond, too, Bill, with the Savior. Do you see that?"

The doctor said nothing. Jacob decided he should probably stop trying to explain. "Goodbye, my friend." He turned away, checked the hitches and buckles of his wagon one last time, and hopped up onto the wooden seat. The buckboard had belonged to his father for as long as he could remember. His father had called it his "old four-wheeler." There was more than a little irony in that his father's transportation, which probably had never rolled outside of Skanoh Valley, would now carry Jacob into unexplored territory.

"Jacob, I don't know what to say. You're my best friend in the world. How can I just let you go?"

Jacob smiled. "You have no choice but to let me go. You can wish me well, though, and you can know that I am happy."

Bill frowned. "Be careful. Please, be careful. And come home soon."

"Stop worrying. You're worse than Betty Louise."

Jacob snapped the reins. Floyd, his mule, moved forward with no great haste. Slow and sure, that was Floyd. He would have made a good Christian, taking careful steps, never complaining, doing only what was expected of him. The man and his mule were very much alike. Had been very much alike. Jacob's life was about to change—swiftly and drastically. His life, now, was about answering a call.

He glanced back over his shoulder at his old friend, who stood motionless beside the road, his horse gently nudging him. To Jacob's surprise, he felt tears well in his eyes, tears of sorrow, tears of joy.

"Goodbye, Bill," he whispered, setting his gaze upon the dirt path ahead of him. He must not look back. Now there was only the road ahead and the lonely life of a prophet. He must never look back.

Tink Puddah stood over his workbench in the back room of Mr. Emery's gun shop, working on the inlay for another rifle stock.

Mr. Emery was a gunmaker. He bought his rifled barrels from a factory in Pennsylvania, had them ferried to Palmyra, and delivered by horse cart to his shop some twenty miles east to Fayette Township. Then he cut stocks out of cherry wood and put the guns together in his shop by securing the barrels to his stocks, attaching simple lock and trigger mechanisms he purchased from a local blacksmith, and carefully calibrating the sights. For years he'd sold his guns for a meager profit.

That was before Tink arrived. Once Tink began working for Mr. Emery, the man began to see much larger profits. Tink only knew about the money from overhearing Mr. Emery's conversations with the other men he called buyers. They wanted the fancy designs that Tink carved into the stocks, and they were willing to pay "top dollar" for them.

"Buyers are on their way," Mr. Emery said to Tink in the back room, in the middle of the afternoon. "Which means I gotta hide you in the vegetable cellar." There was neither regret nor antagonism in Mr. Emery's words. He was a man of many thoughts. He was always thinking out load about how to make more money, expand business, where to sell, and how much he could get for his product. When he talked of hiding Tink in the basement, it was just another fact to consider.

He unlocked the chain that bound Tink's leg to his workbench, led Tink out the back door and down into the vegetable cellar, and secured the chain around a thick pine beam driven deep into the earth.

Mr. Emery was wearing a dirty shirt and pants. Sawdust clung to the thin hair on his head and arms and eyebrows. He did not clean himself nearly enough. He stank of toil and whiskey. His chipped front tooth gave him the look of a lean predator, a hungry one, dangerous.

Mr. Emery locked the cellar door behind him as he did whenever his buyers came calling, and told Tink not to "make a peep" or he would whip him to a "bloody pulp."

He had never harmed Tink or even raised a hand against him, but he liked to threaten. Tink didn't care about the threats. Mr. Emery would never hurt him because of the money. Without Tink Puddah's inlay work, Mr. Emery would not be making the profits he seemed to care more about than anything else in the world. It was the most beautiful inlay work Mr. Emery had ever seen, he'd told Tink. It was so beautiful that Mr. Emery was afraid of it. Tink could feel the man's fear every time he looked at Tink's engravings, or ran his fingers across one of his designs.

Tink wasn't sure what Mr. Emery was afraid of. He knew, at least in part, that Mr. Emery was afraid of losing Tink, therefore his profits, therefore his dreams, whatever those dreams might be, for didn't all men have them? He was so fearful that he kept Tink chained to the workbench. Tink was not a slave, or so Mr. Emery insisted. He paid Tink a few coins every week, made a point of showing Tink how he placed the coins in a small bag and where he kept the bag in a chest in his office. Mostly he did this, Tink decided, to assuage his guilt, for what little remorse the man felt quickly dissipated when he put the coins in the bag and ordered Tink back to work.

But there was something other than the fear of losing Tink that haunted Mr. Emery. Mr. Emery feared the designs themselves, designs that did not really belong to Tink Puddah, but belonged to his parents.

Tink had discovered that he could reach into his own mist and find the Wetspace it contained, and then take up the thin, sharp woodcarving implement in his hand and engrave the images he saw there. To men, Tink thought, these engravings were probably eerie, alien designs, warped patterns, convoluted in both their meaning and their attraction, that seemed almost random, never quite connecting in physical form or in the proper perspective of the mind's eye. But they were beautiful, he knew, and it was this beauty that drew the men and their money and also their fear. Fear drew men, Tink had learned, and left them wanting.

But Tink did not care about that. He did not care about the shackles around his leg or the way men felt about his carvings. Tink knew only that he must engrave and learn, that was all. Find the designs within him, carve them, let them live.

So he cut. And he inlaid with metal and silver his alien depictions, smooth and liquid representations of what Tink came to understand as pictures of his ancestors—his otherselves—soft, sentient pearls moving through an ocean of warmth and light and nutriments they called Wetspace. Their mind—their Wetspace—could reach beyond its liquid shell, its liquid world, and explore other places, other planets, other times. This is what he'd learned from his parents as he cut into Mr. Emery's cherry wood gunstocks. Patterns, memories, visions, lives.

Tink knew that so many more patterns yearned to be carved by his careful, patient hand, enough patterns to exceed his lifetime here on Earth. He would have to decide when he had carved enough, learned enough to give himself peace of mind, and then he would move on, for the alien light that was a part of him needed to reach outside as well as inside. Stopping. Stopping would be the most difficult part for him.

Tink heard the hooves of horses approach, the animals snorting, and the slap of leather as the men dismounted. Mr. Emery's buyers had arrived. Tink had learned to take solace in these quiet moments when Mr. Emery was talking to his visitors. He could rest his weary muscles and his tired mind. It was mentally and physically exhausting work for him—the searching of his mist, the interpretation, the carving and inlay—so he liked it when the man physically moved him from the workbench in the afternoons to feed him, and at night to chain him to his small bed, and then again when he saw his buyers riding up the road from Palmyra.

Tink also liked the vegetable cellar and its smells of dirt and mold and cedar, onions and potatoes and apples. He liked its dampness and darkness and the things that crawled in the dirt, the spiders and centipedes and worms, and he liked the deep, sonorous echoes of the men's voices he could hear through the pine floorboards.

"Afternoon, Em," came a man's echo from above. Mr. Emery's buyers always called him Em.

"Why did you bring *them?*" Mr. Emery asked in a gruff voice.

"They're friends of mine."

"I didn't invite any of your friends."

"Well," said the man, "my associates have some concerns."

There was a long pause. Tink heard feet shuffling, chairs sliding in and out as the men sat. He could smell their cigar smoke. Tink thought there were at least four men who had come.

"Look, here, Rollins," Mr. Emery said. "I don't know what you're trying to pull, but I don't like it. I said I wouldn't have anything to do with *them* or their kind, didn't I?"

Tink did not know what Mr. Emery meant by "them or their kind," but he could feel the fear now, Mr. Emery's familiar fear, and a different kind of fear coming from the others—maybe not fear so much as anxiety, the tightness of animals barely kept in check, like the dogs, Darryl's bear dogs.

"Sorry, Em, but my associates wanted to send their own representatives. They wouldn't do business otherwise."

"Associates? Representatives? Awful fancy names for these no-good filthy scum. I said I wouldn't do business with 'em, so I guess this means the deal is off. Get out of here, all of you."

"Oh, now, don't overreact, Em," Rollins said.

"Get out now!" Mr. Emery pounded the top of his desk with his fist.

None of the other men—Rollins' friends—had said a word yet. Nor did Tink think they would. They had not come to speak or to meet with Mr. Emery. They had come, Tink suddenly felt certain, because the man Rollins had hired them to do so, or perhaps someone else had ordered them to come.

"Look, Em," Rollins said, "the fact is you're asking an extraordinary amount of money for these guns, so naturally—"

"Naturally nothin'. You're acting as their buyer. If they don't trust you, why did they hire you? They've seen the product. Course it's expensive. Nobody else in the entire country is doing work like this. It's the best dang work they've ever seen."

"Well, now, Em," the man named Rollins paced across the floor as he talked, "that's one of the things that concerns my associates. They're collectors, you know, collectors of fine things, and they're kind of curious as to who else you would be dealing with. I mean if they're paying prime dollar, we would expect an exclusive contract."

"Ain't got no such thing as an exclusive contract. I'm selling piece by piece to the highest bidders. You know that. Maybe this time I sell to you, maybe next time somebody else pays more. Now you and this scum can kindly get out of my shop. And you can tell your clients this little show is going to cost them five percent extra this shipment, and there might not be a next time if they pull another stunt like this."

There was no bending in Mr. Emery's voice. There was only fear and fury. Blind fury. Anybody could have seen what was coming next, even Tink. Perhaps it was the fear that was blinding Mr. Emery.

"I'm real sorry to hear that, Em."

The chairs slid as the men stood.

A moment of silence.

Mr. Emery laughed. "What's the matter?" he said. "Never seen a Colt Army .45? Didn't think I'd be ready for you? I ain't no fool. Now back on out of here real slow, all of you. I figure I can kill at least two, maybe more, before you kill me. Now get!"

"Em, hey, come on, put that gun away. We're not even armed. Look."

"More ways to kill a man than with a gun. I told you to get so—"

There came a sudden *thwack!* So sudden Tink gasped. Followed by an unnatural silence.

Mr. Emery grunted.

A bullet fired.

Feet scrambled.

Tink heard the sound of a knife plunging into flesh, and another knife, stabbing, stabbing. There was pushing and shoving and grunting from everyone. Tink felt sick to his stomach.

"For chrissakes," Rollins said, "try not to get his blood all over you."

"He's still alive, I think," one of them said.

"Show a little mercy," Rollins said. "Slit his throat."

Tink put his hands over his ears. He did not want to hear the slitting of a man's throat. He closed his eyes, too, although he could not see anything that was happening. He closed his eyes against the memories. Another mercy killing. He did not understand. So much killing, so little mercy.

When he took his hands away from his ears he could still hear the men upstairs in Mr. Emery's office, and in the back room, now, along with the knocking sound of wood against wood, the men collecting all of Tink's gunstocks, no doubt. They were working quickly, clumsily, desperate thieves. Then Tink heard footsteps coming down the wooden planks to the vegetable cellar. One set of footsteps. The man tried the door, yanked at it, threw his shoulder against the wood, perhaps hoping to break the lock or the door itself, but both held firm.

"Hey," he shouted. "We got a locked cellar down here! Maybe there's more!"

"Shoot it open!" another man called.

"No! Don't be stupid!" That was Rollins. "Emery already fired one shot. If somebody heard it they'll be on their way. In case you've forgotten, the penalty for killing a man is the rope. We got to get the hell out of here *now*."

The man at the cellar door ran back upstairs. A few moments later they were all out on their horses. Tink heard the horses stamp their hooves, heard the men say some words that sounded too muffled to make out. The horses galloped away. Eventually all was quiet.

Tink didn't really want to move. He felt safe down in the dark and quiet vegetable cellar. But he knew, eventually, other men would come. Not right away, as the buyers had feared. It was often days before anyone stopped to see Mr. Emery. But when they came they would find Mr. Emery dead. They would ask Tink all sorts of questions. They would probably be suspicious of him, although it was obvious he'd been chained in the cellar and Mr. Emery had treated him like a slave. Men had a way of turning truths into lies. Tink had seen enough to know this. Besides, he did not want to wait too long if he was going to pardon Mr. Emery.

He reached down and touched the pin that secured the shackles around his leg. He tried to bend it. At first it refused to bend, but then as he reached inside its core with his mind, he felt where it was strong and where it was weak, and he felt that the iron pin would cooperate with him if he pushed it just so, in one particular place, over and over. After a time the pin bent enough for him to free the shackles from around his leg. Tink did the same thing with the door. Not bothering with the lock, he worked on the wood and was able to loosen its lowest board and crawl out the bottom. Tink was free.

He climbed the stairs and went in the back door of Mr. Emery's gun shop. The men had stolen all of the cherry wood stocks. They'd overturned Tink's work bench. The men had not touched any of the gun barrels, probably because they were too heavy and there was nothing special about them. Tink went into the front room, where Mr. Emery kept his office. The floor was slick with blood. The room smelled of feces and something else raw and terrible.

Tink took careful steps, trying to avoid the blood. He wasn't sure if it was the smell that sickened him or the blood. Mr. Emery lay sprawled next to his desk. Tink saw that he would not be able to avoid the blood altogether if he was going to save Mr. Emery. He stepped to his side and turned him slightly so that he could touch his chest, feel the essence of the heart beneath it, and search for the misty substance at Mr. Emery's core that he hoped was not too far gone to call back.

He concentrated, looking for the mist. Where was it? Where? Was he too late? No, he was not too late. There should still be mist. Tink searched deeper. What he found was not very pleasant. He found a small, hard knot. He probed the knot with his mind, trying to soften it, loosen it. He worked at its tightness, sensing the mist was near. That was when Tink realized that the knot *was* the mist. The man's mist had been so tightly corded inside him that Tink could not slacken it. The mist kept tightening and closing in upon itself. It was a bitter, foul mist.

Tink tried to work it, relieve it, set it free, but it fought against him. Suddenly he had a clearer understanding of Mr. Emery; his polluted mist had the ability to control him. Tink tried to pull the knot up inside Mr. Emery's body to see if he might work with it better there, or at least begin the pardoning of injury as he had done with the railroad worker, ol' Jimmy. But the harder he tried, the more he realized that the man's mist was obstinate and angry at Tink's intrusion.

The man's knot wanted to die. The man's knot hated its own ugliness so much it would gladly kill itself. The ugliness of the knot brought tears to Tink's eyes. It was awful. How horrible to bear the weight of such a malignant force. Tink had no choice but to let it go.

He felt weak from his efforts. There was a limit to what he could do. There was a limit. Mr. Emery was stubborn even in death. His chipped front tooth no longer made him look dangerous. Now he looked more like an extinct animal, sad and skeletal. Tink wiped the blood from his hands onto his work pants and said, "I'm sorry, Mr. Emery, I cannot save you."

He went to the box behind Mr. Emery's desk where the man kept Tink's wages. He removed the bag of money he had earned and put it in his pants pocket. He returned to the back room of Mr. Emery's gun shop and picked up his sack, the sack with his shotgun, the weapon that he had carried with him on the bear hunt, the gun that had killed the man named Darryl. He slid the big hunting knife into the sack too, the knife he'd carried with him ever since he and the bear had wandered into the frigid woods of Pennsylvania. He slung the sack over his shoulder. He knew that he never wanted to lose these things. They reminded him of the harsh life on this planet, something he must never forget.

Then Tink thought it might not be such a good idea to leave just yet. Maybe he should wait until dark so he wouldn't be seen on the long, dirt road leading away from the gun shop. Besides, he was hungry. Famished. He had spent all of his energy trying to save Mr. Emery. He went downstairs into the vegetable cellar, took some tomatoes from a basket, and ate them, chewing on the seeds and sucking down the red juice. He had never felt so hungry. He ate some apples and carrots.

When he finished eating it was almost dusk. He could barely stand, his legs were so weak. Trying to pardon Mr. Emery had cost him more strength than he'd anticipated. He couldn't imagine walking all night long. Should he wait? What would happen to him if he waited upstairs in the gun shop? Other men would come and investigate the murder of Mr. Emery, a murder he had not seen but heard, and might describe well enough to lead to the capture of Mr. Rollins and his friends.

No. He felt he could no longer trust men, or the hidden mists that controlled them. He had known this, perhaps, ever since the bear hunt, but there was a difference now in the way he viewed things.

He thought of Claudia, the kind woman with the warm arms, and how he would like to see her right now, sit with her and share some corn bread. But that was not possible. He had once thought the truth would have made things right with her, but in the end she had wanted to kill Tink, too. Perhaps he could never be one with mankind. He could be one with their world, with their earth and substance and nature, more one with man's planet than even man could be, but otherwise he was in danger, constant danger from the humans to whom he was closest.

No one knew that he had been working for Mr. Emery. The gunmaker had kept it a secret. Better for Tink to go. He must walk. But he would have to rest for a few minutes first.

Tink lay down on top of one of the crates in Mr. Emery's cellar and closed his eyes.

\*   \*   \*   \*   \*

Tink came suddenly awake when he heard the loud bark of men's voices. He had fallen asleep on top of the crate. How long? How long had he been asleep?

The men sounded angry. Tink knew the sound of angry men very well. They must have found Mr. Emery dead in his front office.

They ran down the steps to the vegetable cellar. Tink hopped off the crate and looked around for a place to hide. There were crates and sacks of potatoes and onions and bushels of apples, but there were no hiding places.

"There's blood on the steps! Break down the door!" one of the men shouted.

Tink heard the sound of iron on iron, the groaning of wood forced beyond its limits, and then the loud snap of lumber. The cellar door pitched open and bright sunlight flushed in. Tink froze. Three men, four, five came into the cellar.

"Christ, what the heck is that thing?" said the first, raising his revolver and aiming it at Tink.

Two other men raised their guns, too. Tink held up his hands. He didn't know what else to do. He said nothing. He decided just to look fearful. Both these things were very easy for him to do. Let the men look around. Let them figure out that Tink could not have killed Mr. Emery. Maybe they'd figure it out. Wouldn't that be something?

One of the men walked up to Tink and slowly reached out to touch him, the gun trembling in the man's hand. Tink retreated from him. All the men were dirty and unshaven. Sweat stained their clothes and their hats. They looked awkward with their guns.

"Look at this," another man said. "Em must a had that thing chained up down here. Look."

The men gathered around the beam where Tink had been chained.

"How did it get out?" asked another man.

"Don't know—wait—look here—must a bent the iron."

"That little critter? Got to be powerful strong to bend iron. If that's the case, it could a killed Em, for sure. It would be strong enough to kill Em."

"But how did it get out of the cellar to kill him? The door was bolted and locked shut from the outside."

"There's a board broke out the bottom of the door. It might a crawled under the door, then gone upstairs and killed Em, then come back to the cellar."

"Why the heck would it do something like that?"

"I don't know. Maybe Em captured it, figured out how strong it was so he chained it up. Maybe that thing there didn't so much like the idea, and then it gets out and kills Em, just like that."

"But why come back down here? That don't make no sense t'all."

"We don't even know what it is. How do we know what it thinks like?"

"What do you mean, don't know what it is? Can't you see it's a dwarf?"

"A blue dwarf?"

"Look. There's blood on its shoes and pants."

"It was hungry," said another man. "Look, there's a apple core and some potato on the ground. It ate some stuff down here. It come back because it was hungry and then it was gonna run off, I bet, maybe with Em's money."

"Em's coin box was open. Somebody check that thing's clothes to see if it's got any coins."

One of the men eased toward Tink. He was an older man with gray-black hair who smelled like cows. His gun trembled in his hand. The gun's frame was pitted with rust. The other men circled around Tink to make sure nothing bad was going to happen to their friend.

Fine, thought Tink. Shoot me. Kill me. He was so tired of all this.

The man put his hand in Tink's shirt pocket and found nothing there. Then he stuffed his hand in Tink's pants pocket and pulled out the coins. The coins belonged to Tink, of course. He had earned them fairly, by all the rules of men and their vocations.

"What's that?" asked another man, pointing at Tink's burlap sack.

They opened his sack and found his shotgun and hunting knife. "If this don't beat all," one of them said, examining the knife. "Em was stabbed to death, and this thing's got a huntin' knife sharp enough to cut stone."

"All right, what's going on down here?" Another man came down the steps into the cellar. This man was clean. He had a fancy mustache, a neat hat, a brown leather coat, and a lawman's star pinned to his lapel. His boots were shiny and he had his gun holstered. He was much taller than the other men.

"We got Em's killer, that's what's goin' on!" said one of the men.

"Oh, you do? What makes you think so?" asked the clean one.

"We got it all figured, Marshal Braddock. Look—"

"Yeah!" another man said. "That *thing*, whatever it is, busted out of its chains here, look for yourself, you can see it must have knocked out a board and crawled under the cellar door, went upstairs, and took its revenge on poor Em. We figured Em captured it out in the woods or somethin'. Then it cleaned out Em's coin box and came back down here to fill its belly. We figure we nabbed the little runt just before it was about to make a run for it. Look here. These coins was in its pants."

"And the critter's all bloodied up, too. Em's blood, for sure," someone said.

"Settle down, boys, settle down," said the marshal. He looked around, expressionless. He took the coins and stuffed them in his vest pocket.

Finally, the man with the salt-and-pepper hair said, "It had this sack with a knife inside, the knife that killed Em. He was obvious sure gonna run for it. Murderin' varmint. What the hell is it, anyway?"

The marshal took the sack from the man. He stepped over to Tink. He towered over Tink and stared down at him with steady blue eyes.

"Don't get too close, Braddock, that thing has got some kind of evil power. It busted clean out of these here iron shackles."

The marshal knelt down in front of Tink. "You want to tell me what happened here, boy?"

Tink just looked at him. No. He did not want to say anything. Men were too good at turning words around to suit their own purposes. Anything he said would only cause him grief. No. Tink had nothing at all to say.

"Maybe you're afraid to talk. Is that it? You don't have to be afraid. We just want to know the truth. These men won't hurt you."

Easy for mister shiny-boots to say. Tink turned away from the man. He did not like looking into the man's eyes. He had soft, friendly eyes that might compel Tink to speak if he were to let down his guard.

"Do you have a name?" said the man.

Tink ignored him.

"Well, I'll tell you what we're going to do, just in case you can understand me. We're going to ride back to Palmyra together. You can ride right up on my horse with me. Nobody's going to hurt you. I promise. Then when we get back to Palmyra we can talk again in private. Okay? You don't have anything to be afraid of." He held his hand out to Tink.

"Jesus, Braddock, be careful, that thing might rip off your arm for all we know." This was the salt-and-pepper man still pointing a revolver at Tink. His hand was shaking worse than ever. There was dirt embedded so deeply under his fingernails that it would probably never wash out.

"I want you men to get out of here," said the marshal in a calm voice. He reached out and pushed the barrel of the man's gun toward the ground. "Go on."

The men slowly walked out of the cellar. The marshal held his hand out to Tink again. Tink reached out and grasped it. Why not? This was the only man who had ever spoken to him reasonably. What did he have to lose? Nothing. He had nothing to lose.

The man smiled, and they walked out of the cellar, up the steps, into the sunshine.

The other men milled around outside. "We want justice done!" one of them snapped. "That thing killed Em. You got the murder weapon right there in that sack, Braddock."

"Don't worry, I'll find out what happened," said the marshal.

"We're serious. We'll lynch that thing if you don't."

The marshal's face did not change expression. "I don't tell you how to milk your cows, do I, Mr. Hansen? I don't tell you, Mr. Blake, when to harvest your corn. Seems fair, then, I don't expect you—any of you—to tell me how to do my job."

He lifted Tink up onto the saddle of his big horse, then he put his foot in the stirrup and hoisted himself up behind Tink. He tied the sack to the horse's saddle. Without another word to the men, he heeled his horse and started off down the road toward Palmyra.

Tink was shocked. Why had this man helped him? He had never met anyone like him before, someone who had such authority over other men. He had never before felt safe in the company of any human being. Did he feel safe now? Maybe he did. That was probably a mistake. He warned himself not to feel safe. He knew better. Feeling safe on this planet was like asking to be killed.

Tink must have slept a long time in the vegetable cellar because now he was wide awake. He felt every clomp of the horse's hooves. But it was good to feel the man's body hovering over him, and the man's arms around him. This reminded Tink of the woman, Claudia, who had once loved him as if he were her own child.

Tink was glad that it was nighttime when they reached Palmyra. The buildings were low, dark shadows, except for a couple of taverns where oil lamps glowed, and Tink could hear the distant sounds of laughter and piano music. Palmyra was a large town. He had never seen so many buildings strung together all in one place. If the marshal had come riding in with Tink in his saddle during the middle of the day, many people would have seen him. This way, no one would take notice.

Tink was learning that it was better for him not to be seen by anyone. If he got out of this mess alive, he decided, he would build himself a cabin somewhere out in the woods, alone. Just Tink and the animals and the Planet Earth. If he got out alive. He did not need a vocation. Vocations were for men, men who were not blue dwarves, men who were not hated and feared, men who were not Tink Puddah.

\* \* \* \* \*

The marshal helped Tink down off the horse and led him into one of the buildings. It was the jailhouse. The building was not made of wood like most of the other structures. This one was made of brick. Inside there was a desk and some chairs and a large stove with a black pipe that went through the ceiling like a chimney. Some tin cups and plates. An old rifle hung on the wall behind the desk. There were three small rooms to the left, rooms that had iron bars for doors.

Tink did not like the idea of being trapped inside a cell at the mercy of men. He fought down a sudden urge to run. If he ran, what good would it do him? Now that he had trusted this man, he must trust him all the way. How had he gotten himself into this situation? How could he have been so foolish? The marshal's eyes, probably, had lured him in.

"Go ahead and sit down." He motioned to the chair.

Tink went over to one of the chairs and sat.

The marshal squatted on a tall stool beside his desk. He looked at Tink. He didn't say anything. He just looked. His scrutiny made Tink self-conscious. *What?* Tink wanted to say. *What do you want from me?*

"What the hell are you, anyway?" asked the man.

Tink closed his eyes and frowned. He should have expected this.

The man stood up, took off his hat, unbuckled his gun holster, and hung them both on the hat rack behind his desk. He went over to a pan of water and washed his hands and face. His fancy mustache stayed in place even after he'd splashed water on it. "Would you like to wash up? Can I get you a glass of water?"

Tink shook his head no. He was more interested in his fate.

"Well, I'm glad you can at least understand me. You can listen to what I have to say if nothing else. I'm going to be straight with you, stranger, whether you want to hear it or not. That's my way. I'm a straight shooter."

The marshal wiped his hands and face with the towel. "I'm no fool. I can see Emery's been cleaned out of gunstocks. Looks like a robbery and a killing to me. Looks as if Emery had you working for him, maybe even forcing you to work, but I don't figure you for being involved in any crime. How am I doing so far?"

He sat down in his chair and put his feet up on top of his desk. "Of course to those men back in Fayette, it doesn't much matter what you were doing at Emery's gun shop. You're different, and as far as lots of folks are concerned, that's all that matters. What that means is, they probably don't care as much about what really happened to Emery as I do. What that means is—"

"What that means," Tink interrupted, "is that they want to kill me."

The marshal's expression did not change when Tink spoke, as if he'd been expecting it all along. He nodded. "That's about right. So why don't you tell me the truth so I can get to the bottom of Mr. Emery's murder."

"I worked for Mr. Emery. I did the inlay work on his gunstocks. The work was so good that Mr. Emery was apparently selling his guns for very high prices. The men he was selling to were afraid that he would sell his guns to other men who might be willing to pay more. So yesterday Mr. Emery's business associates, he called them buyers, came to visit him. There were four or five of them. They stabbed Mr. Emery to death and stole all of his gunstocks. I heard it all from the cellar. I was chained to the beam in the vegetable cellar. One of the men was named Rollins."

For the first time the marshal's face registered some sort of emotion. Tink could not tell what his expression meant, but he knew that the marshal had recognized the name Rollins. That much Tink could tell for sure.

"All right," the marshal said. "Now I'm going to tell you some things you should know." He sat up straight, pulled some chewing tobacco out of his desk drawer, and tucked a wad into his mouth. "First off, you're a wanted man. There are some folks in Pennsylvania who say you shot a man in the head. You got any recollection of that?"

Tink was afraid that his face showed he knew all about it. The marshal's jaw worked on the tobacco. "I took the man out of his misery," Tink said. "That's all I did. I was being merciful. The bear injured him beyond repair. I thought it was the right thing to do at the time. He was dying, and he was in pain. If I had it to do all over again, maybe I wouldn't be so merciful. Maybe it would have been better to let him suffer. I don't know. Probably they still would have blamed me."

"Probably. Like I said, you're different."

"Yes. So it does not matter whether I did the right thing or the wrong thing."

"That's about it."

Now the man's "straight shooting" was beginning to annoy Tink. What was this Marshal Braddock trying to tell him? Was he going to put him on trial for the murder of the man named Darryl? If so, fine, put him on trial and be done with it. That would be the end of Tink Puddah. He would be hanged after all.

The marshal leaned back in his chair. "I know you didn't kill that man. I was in the area at the time the killing was reported to the law. I went to see the body with one of the lawmen in Alleghany. It was obvious a bear mauled that man to death. He was slashed wide open, there were claw marks all over him, but nobody cares about that. Same thing would happen if I kept you here for Mr. Emery's trial. That's why I'm going to let you go. With you out of the picture, now that I know where to look, I can nail the men responsible, and justice will be served. Do you understand what I'm saying?"

Tink was speechless. He thought he understood. No. Impossible. This was another game. Men liked playing games of power and control. There was no way this marshal was going to let him go, just like that. "Just like that? I can go?"

The man nodded and spat some of his chew onto the plank floor. "I'll probably have a crowd of men around this jailhouse first thing in the morning, at least twenty strong. They'll be wanting to lynch you. That's why I want you to clear out of here tonight. I'll have to tell them I questioned you, and I got some information that will lead me to Emery's killers. They won't be happy about it, but there won't be anything they can do, either. Comes right down to it, they're farmers and family men. Their anger will pass."

Tink stared at the marshal. Could he be telling the truth?

"Normally, I'd want to keep you here to testify against Rollins, but I'll have to try and stick it on him without your help. I won't endanger your life any more. But I want you to know you'll be on your own. If somebody comes after you, I won't be around to protect you. And then there's Pennsylvania, too. Don't go toward Pennsylvania. There's a five-hundred-dollar bounty on your head. I just want you to be aware of that."

Tink didn't say anything for a while. He just sat and thought. He was wanted for murder. People thought him capable of taking a life. People hated and feared him for no other reason than he was different. How had all of these things happened?

"I'll have that glass of water now," Tink said.

The marshal got up and dipped a cup into a bucket of water. He handed the cup to Tink. Tink drank it all. The man picked up Tink's sack.

"Since I'm releasing you, I'm going to give you back your belongings. Your money, too. I take it you earned it."

Tink nodded. That was certainly true.

"The way this works is, I never realized you were wanted in Pennsylvania. Do you understand that? We never had this conversation about a man wounded by a bear and you taking him out of his misery."

Tink frowned. "No one will ever believe that. How many little blue men are wanted for murder? I can tell you. One. Only one. If someone finds out you let me go, you'll be in trouble with your own law."

"I can take care of myself. I suggest you do the same. Now you better clear out of here. You've got a lot of road to cover in a short time. I'm sorry about that. I wish I could help you more."

"You have been a large help. You have spared my life. I am grateful."

The marshal filled a canteen of water and handed it to Tink. "Take this," he said. "Don't worry about bringing it back."

"Thank you. You are a generous man."

"Just one thing I can't figure," said the marshal. "How did you break out of those shackles Emery locked around your leg?"

"That would be difficult to explain."

"Try," said the man.

"I touched them. I persuaded them. I didn't really break out of anything. The shackles let me go."

The marshal shrugged. "I should have expected an answer like that. Walk due west. Stay off the main road come sunrise."

Tink got up out of the chair. He went to the door of the jailhouse and walked outside. The night air cooled him. He strode through town, keeping to the side of the road. Bugs swirled crazily at the edges of the dirt trail. Tink walked.

He would have to live alone from now on, not among men, but around them, on the outside, always on the outside. This saddened him. He was lonely. He knew he shouldn't be. He had his parents inside him, and he could communicate with the world around him—its plants and animals and minerals—like no one else on this planet. But of all creatures, Tink was mostly human, and now he must turn away from humanity. He must fear, always, that some bounty hunter might come and kill him for a five-hundred-dollar reward. So much for being part of everything on this planet. So much for being one with mankind.

The smell of wild weeds and thick, snarly roots refreshed him. He looked up at the sky, watched the clouds pace steadily onward under the soft glow of a pearl-white moon. Bats flapped, crickets and bullfrogs sang, owls hooted. It was night, and the clouds were walking. They walked tirelessly. Tink was beginning to understand them. He had a long way to go himself, not just on this night, but for the rest of his life.

Step,

step,

step,

step.

What could be easier, Tink thought, than to walk alone under the moonlit clouds, hand-in-hand with the creatures of the night?

Palmyra township. Jacob had never seen so many beautiful homes with white picket fences and fine green lawns. Some of the houses were two and three stories tall. Gorgeous poplar trees shaded the cobblestone walks. And the businesses . . . look at them all! General stores, apothecaries, tailor shops, hotels, saddlers, harnessers, shoemakers, blacksmiths, a tinker's shop, even a bookstore, and the print shop where the *Wayne Sentinel* was printed. There was a grammar school in town, two dress shops and a millinery right on Main Street, a barber and bathhouse.

Men and women pushed handcarts along the road, selling cakes and pies and hand-woven baskets and iron pots and pans. And there, and there, and there, the churches! This is where religious revivalism thrived. The Baptists, the Roman Catholics, the Methodists, and the Presbyterians all had churches right in the center of town.

Mormonism was born here. If the people could accept the prophecy of Joseph Smith and his gold plates, they could accept *anything*. Jacob laughed at this thought. Joseph Smith claimed to have been visited by angels of God. Jacob Piersol had been visited by the Savior Tink Puddah, a blue-skinned angel risen from the dead. Who would they throw in the asylum first?

The fact remained that thousands of people lived in Palmyra. Thousands of people who would now hear of Tink Puddah, and how God had sent a very special blue-skinned prophet to serve among men.

Jacob had been thinking about how best to shape his message, how to turn it into something that the multitude could trust and understand. *Ha!* He could think from now until the end of time and it wouldn't matter. *Do your best, Jacob. Speak the truth. The Lord's hand has fallen upon your shoulder. God asked you to serve.* Not even his father had accomplished such a feat. Those who didn't see that, those who didn't believe, well, they would burn in Hell, and there was no better place for them.

Jacob decided to push his tired old mule, Floyd, a few more miles. He snapped the reins and headed his buckboard down toward Erie Canal, on the outskirts of Palmyra Village. He passed a huge mill where wheat was ground into grain, a livery that had to house near a hundred horses, a cow farm and a hen house that looked longer than the main road that ran clear through all of Skanoh Valley.

He rode along Canal Street to the strong, sharp smell of the waterway. Barges moved slowly up and down the canal, hitched to teams of horses plodding along the muddy towpath. Dockworkers loaded and unloaded bales of cotton and sacks of wheat from keelboats. There was a tang in the air of dirty water and sweaty animals, not good air, but heavy air wrought with bad character.

Jacob had heard tales from other preachers about the dockers of Palmyra and their state of abjection. The boatmen and the prostitutes and the shore men lived shameless, bawdy, sinful lives, creating a shanty town of profane denizens only a few miles from one of the most forthright and religious communities in all of America.

Progress—the progress of the canal that ran all the way from Lake Erie to the Atlantic Ocean—brought evil as well as prosperity.

But this is where Jacob Piersol wanted to be, here among the alleys littered with trash, the broken crates and wagon wheels and broken lives, the water snakes and river rats, the smell of dung from the oxen and mules and horses, and the black flies and fat mosquitoes and, yes, even the disease that flourished in the crowded warehouse district along the piers.

Unlike those revivalists before him, this is where Jacob would begin his mission. Here, burrowed in among the sinners, the fallen, the needy, he would first deliver the message of the Savior, Tink Puddah, and here he would begin to make converts. Soon he might be able to build a church of his own in Palmyra, standing right next to the Catholics and Presbyterians. Jacob had done his homework. A man of God needed only three trustees to legally form a religious organization in New York state. Would it be that difficult to find three influential believers? Dare he dream of such a thing?

He settled Floyd and his father's "old four-wheeler" into a wide patch of mud and hay between a barn and a ramshackle rum-hole. This busy thoroughfare looked as good a place as any to preach the Word of the Lord. The sun was beginning to set, and it appeared that most of the day's work along the docks was done. People were sure to be coming and going from the tavern.

"Sisters!" he called, startling three prostitutes out of their chatter. "I have come to you to speak the Word of the Lord."

They smiled and continued on their way, gathering their long skirts and tugging at their short coatees.

"Hear me!" he shouted. "God has sent a messenger to show us the way to Heaven. He sent Him in the guise of a blue-skinned foreigner, a most unlikely Savior, but a man filled with the love and grace of the one true God. Tink Puddah was his name."

The women kept walking, nudged each other, chuckled.

"Laugh if you will, but I've seen Him with my own eyes, risen from the dead! Don't ignore me! Your very souls are in peril!"

But ignore Jacob they did. As did the man with the pea coat, and several more prostitutes, and some horse-keepers. At nightfall a group of dockers already stumbling drunk, singing and passing back and forth a jug of rum, fell to their knees mocking Jacob, spitting rum at his feet, and then at Floyd. "Save us! Save us, oh great and powerful mule!" they shouted at Floyd. The mule wiggled his ears at them and looked away.

Jacob tried to preach to them from Paul's Letter to the Romans, Chapter 9, Verses 27 and 28: "'Though the number of the children of Israel be as the sand of the sea, a remnant shall be saved: For he will finish the work, and cut it short in righteousness: because a short work will the Lord make upon the earth!'" But this only sent them weeping in laughter again. Jacob could see that his labor here would not be easy. God had challenged him, indeed. But he was up to the task.

Long after dark, after the laughter and the sound of the piano and the fiddler from inside the saloon had died away, and the prostitutes no longer walked the piers, Jacob Piersol unhitched Floyd and let the old mule graze on scraps of hay from the nearby barn. Then he curled up in the back of his buckboard with his blanket and pillow to the sound of the water sloshing in the canal, with the Bible that once belonged to his father clutched firmly to his chest.

He gazed wearily up at the stars and fell fast asleep—the deep, restful, dreamless sleep of the righteous and the strong.

*     *     *     *     *

When Jacob woke the next morning his stomach grumbled from hunger, but there was preaching to be done. The dawn brought with it a slew of canal workers. Jacob Piersol stood on the back of his buckboard and read from Mathew 15:

"'And Jesus called the multitude and said unto them, Hear and understand: Not that which goeth into the mouth defileth a man; but that which cometh out of the mouth, this defileth a man.'"

"I'm gonna put a fist in your mouth if you keep yacking!" shouted a man lugging sacks of grain. Others laughed.

"'Do not ye yet understand?'" Jacob preached, returning to Matthew, "'that whatsoever entereth in at the mouth goeth into the belly, and is cast out into the draught? But those things which proceed out of the mouth come forth from the heart; and they defile the man. For out of the heart proceed evil thoughts, murders, adulteries, fornications, thefts, false witness, blasphemies: These are the things which defile a man!'"

Jacob raised his Bible and shouted at the people. "Do you hear the Lord's message, brothers and sisters? Your Judgment Day is coming. You are living unclean lives! You are soiling your souls! But it is not too late. Christ has come to us in the form of a blue-skinned Savior, Tink Puddah. Repent! Hear me! Repent!"

Jacob Piersol read from Mark and Luke and John. He read from the Acts of the Apostles and the Letters to the Romans. Some people ignored him, others sneered, others told him to shut up, others threatened to shut him up.

From the Ephesians, chapter 4: "'Wherefore putting away lying, speak every man truth with his neighbour: for we are members one of another.'"

"You want some truth?" a tall man shouted back at Jacob. He had broad shoulders and a bent nose. He wore a skullcap, a dirty jacket, and a pair of gloves worn thin from lifting. "I'm tired of listening to your big mouth. Shut it up or I'll shut it for you."

Jacob stared at the heckler and turned to another page. "'Be ye angry, and sin not: let not the sun go down upon your wrath: Neither give place to the devil. Let him that stole steal no more: but rather let him labour, working with his hands the thing which is good, that he may have to give to him that needeth.'"

The tall man stopped and stared at Jacob. "Are you saying I don't make an honest living? Are you accusing me of being a thief? I've had about all I can take of you. The docks ain't no place for a village idiot!"

This was just the sort of man Jacob needed to reach. "I'm reading from the Ephesians, brother. 'Let all bitterness, and wrath, and anger, and clamour, and evil speaking, be put away from you, with all malice—'"

The man stepped forward. "I'll get rid of some anger." He scooped up a handful of mud and slung it at him, slopping it all over Jacob's coat and splashing his cheek. The man and the crowd behind him laughed. "Get out of here!" he shouted, turning his back to Jacob and the Word of the Lord.

But Jacob would not be so easily intimidated. He brushed the mud from his coat and read, "'And be ye kind one to another, tenderhearted, forgiving one another, even as God for Christ's sake hath forgiven you!'"

The man turned back to Jacob then. Jaw tight, teeth clenched, he walked up to the buckboard, grabbed hold of Jacob's coattails, and yanked him down into the mud, letting out the roar of a wild beast.

The mob of people laughed.

Jacob was so stunned he forgot himself for a moment, forgot about Nathan Piersol's Bible underneath him buried in the mud, forgot about Tink Puddah's message and his mission of peace.

"You big oaf!" Jacob said, pushing himself up. As soon as he found his feet, he punched the man square on the chin. The man had not been expecting it. He staggered back and bumped into the wagon. Jacob grabbed him by the shirt.

"I said to be kind and tender-hearted, didn't I?" He spun the offender around and hurled him aside with all his strength. The man tripped and fell to his hands and knees. Jacob came up behind him and kicked him in the butt, sending him sprawling. "Soil a man of the cloth, will you? The Lord will not stand for it!"

The man tried to gain his feet, but Jacob rushed him like a bull, shoulders down, hit him full in the ribs and sent him reeling back, back, until the man tripped and fell into the canal with a loud splash.

The people—quite a crowd had gathered by now—howled with laughter.

Jacob stood in the mud, watching two men reach into the canal to help the vile offender out. What had he done? What had Jacob done? He looked down at his clenched fists and forced them open. He'd struck a man in anger—Jacob Piersol, who had never struck another human being in all his life. He turned to the crowd. "I'm sorry, good people. I am a man of God, a man of peace."

"Let's ask Skiles about that," came a woman's voice, clearly amused.

Skiles? Skiles was his name? "I'm sorry, Brother Skiles," Jacob said. But the man would have none of it. As soon as he was out of the canal he pushed aside the men who had helped him and ran off in the opposite direction. No one seemed to care what Jacob had to say after that. The fun was over. The men and women had already begun to disperse.

"I don't know what came over me," Jacob said.

"Larry Skiles came over ya, that's what."

Jacob turned around. An old man with a gray beard and a floppy hat stood in front of him. He smiled a near toothless smile. "Had it comin', he did. He's been bullyin' ever'body down here for too long, looking for a brawl. Somebody was gonna hit him sooner or later. Glad it was you."

"No, no, this was very bad," Jacob said. "I can't believe I lost my temper like that. But the Lord must have had a reason, a purpose. I can't say what it was. He's been difficult to interpret lately."

"You can call me Pike," the man said, extending his hand.

"Jacob. Jacob Piersol."

They shook hands. "You lost this." The old man handed Jacob his Bible. The cover and some of its pages were caked with mud. Jacob wiped them with his coat sleeve.

"I like you, preacher man. Ya got guts." The old man held a bag at his side. He reached inside it and pulled out a big red apple. "Here. I been watching you all morning and you ain't had a bite to eat."

That was true. It had been over a day since Jacob had eaten. He reached out and took the apple. "Your kindness and generosity will not be forgotten, Brother Pike."

"Ha! Brother Pike. I like that. Let me give you some advice, Brother Preacher Man. You can shout all you like down here about religion 'til your throat is dry as dirt, but ain't nobody gonna listen or care unless you got yourself a gimmick."

"A gimmick? God needs no gimmick, sir."

Pike shrugged. "Maybe God don't, but you do."

"People who do not wish to hear the Word of God will burn in Hell."

"Whatever you say, preacher man, but it's your job to make 'em listen, ain't it?"

Jacob bit into the apple and tasted its sweetness. He had no idea until this very moment how famished he was. "What do you mean by a gimmick?"

"The people down here live hard lives, work like dogs. They're tough, body and soul. Get what I'm sayin'?"

Jacob nodded. Tough of soul. Yes, that made sense. People who lived hard lives, lives without loved ones or people to care for them, were not so easily won over by God's message of love.

"Talk is cheap," Pike said. "Get yourself a soup cart, or some corn meal to dish out from the back of your buckboard there. If you're preachin' over a bowl of slop, people will listen, at least for a little while. Go into the village and ask the locals for whatever they can spare. Fruit, vegetables, milk, soup, don't matter, might be something different every day. Soon as the locals see you're a man of the cloth, they'll donate to your cause. They all want somebody to clean up this section of town, just don't want to sully their own hands doin' it."

Jacob thought about it. It wasn't such a bad idea, old Pike's suggestion. There was nothing wrong with using a little ingenuity in the service of the Lord.

"Besides, you gotta eat, too, I imagine. Ain't nobody gonna throw money at ya down here, friend. No, sir."

Pike had a broad smile, chapped lips, and a sparkle in his eyes. He was wearing torn clothes, and the cloth sack over his shoulder looked about a hundred years old, only slightly more weathered than Pike himself. This man was a survivor, Jacob decided. He knew of what he spoke. Perhaps he had even been sent by the Lord Tink Puddah to help him.

"Take my advice," Pike said. "When you go asking for handouts, I wouldn't mention this here blue-skinned savior of yours. The people of Palmyra are pretty fierce about their religions. A man says his church is right, that means everybody else is wrong, if you get my meanin'."

"If they ask me, I will tell them all about the Savior Tink Puddah. That is my mission."

"Yeah, well, maybe so, but folks aren't likely to ask because they don't want to know. Just don't go offerin' anything up. Believe me, you'll have an easier go of it. I ain't steered you wrong yet, have I, preacher man?"

He winked, cackled, and walked away, whistling a tune, leaving Jacob Piersol standing there dripping mud, holding his apple in one hand and his father's soiled Bible in the other.

People don't want to know, thought Jacob. Yes, that was probably the truth, the very sad truth. But that was something Jacob Piersol was determined to change.

# THE BOOK OF RESURRECTION

Tink Puddah built his own cabin on a hill overlooking Skanoh Valley.

Most men would have needed help building a cabin. It was not an easy job. But for Tink it was not so difficult. He was one with the earth and stone and wood and land, and he was growing more one with them every day. Where men helped men, nature helped Tink. Nature led him to the stones he needed for the foundation. Tink hand-picked and set each stone himself and, as varied in shape and size as they were, each stone fit neatly and perfectly together until he had a foundation one leg high over which to place his sills. Nature led him to the northern hardwoods he needed to log for his cabin walls, and nature guided his broadax to cut smoothly and effortlessly through the wood.

When Tink began to build his cabin, the structure itself seemed to guide him in notching and setting the poles, in levering and lifting the logs that should have been too heavy for him, in pounding the nails and locust pegs he'd purchased in the nearby town with some of the money he'd earned from Mr. Emery. It was nature and the cabin that showed Tink Puddah how to lap joint, fashion the walls log by log, fit the rafters and joists and gables with ropes and pulleys, lay the ceiling and the floor. His oneness with the planet helped him more than ten good men.

He constructed his own chimney and fireplace out of fieldstones and creek rocks, carefully throating the chimney and balancing its foundation.

This was a more difficult task, because the wood seemed to fight him along the way, as if it knew that the chimney would one day house its greatest enemies, smoke and fire. But when Tink finished, it was not a crude job at all, for the stone and the wood had found their own symmetry, perhaps knowing that in the end one must support the other or both would suffer.

Soon he was finished building his first home, and Tink Puddah was much pleased with what nature had provided.

The planting came next. At first he planted only a small garden of corn and squash and tomatoes and onions. Tink did not eat meat other than the occasional bird. He did not need much to keep him alive. In time, he would harvest some other fruits and vegetables, but in the beginning a few things would be enough. In time, there would be many things he'd like to do. He would like to build a cider press like the one he'd seen in Fayette, for he loved the sweet taste of crushed apples. He would like to have a vegetable cellar and a smokehouse and an icehouse, and maybe next season he could purchase a mule to help with the plowing. It would be nice to have a mule to keep him company. But for now he would make do. He could store and preserve some food to help him through the cold season, and he loved to eat chestnuts and acorns, and he knew he could always find tasty barks even in the dead of winter.

So Tink Puddah tended his small garden and cabin, dug a well for fresh water, picked wild berries and apples, built himself a quern he would need to grind corn, and spent his days and nights in quiet comfort, alone, until one day the man named Jacob Piersol came to visit.

\*   \*   \*   \*   \*

"Hello! Is there anybody here? My name is Jacob Piersol. I'm the preacher from Skanoh Valley. Hello!"

Tink was inside by the fireplace, stacking some wood. He heard the preacher walk from the front of the cabin around to the back. Tink did not like introductions. When men first met Tink they did not know what to make of him. They often stammered, gave him strange looks, asked odd and uncomfortable questions.

Tink stepped outside. "Hello," he said in his friendliest voice. Tink's voice could be musical when he tried.

The man named Jacob Piersol stared at him.

"My name is Tink Puddah. I just built this cabin. I'll be farming some vegetables. Not much for now, as you can see, but enough to keep me well."

The preacher stood motionless, gripping a book in his hands. He seemed lost for words. This was all right with Tink. Tink preferred it this way. Let him gawk for a few moments at the little blue-skinned man, and when he came around things would be better.

"I am pleased to meet you," Tink said, stepping forward, offering a handshake. This seemed to break the spell.

"Yes, yes," said the preacher, blinking, shaking Tink's hand. He stared as if Tink were an intricate painting. "A pleasure. Forgive me, it's just, I—"

"My look is very different, I know, but I am really quite harmless."

"Of course. Forgive me for staring. How rude of me."

"Not at all rude," Tink said. "May I offer you a cup of water?"

"Yes, thank you."

Tink went to his cistern and drew a cup of water for Jacob Piersol. He thought the man had done very well in recovering. Better than most, in fact.

The preacher drank from the cup. "I came to welcome you to the area. Do you have a wife and family?"

"No, no family. Just me."

"That's Skanoh Valley down there." Jacob motioned down the hill, toward the east. "Skanoh is an Iroquois Indian word. It means peace. We call it the Valley of Peace."

"The name is very beautiful, and so is the valley. It seems like a pleasant town. I bought some supplies there."

Jacob smiled. "Not many folks, but we've got a blacksmith and a small mill. The mercantile carries some staples you might find useful. Most people around here are farmers. The land is rich, arable, cradles a good crop."

Tink nodded. "And you are the preacher."

The man seemed suddenly to remember his purpose. "Yes. I came to introduce myself, and I brought you a gift, just a small gift. I do it for all the people who settle in these parts." He handed Tink the book he'd been clutching.

Tink accepted the gift. It was a magnificent, leather-bound book.

"Do you know how to read, Mr. Puddah?"

"Yes. I was taught to read."

"Good. In that case, I'm sure you will appreciate my gift. I ordered it special from the printing press in Palmyra. It's the Bible, the King James Bible."

"It's beautiful," Tink said. "I am sure I will enjoy the story."

"Oh, it's more than a story, Mr. Puddah. It's a book about the life and death of our Savior, the Lord Jesus Christ, and the record of God's New Covenant with mankind. It is the Good News."

Tink Puddah turned the Bible over in his hands and made a show of studying it. "Yes, it is wonderful. Thank you."

The preacher gave him an encouraging nod. "I should say that what I'm offering you is more than a book. I'm offering you the gift of our Lord, Jesus Christ. I hope that you will read the Bible carefully, hear the Lord's message, and accept His gift."

"Yes, certainly, thank you for such an attractive and thoughtful present. It is very kind of you. I will read it."

"I'd also like to invite you to our church. This is a community of fine upstanding Christians, and of course I would like to have you join us for Sunday morning services." He smiled, sipped again at the water.

Tink felt better now that the man was relaxing. He had never been invited to church before. It was a kind gesture, but he really saw no need for it.

"Thank you for your gracious invitation, but I am not a religious person."

"Not a religious person?"

Tink shook his head. "No. Religion to me is . . . how can I explain this . . . ?"

His parents, during their solidification, had discovered the religious impulse as part of the collective subconscious architecture of men, but they had rejected it. *Prayer, faith, theology . . . intellectual perception . . . ideational content . . . unconquered characteristics of inherited mental life . . . phylogenetic development . . . non-essential influences . . .*

"Philosophical beliefs of men," Tink finally said. "I do not have the religious impulse."

"Every man has feeling for God, Mr. Puddah, whether or not he knows or understands it. That's one of the great joys and mysteries of God's relationship with mankind."

"Perhaps. But religion is not for everyone, wouldn't you agree?"

"No, I would not. God sent us His son Jesus who died for our sins and was resurrected from the dead." The preacher's voice had become unfriendly, and his expression had hardened.

"Well . . . I am not from here. Where I come from—I should say where my people come from—there is no spiritualism directed toward a God. We do not need to seek things outside ourselves."

"You don't believe in *anything?*"

Tink tried to think of the best way to end this conversation. He feared he was close to insulting the preacher. "I am a foreigner," he said, hoping that would end it. He found that sometimes if he stated this plainly, standing in front of someone, it was surprisingly easy for a human being to accept him and his blue skin and his tiny body, and in fact accept all that was strange about him, without fear or expectation.

"A foreigner," the preacher said. "I figured that just from the looks of you. Where are you from?"

"A small village overseas. Very far away."

"Are your people savages?"

"What do you mean by savages?"

"Primitive. You don't believe in God. Why not? Aren't you familiar with the God of man, or with Jesus Christ? Is that it? You don't know about the Resurrection?"

So being savage was disbelieving in God. Tink did not think this was exactly right. "I know about your belief. But there is no God."

The man drew back. Tink felt suddenly wicked. He shouldn't have said that, he knew it as soon as the words had passed his lips, but he had never discussed God with any man before. He would have to learn what and what not to say.

"You poor, sorry, wretched heathen," Jacob Piersol said, without sounding at all sorry for Tink Puddah. "I advise you to read that Holy Bible very carefully, word for word. You need it, Mr. Puddah. You need God in your life, whether you know it or not."

The preacher turned around stiffly, chin up, spine straight, and marched around to the front of the cabin, not even glancing back or saying goodbye.

Tink watched him walk down the trail toward Skanoh Valley, the Valley of Peace. He thought that it had been nice of the preacher to come. Tink did not mean to insult him. He must remember not to discuss religion with men from now on, or he must at least remember not to tell them the truth about it.

He brought the Bible inside his cabin, set it on the mantle of the fireplace, and returned to stacking wood. It was a fine day, clear and cool, and Tink had many chores to finish before sunset.

Tink Puddah walked briskly with Miss Anna Goodlowe toward the grandstands where the boars would be judged. Tink found himself smiling, always smiling, around this girl who was so full of joy. She wore a long cotton dress and bonnet the color of Tink's blue hair. Tink had donned his overalls and his best wool shirt. The Rochesterville County Fair, Anna had told him, was "the event of the fall season."

And so it seemed. Huge red-and-white striped tents stretched across acres of open fields. Women sold their preserves and pies and cookies and breads, their hooked rugs and doilies and embroidery. Chicken farmers sold eggs for three-cents-a-dozen. Bands played wind and string instruments and snare drums. Livestock stood on display, their anxious owners vying for blue ribbons. Men competed in tournaments of horseshoes and ax hurling and black-powder rifling.

Tink could smell roasted peanuts and an enormous pig burning on a stake, as he and Anna strode past a dozen families filling their plates with potatoes and squash and corn biscuits, the mothers trying to get their children to sit and eat, the men battening their hats against the wind. The sky was bright, the air brisk with the spice of the season. Near the stables, Tink could smell the cattle, the cow dung, and the rank odor of milch goats. They hurried past a pen where prize hogs bathed in shallow mud.

"Look at those shoats!" Anna said. "Oh, wait, Tink, look over there." Anna pointed to a small tent between the pens. "Mrs. Gish is here. She's a phrenologist. She's wonderful, absolutely *wonderful*. Let's go!" She pulled Tink toward the tent.

"What is a phrenologist?" Tink asked.

"She can tell your future by reading the bumps on your skull. Well, she's not an expert yet, but she's been taking instructions once a month in Albany because her husband travels there for business meetings—Mr. Gish is a banker—and she's getting quite good."

Mrs. Gish had a sign hanging on the outside of her tent. *PHRENOLOGY! LEARN YOUR FUTURE! 2 COPPERS.* Anna pulled back the tent flap, and she and Tink stepped inside. It was dark and smelled sweet and floral. A table sat in the middle of the tent with one candle on it. Mrs. Gish stood just inside its glow. Tink could see the folds of her white, frilly robe, and she was wearing a flat black hat with a wide brim. Her jewelry jangled when she moved.

"Anna, my best customer," Mrs. Gish said. "How splendid to see you again. But haven't you seen enough of your future?" Mrs. Gish and Anna laughed and hugged.

"You can never see enough of the future," Anna said. "But today I brought someone else I'd like you to read."

"Ah, excellent, a new skull." Mrs. Gish motioned for Tink to sit in a chair beside her table. Tink reached in his pocket for two cents. "Oh, no," said the woman. "No payment until after your reading, if you're satisfied with my skills."

"Of course he'll be satisfied, Mrs. Gish," Anna said.

"*Madam* Gish," said the woman.

"Oh, I'm sorry, I forgot. Tink, when Mrs. Gish is in her tent, she's not really Mrs. Gish. She's to be referred to as Madam Gish." Anna walked over to the woman and touched her lightly on the arm. "Madam Gish, this is my dear friend, Mr. Tink Puddah. Tink, Madam Gish."

"It's a pleasure to meet you, sir," said the madam. "My, you certainly have a different look about you. Where are you from?"

"Very far away," Anna answered for him. "Can we just get a brief reading, Madam? We need to rush over to the grandstands to see the boars."

"Of course, quickly then, let's see," Madam Gish said. "Everyone likes to know about life and love, Mr. Puddah, so I will read your life line and your love bumps."

"Thank you, that would be fine."

The woman came up behind him and placed her fingers on top of his head. Tink looked up at Anna. She smiled at him.

"Just relax," Anna said.

"What an interesting skull," said Madam Gish. "I've never felt a head quite like this. No two heads are alike, of course, but this one is softer than most, but firm, yes, firm, almost like clay. I've taken some ironstone pottery classes, too, Mr. Puddah, you might be interested to know."

Anna said to Tink, "Mrs. Gish—oh, I'm sorry, *Madam* Gish—is wellschooled in lots of things." And then to Madam Gish, "What do you see there for love?"

The madam's fingers probed Tink's skull. "Well, he has many bumps. But their shape doesn't suggest love, exactly, and yet, well, they're not worry bumps, either, and I can't say they're disaster bumps because I haven't learned quite enough yet about catastrophe. But isn't this strange? I've never felt anything like this before."

Anna's eyes opened wide. Tink saw the candlelight flicker in them. "What? What?" she said.

"Mr. Puddah's life line is slanted at an odd angle. I've never felt such a sharp backward pitch. I might have expected to see something like this on a very old man, someone who has left a long life behind him, but Mr. Puddah, well, he doesn't appear to be old. Are you an old man, Mr. Puddah?"

"Oh, no, he's not old at all," Anna said. "He's a young man."

"Ah! It must be—" the woman's fingers tightened around Tink's head; he felt her short fingernails digging into his scalp.

"What? What?" Anna asked.

"Previous lives!"

"Oh. Are you sure?" Anna sounded just the slightest bit disappointed. "Nothing about love?"

"Well, I'm almost sure. His love lines are very elusive. I'll have to discuss this with my instructor in Albany. When you have more time, Mr. Puddah, perhaps I could get you to come back for a more thorough reading, free of charge."

"Perhaps," Tink said.

"Can you tell us anything else?" said Anna.

"Not without more time, I'm afraid."

Anna frowned. "Well, we really must be going."

The woman let go of Tink's head and he stood up, relieved to be set free. He reached into his pocket and put two cents on the table. "Thank you, Madam Gish."

"Oh, no, I couldn't take your money. I haven't given you a full reading."

"I am pleased with your skills," Tink said.

"I could have done much better if I'd had more time. You will come back, won't you?"

Anna pushed the tent flap open. "Goodbye, Mrs. Gish. We'll come again."

"Madam!" the woman called, as the tent flap closed behind them.

Tink blinked at the bright sun, glad to put the overwhelming scent of opium perfume behind him. "You were displeased with the reading?"

She shrugged. "No. Well, maybe a little."

"I'm sorry."

"Don't be sorry. It's just that a woman likes to see a lot of love bumps. For a man, it probably doesn't matter. Besides, we've got boars to watch. Let's go."

They ran across the field. The grandstands loomed before them. Long benches stood in rows stacked forty feet high, circling a dirt field, with bright rainbow flags flapping in the breeze atop tall wooden posts. The enormous structure could hold hundreds of people. Later there would be buggy racing and a tightrope-walking contest inside the grandstands, and earlier in the morning there had been clowns dancing for the children. But now the judges would select the best boar of the fair. This, according to Anna, would draw the largest crowd.

"C'mon, Tink," Anna said, pulling him along faster by his shirtsleeve.

They passed through the main gate, and Anna led him up the steps to a bench on the upper tier.

"You can see everything from here. Look!" She stood on the bench and looked out over the fairgrounds.

Tink could see the Genesee River far off in the distance. He hated the river. It frightened him. He could not achieve the oneness with the water on this planet the way his parents had in Wetspace. Here, on this planet, Tink was an intruder in the water. He did not belong. The water could easily swallow and drown him. On Earth there was land and water, and he could truly belong to only one or the other. Man belonged to land, and Tink was more man than anything else.

He looked out at the crowd. He would normally have avoided a gathering of so many people, yet now he was not nervous. He was not afraid, as he normally might have been if he were alone. Anna's presence—her charm, her life force—had given him comfort. He felt safe with Miss Anna Goodlowe. He felt free.

The competitors marched out their prize boars to the sound of blaring bugles. The people in the grandstands cheered as the boars circled the dirt arena. Anna sat on the bench and turned her full attention to the contest.

"Look at those Hampshires," Anna said. "They've got to weigh a thousand pounds each! One of them will win for sure."

"Yes, certainly."

"Papa asked a man last year how much a good Hampshire boar cost, and do you know what the man said?"

"No."

"The man said five hundred dollars! Can you imagine that much money? But look at them. They're like kings, don't you think? So proud and majestic."

"Yes," Tink said. "And arrogant."

Anna laughed, her voice a flock of delighted birds. They laughed together then. "Why don't you ever talk about yourself?" she asked. "All I know about you is that you're from very far away. I don't even know where."

Tink hesitated. No one had ever really been interested in Tink Puddah before, and Tink had never been anxious to talk about himself. He was different; he was a foreigner. That was usually enough for people to know; that was all they ever really wanted to know. Tink was always shrinking away from human beings, even those he felt were not a threat to him, but it was not so with young Miss Anna Goodlowe. She had a way of making him relax. Her presence here, now, made him feel things he could not explain.

"I was born here," he said. "But my parents came from a faraway place. I don't know where exactly."

"You don't know where your parents came from? That's odd. Why didn't they tell you?"

"They died. They both died the day I was born."

Anna looked stricken. "Oh my God, I'm so sorry. I had no idea."

"It's all right. Death is not the same thing for us, for my people, as it is for yours. My parents—how can I say this?—I feel them inside me. They are always here for me. Sometimes stronger than others, but always here." He put his hand over his heart.

"That must be a wonderful feeling. I sometimes think I can feel my mother inside me, but I can't, not really. It's just that I wish it so hard sometimes I can fool myself."

"My parents have always been able to tell me things," Tink said. "I've learned from them about the place where they were born."

"Really? What have you learned? Tell me about it."

She seemed genuinely interested. Why not? Why not tell her? "My parents came from a place not at all like this one. I don't think I will ever fully understand it, but from what I can tell . . . " he hesitated.

How much could Tink say to Anna Goodlowe? Tink's people were pearls, pearls that could communicate with one another just by thinking, and they could swim through Wetspace, open their cells to it, and their Wetspace would sustain them, feed them and keep them healthy and strong, and they in turn would nourish their world with their own nutrients. How does one explain such things? Could he tell her that Wetspace was formless, and yet firm, and was always moving, like a wave through space and time? Could he tell her no one was ever alone there, not even after death? No, if he told her too much, she would not understand. He might even scare her.

"My people live near the water," he said, "and the water is everywhere. Where my parents are from . . . I guess you would say everyone knows each other the same way they know themselves. The wants and needs of one are the wants and needs of all. There is no fighting, no hurt, no loneliness."

"Oh, Tink, that sounds so beautiful."

Tink glanced out over the crowd. The grandstands were filling up. Children laughed, men and women held hands and talked quietly to one another. In the distance, a musical band played songs interrupted by gusts of wind. "Sometimes it is beautiful here, too."

"Why did your parents leave their home?" she asked.

Tink had been searching inside himself for the answer to that question for a long time. "I'm not sure. I sense that it had something to do with my father. He wanted to come here very much, to explore, although I don't know why. I don't believe my mother wanted to come at all. She came anyway, for my father, for all of us, so that we could be together. I feel pain for my father. I think he wanted and needed something outside himself, which is unusual for our people. When he died, he knew he'd made a terrible mistake."

"Lord have mercy, you've been here all alone since the day you were born. How did you survive? How did they die?"

"They were . . . they were involved in an accident," Tink said, smiling to defend himself against the memory. He did not want to talk about the past anymore. He was here with Anna Goodlowe, and he was happy, and the now seemed much more important. "Please, tell me about the boars. I want to hear about them."

Anna looked down at the field. "Papa took me right down on the field last year, and one of the owners let me touch a Hampshire. You would not believe the strength in those hocks until you've seen them up close." She reached out, as if she might curl her fingers around the moment.

Tink took hold of her hand then, without even thinking about it. She looked surprised. Tink was surprised, too. He was about to let go of her when she squeezed his hand and smiled. They looked into one another's eyes for a moment.

Suddenly, from the benches below, someone yelled, "Boar war!" and the crowd roared in unison.

Tink glanced down at the field. Two boars in a cloud of dust thrust furiously at one another. Anna gasped. The two owners tried to distract their animals, slapping at them with short whips, but the boars ignored them and wrestled out to the middle of the field, spinning round and round, snorting furiously.

"Oh, no," Anna said. She stood, grasped Tink's hand tighter. Most of the people in the grandstands had jumped to their feet. Anna pulled Tink out of his seat, and the two of them ran down the steps hand-in-hand. Anna pushed her way through the crowd to the railing, dragging Tink along behind her.

The dust on the field swirled. The men were now trying to put a large, wooden shield between the two boars to separate them, to blind them. But the beasts fought on. Tink was amazed at their speed and fury.

"They must have caught each other's scents," Anna said. "Male boars challenge for dominance. They don't know any better."

The men trying to intercede were in danger of being trampled. They circled the dueling boars, unwilling to give up, but the boars were unwilling to give up too. The beasts reared, lowered their heads, and charged.

Anna turned and pressed her head against Tink's chest. The beasts clashed, tusks surging forward. Blood spewed from one of the boars and the animal shrieked in agony. Tink felt the press of bodies behind him. He pulled Anna away from the railing, back through the throng.

"It's all right," Tink said as they cleared the mob. He held her close to him. She trembled in his arms.

When Tink looked up, he was surprised to see Papa Bear Goodlowe standing in front of them. Anna had said her father was off selling corn and would not be able to attend the fair this year. She'd asked Tink to accompany her instead. Papa Bear looked puzzled, too.

"Anna?" he said.

Anna glanced up. "Papa? I thought you were in Bloomfield."

"Yes, I was. But I sold the crop early, and I was on my way home, so I thought I'd stop and buy you a gift from the fair." Papa Bear's voice had an edge to it. He was holding two folds of fine jade cloth under his arm. He glanced soberly down at the material. "And I thought you were at home tending to chores."

"I was. I finished my chores, and since you couldn't make the fair I thought I would ask Mr. Puddah to accompany me."

"And this is how Mr. Puddah accompanies you? By holding your hand in public and hugging you?"

Papa Bear had not addressed this question to Tink, but Tink felt compelled to answer. "Miss Anna was upset," Tink said, "about the boar fight." He let go of her.

"I'm talking to my daughter!" snapped Papa Bear, glaring at Anna.

"Father, don't—"

"Don't talk back to me, child. I'm your father. Is this how you repay my trust in you? While I'm away you go out calling, is that it?"

"Papa, stop!" Anna said. "This is Tink Puddah. What's wrong with you? Have you forgotten all he has done for us—"

"What's wrong with *me*? What's wrong with *you*, Anna? Use your head. Tink is a foreigner. What are people going to say when they see you out with him? What are they going to think? What are the *young men* going to think? Didn't you consider your reputation?"

"Papa! You're making a scene."

Tink noticed people staring at them. He wanted to run. He wanted to disappear.

"We'll discuss this at home," Papa Bear said. "Come with me." He held out his hand to his daughter.

"Papa, don't do this to me," she said.

"Now!" He still hadn't looked at Tink, not even a glance in his direction.

"I wanted to see the twenty-foot cornstalk," Anna said, but her voice had turned small and injured. "There is talk of a twenty-foot shoot in the competition."

"Now," Papa Bear repeated.

"And a pumpkin two feet wide," she said.

Papa Bear glared at her. "*Now.*"

"And the buggy races and the tight-ropers." There was a catch in her voice. Anna did not reach out for her father's hand, so Papa Bear stepped forward and grabbed her roughly by the arm.

"Mr. Puddah," he said, still refusing to look at Tink. "You are like a son to me, but this will not happen again, do you understand? I love you like a son, I'm telling you, I want you to know that, but you can't make me compromise my daughter's reputation. Someday she will want to marry. This will not happen again. Do you understand?"

Anna was crying now. "Papa, stop, you don't know what you're saying!"

"Mr. Puddah," Papa Bear said, looking out across the field, up into the grandstands, his jaw tight as corded wood. "I love you like a son, but this is my daughter, do you understand?"

"Yes," Tink said, "I understand."

Papa Bear yanked Anna by the arm, half-dragging her away from the crowd.

Tink stood by himself as the mob disbursed. He looked out across the dirt field. The boar war was over. The boar that had been speared by the other was dead, lying flat out in its own blood, covered with dirt from the battlefield. The other boar was injured, hobbling badly, unable to stand on its left front leg. The leg dangled, tick-tock-tick-tock, like the arm of an antique clock.

A man came out onto the field with a shotgun. He put the gun barrel to the head of the wounded boar and pulled the trigger. The blast echoed through the grandstands. The boar toppled over. The earth shook when it landed. Another mercy killing.

Two angry men—the owners of the dead prize boars, no doubt—had to be held back from fighting. They shouted curses and accusations.

Let them go, Tink thought.

Let the savages kill one another.

Tink turned away, alone, and walked out of the grandstand.

Jacob Piersol brought old Floyd and his buckboard to a stop in front of the docks down on Canal Street. Brother Pike waved to him and smiled his near-toothless smile. The old docker would surely be among the saved come Judgment Day, thought Jacob. His advice had been sound.

The locals were willing to donate food to Jacob's cause each morning, sometimes cornmeal, other times day-old breads or fruits past their prime. One of the hotels, twice a week, gave him a huge pot of soup. He told the locals he was reading from the Bible and offering the food to the hungry dockers, and they applauded his efforts and skirted the topic of his religious preferences. For almost a year now they had supported him.

So Jacob would load his spoils onto the back of his buckboard, travel down Canal Street, and set up with old Floyd every afternoon in the same spot so that the dockers knew they could count on him being there. Each day Brother Pike helped him serve the daily meal while Jacob read aloud from the Bible and related his experiences about the Savior, Tink Puddah.

In this way, for a few precious minutes out of every afternoon, the people came to him, and he spread the Word of the Lord. This was his mission, after all, his purpose, and he was happy.

But in another way he was not so happy. Although he preached, no one really listened. They came for the soup and cider; they came for the cornmeal and bread. If they heard Jacob's words, those words did not seem to make any noticeable difference in their lives.

The same men who frequented his cart each afternoon continued to frequent the saloons come dusk and the prostitutes come dark. The women, hungry for food and lacking Christian decency, thanked him and smiled up at him as Pike filled their bowls, but come sundown, they strolled away with the men who paid them for their favors.

For a year he'd been preaching, and still nothing had changed. He was beginning to think he'd made the wrong decision, starting here, in the midst of such avarice. Perhaps the early revivalists had been right. The Word was better spent on those more inclined to hear it.

Brother Pike hopped up on the back of the buckboard. "What did you get?" He took the lid off the huge iron pot and a cloud of steam escaped. "Ouch!"

This was a daily ritual, Pike picking up the lid and burning his fingers. Jacob laughed.

"Oatmeal!" Pike announced.

Jacob tied up Floyd's reins and joined Pike on the back of the buckboard. "And maple syrup," he added with relish. "Praise the Lord!"

"And some elderberry juice from the Presbyterian parson," Jacob said.

"Saints be praised!" Pike performed a ridiculous shuffle and began waving people to the buckboard. "Come and get it!" he yelled.

Jacob opened his Bible and cleared his throat. Already the dockers had gathered. It was overcast and uncomfortably humid for late summer, but that would not deter the hungry. Many of them now planned their day around his appearances.

"Brothers and sisters!" he hollered, "welcome, and let us rejoice! God has sent us a messenger in the name of Tink Puddah. I am here to give you my testimony. I have seen the Savior risen from the dead. I have touched him with my own hands. He lived a small life, but a remarkable one, a life of kindness and charity. Let us learn from his example of peace and love. Today I shall read to you from 1 Corinthians, Chapter 11."

"'For I have received of the Lord, Tink Puddah, that which also I delievered unto you, that the Lord the *same* night in which he was betrayed took bread: And when he had given thanks, he brake it, and said, Take, eat: this is my body, which is broken for you: this do in remembrance of me. After the same manner also he took the cup, when he had supped, saying, 'This cup is the new testament in my blood: this do ye, as oft as ye drink it, in remembrance of me.'"

"Hey, preacher, you sure that part about Tink Puddah is in your Bible there?" said a man in the crowd. "I've heard a lot of preachin' in my day, but I ain't never heard that."

Another man yelled, "Give us a break from your Tink Puddah Jesus. We already got too many churches in this damn town!"

Laughter came from the crowd. The preacher glared right at the heckler and said, "'Wherefore who shall eat this bread, and drink this cup of the Lord, *unworthily,* shall be guilty of the body and blood of the Lord. But let a man examine himself, and so let him eat of that bread and drink of that cup. For he that eateth and drinketh unworthily, eateth and drinketh damnation to himself, not discerning the Lord's body.'"

"Oh, now I'm an unworthy sot, am I?" the man said, playing to the crowd. "Look, everybody, I'm unworthy!" He cocked his hat, pointed his nose in the air, and marched around in a circle, much to the delight of the others standing in line for food.

And so it went through most of the meal.

Soon, almost as quickly as the dockers had gathered, they dispersed, having filled their bellies, leaving their wooden bowls and tin spoons in the back of the buckboard. Brother Pike took up the large ladle and scooped himself a bowl of oatmeal. He smothered it with maple syrup and began eating.

"You don't look so good today, Brother Preacher Man," Pike said around a mouthful of food.

Jacob tucked his Holy Bible away inside his sack of personal belongings. "I'm just not so sure I'm doing any good here."

Pike swallowed a thick lump of oatmeal. "Nonsense. Look here all the people who come to hear you preach every day. How many preachers can claim that? You can't get upset by the monkeys in the barrel. There's always gonna be a fool or two."

"It's not the monkeys who bother me. It's the barrel. They don't come for me, they come for this." He rested his hand on the pot of oatmeal. "Even you come for this."

Pike put down his bowl. "That ain't true. I want to help. You're doin' a dang fine job here. It's just gonna take some time. I ain't steered you wrong yet, have I?"

"It's not up to you to steer me, it's up to the Lord Tink Puddah, and if I am not best serving the Lord's plan, it's my responsibility to figure out what I'm doing wrong and how to fix it."

Pike frowned. "Every great man goes through doubts."

"I am not a great man. It is the Lord who is great. Let me ask you something, Brother Pike. Do *you* believe me? Do you believe that God sent the Savior Tink Puddah among us to show us the way, and that He rose from the dead?"

Pike hesitated.

Jacob felt a sad smile crease his lips. "There, you see, not even you."

"No, no, I was just thinking about it. I mean, I never much thought about it before . . . you know . . . about how I figured it. Sure, I believe you. If the Savior has come, who am I to say it ain't so?"

Jacob considered this. "You are one of them," he said, meaning the dockers, and then he went about collecting his bowls and spoons.

Brother Pike must have felt a little guilty, which was something for Jacob to cling to at least, for he helped the preacher clean up the buckboard. Usually after he ate, Pike had urgent business to tend to. The two men knelt at the bank of the canal to wash out the bowls and utensils. Pike whistled a tune and every once in a while said, "Cheer up, Brother Preacher Man, smile, smile . . ."

As Jacob Piersol leaned over to wash out the last of the bowls, someone kicked him from behind, and he splashed head first into the canal. He barely had time to close his mouth before he hit the water. When he rose to the surface, a crowd of onlookers stood laughing.

He who laughed the loudest was Larry Skiles.

"Oh my oh my oh my!" Skiles said. "Excuse me, Preacher. I must have accidentally bumped into you. I'm soooooo sorry." Skiles took off his skull cap and took a stage bow for the crowd.

Jacob swam to the canal bank. Pike helped him out of the water. Larry Skiles turned and nodded to the two men who stood just behind him. They all walked over to the preacher's buckboard.

"Well, well," Skiles said. "Looks to me like your wagon is a mite unbalanced. What about you folks? What do you think?" he shouted to the people. "Does it look like the preacher's wagon needs some fixin'?"

Jacob stood dripping river water and weeds as he watched people cheer Larry Skiles on. He stared at the faces in the crowd. These were the very same people he had been preaching to and feeding for so long. And here they were, chiding him, throwing in with the likes of Larry Skiles. He felt the blood rising in him. How could they?

"Look, here, Skiles," Pike said. "You done dunked the preacher, now get lost. You ain't got no cause for bustin' up his wagon."

"Oh, is that right? Well, everybody else seems to think it's in need of fixin'."

Skiles nodded to his two friends. They braced themselves against the side of the buckboard, and the three of them heaved and lifted, easily tipping the buckboard over onto its side. The kettle of oatmeal fell into the mud along with Jacob's sack of personal belongings. Jacob, drenched, walked over to calm old Floyd, who hawed and fussed at the commotion. Everyone guffawed.

"There weren't no need for that!" Pike shouted.

Jacob knelt beside his sack and retrieved his Bible. This was the second time the evil Skiles had muddied the Lord's Word. If there was ever a sign of his allegiance with the archfiend Beelzebub, this was surely it. Jacob brushed off the book and tucked it inside his coat pocket.

Pike ran up to Skiles and shoved him, but the man just laughed, along with all the rest of the folks. Skiles grabbed hold of Pike's shirt and lifted him into the air. The people howled, "Dunk him! Dunk him!"

That surely proved the power of Lucifer, Jacob thought. Who else could take control of a crowd in such a way? He'd shown these people nothing but kindness, and they had turned against him without a second thought. He felt such a mix of rage and impotence that he couldn't move. The Savior, Tink Puddah, must have felt this way, confused and alone in His virtue, standing in the face of God's children gone mad.

Skiles walked Pike over the edge of the canal and dropped him in. Pike screamed and splashed helplessly. When he tried to scrabble up the bank, a group of dockers kicked him back in. The throng found this uproariously funny.

Skiles turned toward Jacob. "I don't think me and the preacher made our peace yet. What do you think, boys?"

"No, I don't think so," his friends agreed. "Not yet, Larry. You best make peace with your savior-man."

"Ha! Where's your God now, you crazy old fool!"

Larry Skiles came up to him, fists clenched, broad shoulders hunched forward, his neck thick and straining at the collar of his filthy shirt.

Jacob, still kneeling, reached inside his sack. He drew out the shot-gun—*the shotgun?* Yes, yes, he'd brought his shotgun with him, although he couldn't remember ever owning a shotgun, but it was here, now, when and where he needed it, almost as if the Lord Himself had provided it for him, almost as if the Lord was putting it right in his hands, asking him to use it. Jacob glanced up and saw the sudden look of fear in Skiles' eyes. He braced the shotgun in the crook of his arm and cocked the hammer.

"Easy there, preacher," Skiles managed to say, his voice more than a little strained.

Yes, thought Jacob, the foul soul should be afraid of the Lord's power, the Lord's wrath, the Lord's gun.

"You can give me that gun now," Skiles said, reaching out. "I know you don't want to use it, you being a man of peace and all."

"Yes, I'll give you the gun," Jacob said. "I'll give it to you just the way you deserve it."

And he pulled the trigger.

The blast echoed like cannon fire. The slug lifted Skiles clean off his feet and plopped him down with a smack in the mud. Blood slogged out of his belly, and his head settled back. He coughed up a red stain, and then he lay motionless, eyes round with shock. The smell of smoke rose into the air, and the heat of the blast stung Jacob's eyes.

The Lord's wrath is mighty indeed, Jacob thought, glancing at the gun and then back at the devil's fallen disciple, Larry Skiles. The Lord's wrath is terrible and righteous and blue—the blue of the Savior, Tink Puddah, in whose name he had just killed.

Jacob stood, shotgun still warm in his grip. The crowd ran away screaming. Jacob didn't care. Let them fear the Lord, let them all fear, as well they should. It was about time they took notice. It was about time.

Jacob walked over to the dead heathen and said, "In the name of the Lord Jesus Christ our Savior Tink Puddah, I condemn your evil soul, Larry Skiles, to eternal damnation. May you burn in Hell!"

It rained. Suddenly and without warning. Where the skies had been peaceful just moments ago, rain burst forth with a vengeance. A cleansing rain, thought Jacob, for the Lord surely wanted to wash him clean of the foul spirit he'd been asked to destroy. Yes, he'd had no choice. God had asked him to kill. Jacob lifted his face to the rain. He was only vaguely aware of the dockers screaming, and then someone tugging on his left arm.

"Preacher man!" Pike hollered. "You gotta get outta here! Go on, run for it!"

Jacob glanced at Brother Pike. He smiled and brushed back Pike's wet hair. "We have done well here this day, my brother. We have defended the Messiah, Tink Puddah."

"Look, the marshal will be comin' down here right quick. He's gonna lock you up for sure. He's gonna think you're as crazy as a caged bear. You best get out of here and let 'ol Pike smooth things over."

"We've done nothing wrong here. I can speak for myself."

"That's what I'm afeared of. You start talkin' 'bout that foreign Savior and that'll be the end of your church—that's right—no more food for the hungry—no more church of Tink Puddah. You know how you always been wantin' that church. You best run for it and let ol' Pike handle this. Go on, now, go on! Follow the canal west and hide out in the hills, and I'll come looking for you later. I ain't steered you wrong yet, have I?"

"Brother Pike, I think this time you might be wrong. Now I see why the Lord sent me to these docks. It was a test, a test of faith. God wanted to know if I had the strength and courage to face the devil, to do what needed to be done. And I've done it. I've succeeded."

"I seen that. I seen what you done. But if you want to keep preachin' you best—"

"I'd best preach," Jacob Piersol said. "The good people of Palmyra await me." He slung his sack over his shoulder and walked over to the buckboard, his shotgun still firmly in hand. Old Floyd stood hitched up in front of the tipped wagon. Jacob laid his shoulder into the flank of the cart and heaved with all his might. The buckboard turned upright onto its wheels with a splash. "Ha! God has given me strength, Brother Pike! Do you see? I can do anything!"

But Brother Pike was gone. Jacob squinted, searching for him through the downpour. There was no sign of the man anywhere. Run off with the rest of them, most likely. That was all right. Jacob Piersol had served his purpose here, and so, he supposed, had Pike. And the evil Larry Skiles, too.

Jacob looked down at the dead messenger of Satan. Perhaps God's rain would wash clean the man's unworthy soul. Yes, he liked that thought. Forgiveness, even for the beasts.

*   *   *   *   *

Jessie Braddock was not in the least bit surprised when he saw Doctor Bill Oberton walk through the front door of his jailhouse. In fact, the marshal thought he'd see Oberton sooner than this. The man had waited nearly a year before coming to Palmyra.

"Marshal Braddock, my name is Oberton, Doctor Bill Oberton, from—"

"From Skanoh Valley—of course, of course—I remember you. Come right in and sit down. Can I offer you some whiskey?" Braddock rose from his chair and shook the doctor's hand.

"Yes, thank you, I'd appreciate that. It's been a long ride. And it's so humid out there today. I'm hoping this rain will break the weather."

Oberton shirked his long black coat, shook the rain off it, and hung it on a wall peg. He was a tall man, a few fingers taller than Braddock himself.

"A storm is always good for a change of one sort or another," said Braddock, handing the doctor a tin cup of whiskey.

Oberton thanked him and sat down. "Glad I made it as far as Palmyra before the downpour. Nothing more miserable than a long ride in the rain."

Braddock stepped around his desk and sat opposite the doctor, regaining his height advantage. The marshal had his desk sitting on a six-inch riser. He found that it gave him an advantage in conversation—or more importantly, interrogation—when he could look down into a man's eyes.

"So, how have you been, Doctor?"

"Fine, thank you, fine, and you?"

"Very well," Braddock said, assuming Oberton needed the pleasantries to get comfortable. When he was ready and willing to talk about what was really on his mind, Braddock would be ready and willing to listen.

"Good." The doctor raised his cup and drank eagerly, maybe even nervously, Braddock thought. Oberton's gaze moved toward the rifle hanging on the wall behind Braddock's desk. "That wouldn't be a Revolutionary War rifle, would it?"

"You've got a good eye. That there's a Brit gun. I bought it from a man in Vermont whose grandfather took it off a dead Red Coat. Did you know that those fancy Brit rifles probably cost England the war?"

"Is that right?"

"Yes. You see our American guns were much lighter, and the butts were cut short so we could brace them against our shoulders and put a sight on the enemy. Those old Brit rifles were heavy as stone and built to put the butts under your arm, so you couldn't aim very well, you just had to point it in the general direction of your enemy and hope for the best. Let me show you."

Braddock pulled the rifle off the wall and tucked the butt under his armpit, holding it about chest high. "As you can see, a very inefficient way of discharging a firearm. What good is a gun that looks fancy if it doesn't do the job of killing?"

"I see your point." The doctor set his cup down on the marshal's desk. He fussed with the brim of his hat.

Braddock put the gun back up on the wall and let the doctor be uncomfortable for a moment. He liked watching people. A man could learn a lot from observation. He sat down behind his desk and reached for some chewing tobacco. He'd made the chew himself. Ollie West, the trapper who'd taken him all the way from Chicago to Vermont when he was just a boy, had taught him how to make his own chew. He remembered watching Ollie dig a hole in a chunk of birch, pull the veins out of a handful of tobacco leaves, and stuff the meat of the leaves deep down into the hole. He could see Ollie clearly in his memory. He wondered why, now, Ollie should come back to him so vividly, and he decided it was the doctor's fault. Bill Oberton looked a lot like Ollie West. The sunken chest and fleshy throat, the craggy face, the pleated forehead. But it was the eyes that did the trick, as bright as new coins, completely out of place, a sign of life in an otherwise spent body.

Braddock took a pinch of tobacco and stuffed it between his cheek and gum. "Well, what can I do for you, Doctor Oberton? I'm assuming this is not a social call."

The doctor crossed his long legs and perched his hat on his knee. Outside, thunder struck, and rain hammered down on the jailhouse. "You're right. This is not a social visit. I'm here to talk to you about my good friend, the preacher Jacob Piersol. Perhaps you remember him."

"Oh, yes, I remember him well. A good host, your preacher, with a mighty deft cook in his employ, if memory serves me."

"Yes, well, I'm a little concerned about Jacob. Awhile back he left Skanoh Valley to come here to your town of Palmyra. It seems he got the notion in his head to preach directly to the people here, broaden his horizons, so to speak." The doctor paused, thinking for a moment. "I remember the day he left the valley. He talked sort of crazy about Christ the Savior. He didn't make much sense at the time, but he was . . . well . . . he was adamant."

Braddock worked the tobacco in his mouth for a moment, thinking maybe it was time to level with the doctor. "Let me ease your burden a bit. I know why you're here. I've been watching your preacher. He's been railing on about that blue boy of yours who was killed in your town, calling him the Savior, the Messiah, the Son of God, preaching how we all better repent because the end is near. I hate to say it, Doctor Oberton, but I believe your friend has lost a fair portion of his wits."

Oberton sighed heavily and finished off his whiskey. He reached inside his pocket, removed a handkerchief, and dabbed a line of sweat from his brow. "Marshal, I came here because, frankly, I don't know what to do. I was hoping Jacob would have come back to the valley by now, come to his senses, but now I'm afraid I've lost him for good."

"Maybe not," Braddock said. "Maybe we can talk to him together, see if he'll listen to reason. We might be able to talk him into getting some help. There are places he could go to rest and recuperate."

"Are you talking about an asylum, Marshal Braddock? Let's get one thing straight. I won't have Jacob Piersol locked away in some institution."

"No, no, of course not. I was thinking more along the lines of some spiritual guidance from a formal church organization, a retreat where he might go and rest and commune with God and other clergymen. I've spent some time looking into it. Some of the pastors here tell me they know of such a place in Ohio, called Willowbrook. Maybe I could ask them to pull some strings and get your preacher friend in there for a visit. You think he might submit to something like that?"

The doctor shrugged. "Hard to say, but thank you, Marshal, for suggesting it. Might be worth a try. A retreat could be just what he needs. We'll have to put it to him delicately. He's very definite in his beliefs."

Braddock sat back in his chair. He didn't often feel sorry for people. Life was difficult for everyone. Life, sometimes, was hell. But he felt bad for Bill Oberton. Braddock knew what it was like to feel as if he'd failed someone. He often thought about the time he had Tink Puddah right here in his lockup, and he wondered if he might have been able to do something more for him than just cut him loose into the world to fend for himself.

"It might please you to know that your preacher friend has been doing some good work down at the docks. Why, every day he's been able to get the local businessmen to donate food to his cause, and he's fed some of the hungry people down along Canal Street. He hasn't exactly been wasting his time. You might even say he's been doing the Lord's work."

"That's good to hear, and I'm sure there are people in need who are grateful for his efforts, but at what cost? Jacob Piersol is a sick man. He's losing himself. He's been caring for people his whole life, Marshal Braddock. He doesn't realize that. He has never seen the good he's done right in Skanoh Valley. Maybe it's time somebody cared for him."

Braddock nodded. He sat thinking for a moment. The wind pushed the rain hard against the tiny jailhouse. "I'd like to tell you something you might find interesting, doctor, about Tink Puddah."

The doctor took a slow drink of whiskey. "Mr. Tink Puddah? What about him?"

"Did you know that Tink Puddah was accused of murdering two men?"

"What? That's ridiculous. He was as gentle a man as I've ever met. And if you'd ever seen him yourself, you'd have known he wasn't capable of injuring a fly."

"I agree with you," Braddock said. "I did meet him once."

The doctor looked at him, and his eyebows twitched the slightest bit. He had the skin of a very old man, Braddock couldn't help thinking, loose and weather-beaten, like a worn-out pair of leather boots. "You met Tink Puddah?"

"He was accused of murder in Pennsylvania, of shooting a man in the head. He did shoot that man, but only after a bear had clawed him near to death. Puddah took the man out of his misery, but the locals didn't quite see it that way."

"That's remarkable. I can hardly believe he'd have the strength to fire a gun."

"Then there was a man stabbed to death over in Fayette. A mob of angry men wanted to lynch Mr. Puddah for it, although it was obvious he wasn't guilty. So I brought him back here, talked to him for a bit, and suggested he clear out of town, told him to put as much distance between himself and here as he could get."

"Apparently he didn't put quite enough distance. Somebody found him and killed him. Why didn't you let on that you knew Puddah when you came to investigate his murder in Skanoh Valley?"

"I didn't see any reason to let on. I was investigating a murder, after all. I've found it's always best not to say anything about a case while I'm working on it. I assumed when the poor little fella turned up shot to death, a bounty hunter had caught up to him. There was a five-hundred-dollar bounty on his head. I was a bit surprised nobody came to claim it. That was when I started thinking maybe somebody from Pennsylvania or Fayette might have got to him, bent on revenge."

"Makes sense," the doctor said. "I suppose."

"Yes, it does, until one day your preacher shows up acting all crazy, telling people the Lord Tink Puddah is the Messiah risen from the dead."

The doctor frowned. "What are you getting at, Marshal Braddock?"

"I'm thinking maybe he knows a little more about that killing than—"

The jailhouse door burst open, letting in a rush of wind and rain.

A man stumbled inside, a fragile old man with a wet, gray beard. He fell to his knees, drenched and gasping for breath.

"Marshal!" he shouted. "Marshal! That preacher man done gone mad as hell! He shot Larry Skiles down at the docks, shot him right in the chest with a double-barreled shotgun, shot him dead, he did, saw it with my own eyes!"

"What?" The doctor jumped to his feet.

Braddock ran around his desk and sat the man down on a bench. He knew him. He'd seen the old coot down at the docks. "Your name is Pike, isn't it? I've seen you with the preacher, helping him out."

"Yeah, yeah, except now he's gone crazy as a drunken rooster, killed a man, I tell ya!"

Pike was covered nearly head-to-toe in mud. "All right, take it easy," Braddock said.

"He's lying," Oberton said, his voice hardening. "Jacob Piersol doesn't even own a gun. He's a man of God. He would never kill anyone. *Never.*"

"I saw it with my own eyes, I tell ya! And he's headed this way. He's got the gun, and he's headed into town."

Braddock went over to where his revolver hung on the wall, buckled on his holster, and snatched his hat. He'd been afraid something like this might happen. He'd had a terrible feeling about it. The fact that Jacob Piersol was a preacher might have made him ignore that feeling. Now he had a feeling of another sort: anger. Anger at himself for being so blind.

"Where do you think you're going with that gun?" the doctor demanded.

"Doctor Oberton, I think if we're going to have that talk with your friend, it had better be now."

"I can't believe it," Oberton said, pulling on his coat. "I *won't* believe it."

Pike was still gasping for breath. "Marshal, what about me?"

"I want you to say right here. I'll need to question you later."

"No, I mean what about me turning in the preacher? Ain't there some kind of reward?"

Braddock went over to Pike, grabbed him by his sopping wet shirt, and half-dragged him into the nearest cell.

"Hey, you can't jail a man for reporting a killin'!" Pike clutched at the iron bars. "Let me outta here!"

Braddock ignored him.

Anger.

First he'd let Tink Puddah go, and then he'd ignored his suspicions about the preacher, Jacob Piersol. Two mistakes, two deaths. Life, sometimes, was hell. "Let's go, Doctor Oberton."

The two men stepped outside into the tempest.

*  *  *  *  *

Jacob Piersol hopped up onto the seat of his buckboard, howling like a schoolboy. He snapped the wet reins, sending a string of rainwater skittering across his mule's slick back.

"Onward, faithful Floyd, onward ho! It's time to bring the Word of the Lord Tink Puddah directly to the Village of Palmyra!"

Floyd started forward with no great haste. Jacob Piersol laughed at this. He laughed long and hard. "A newborn babe could crawl faster than you, Floyd!"

Jacob rejoiced in the feel of his laughter and the heavy rain thundering down on him. A baptism of sorts, he decided. The Lord had chosen to baptize him with rains from Heaven.

He guided Floyd up Canal Street, past the blacksmith's shop, the mercantile and dress shop, into the village proper. The streets were deserted in the face of the storm. He brought Floyd to a halt in the center of the village square, where he stood up on the back of his wagon, reached inside his coat for his Bible, and pulled it out with his right hand. In his left hand—this was odd, he thought—in his left hand he held the shotgun. He seemed not to be able to put it down. *Jacob, put down the gun,* he told himself. But it was almost as if the gun refused to be let go.

No matter. His Bible in one hand, the gun in the other. So what? His words were important, even more important than the Bible. He wondered if his father would have understood that. It's the Word that matters. It's the truth.

"Hear me!" Jacob shouted into the rainfall, into the gusting, howling wind. "Hear me speak of the Lord our Savior Tink Puddah, the Messiah! I give testimony to you. God has sent a blue-skinned angel among us to show us the way. I have seen him risen from the dead with my own eyes. Believe me!"

He held the gun high over his head. "The second coming of the Lord is approaching, brothers and sisters, one thousand years of peace and love and joy is promised at the second coming of Christ to those righteous souls who have lived with virtue and honesty and faith in their hearts. These people will inherit God's kingdom. Believe me!"

"I believe you," came a voice.

Jacob looked down. Two men stood in front of his buckboard. Jacob thought he recognized the man who spoke, but he couldn't be sure. He couldn't get a good look at the other man, half-hidden behind the first. He was wearing a long black coat with the collar turned up and a hat low on his forehead.

Jacob blinked through the rain. "Who are you, brothers?"

"My name is Braddock. I've had the pleasure of your acquaintance once before, down in Skanoh Valley."

Skanoh Valley, the valley of peace. His old home. Braddock? Yes, the name sounded familiar. "You are a believer?"

"Oh, yes, yes, Minister, I'm a believer, all right." The man's cheek swelled with chewing tobacco. He spat a thin line of it out from under the brim of his hat, into the mud, with a *squelshing* sound.

"How do I know you?" asked Jacob. He didn't much like the man's demeanor. And he'd called Jacob a minister. He didn't like being called a minister.

"I'm the marshal here in Palmyra. I paid you a brief visit last year, had some of your rabbit stew, a fine cigar, and a touch of bourbon if I'm not mistaken. I was investigating the murder of your good friend, Mr. Tink Puddah."

Tink Puddah's murder? Yes, now Jacob remembered. "Braddock. Marshal Braddock."

"That's right, Minister."

Jacob frowned. The rain, he noticed, had ebbed to a drizzle. "I prefer to be addressed by the title of preacher. My father was a preacher, and so am I."

"Preacher," the marshal said. "I hear you've been addressing Mr. Tink Puddah by the title of Jesus Christ, is that right?"

"I hope you haven't come here to slur me or the Good Word. God sent the Savior Tink Puddah down to save us, Marshal Braddock. I've seen Him with my own eyes, risen from the dead."

The man standing next to Braddock whispered something in the marshal's ear.

"Who are you?" Jacob Piersol asked. "Don't be afraid, Brother. Step forward."

The man stepped forward, turned down his collar, and lifted the brim of his hat. Jacob finally got a good look at the man and recognized him immediately.

"Bill! Bill Oberton! What are you doing here? It's good to see you, old friend."

"Jacob," Bill said plainly, with no great measure of familiarity. "Where did you get that shotgun? I've never known you to own a gun."

"The Lord provides, Bill. What's the matter? Why so formal?"

"Would that be the Lord Tink Puddah who provides?" Braddock asked, smiling. Jacob decided it was a false smile.

"That's right."

The rain had all but stopped. Jacob could smell the freshness of the passing storm. The sun peeked out from behind a bank of clouds and brightened the village square. The dark clouds moved westward, and Jacob felt the wind push against him, as if he were intruding upon it. He noticed a few people emerging from the surrounding buildings. A man began loading his cart with grain. Two women stepped out of the millinery.

Jacob narrowed his eyes. He suddenly had a piercing headache. He lifted his Bible and opened it to no place in particular. He didn't care where: "'Son of man, I have broken the arm of Pharaoh king of Egypt; and, lo, it shall not be bound up to be healed, to put a roller to bind it, to make it strong to hold the sword—'"

"Minister," Braddock interrupted. "I hear there's been a killing down at the docks. You wouldn't happen to know anything about that, would you?"

"*Preacher,*" Jacob said. "I'm a preacher, and I came here to preach."

"He did it!" screeched a woman moving quickly down the street, pointing at Jacob. "I saw him shoot Larry Skiles in cold blood!"

Marshal Braddock turned toward the woman. "Step back, if you would, ma'am."

She didn't move at first. She stood in her threadbare dress and stared at Jacob Piersol. Jacob stared back at her. He recognized the woman. She was one of the whores who had come to his buckboard every day for something to eat.

"Step back!" repeated the marshal.

The woman finally moved slowly away, but more people came forward.

"Down at the docks," Jacob said. "Yes, I remember. I was defending myself and the Lord, Tink Puddah. Bill, what's going on? What's wrong with you?"

"I want you to do me a favor, Preacher," Braddock said, his voice as slick as snakeskin. "I want you just to hand me that shotgun. Can you do that for me?"

Jacob glanced at his shotgun. He was pointing it out at the street, his finger on the trigger. He narrowed his eyes and glared at the marshal. What was going on here? What did the marshal really want? And Bill certainly was acting peculiar, wasn't he? Jacob felt himself growing irritated.

"I want you to do me a favor, Marshal Braddock. I want you to leave me alone. Can't you see I'm trying to preach? If you haven't come to listen, why are you here? I have important work to do, the Lord's work, and you're frightening away the people."

Bill Oberton frowned at him and said, "Jacob, where did you get that gun? I want you to think about it. Where did you get it?"

"Why are you acting so strangely, Bill? I told you. The Lord Tink Puddah gave it to me."

"When? Where?"

Jacob snapped his Bible shut. "I . . . I don't know. It was in my sack. What's the difference where I got it?"

"Think about it!" Bill insisted. "Think! Where did you get the gun, Jacob?"

Tink Puddah offered Jacob Piersol a cup of water and some apples and wheat bread, just as he'd offered the last time the preacher had visited him a year ago, and the time before that, and the time before that. As always, the preacher accepted the water and refused Tink's other overtures. Not much had changed between the two men over the years, although Tink noticed that Jacob had put on some weight. In fact, Tink decided he looked a little bit like a stuffed turkey.

The two of them sat quietly in Tink's cabin for a while. Winter had broken and spring was upon them, the trees reaching for their thick, dark leaves, the early flowers blooming, sparrows chirping and cardinals singing. Tink had not ventured down into Skanoh Valley since last fall.

It was Jacob Piersol who broke the silence. "Why won't you at least come to church and listen? You have yet to step foot inside my church."

Tink Puddah wanted to be polite, of course. He did not want to insult the preacher as he had during their first visit. Since then he'd done much better at keeping their conversations trivial. But the preacher should know by now that Tink wasn't interested in attending church. He did not want to be involved in any of the affairs of men; too often they had turned against him.

"Easter service is coming up soon," Jacob said. "This is a time of year for good Christians to renew their lives, to celebrate God's mercy and the New Covenant."

"Your favorite time of year, as I recall," Tink Puddah said pleasantly.

"Yes, my favorite season. Do you know why?"

Yes, Tink knew why. Each spring when the preacher visited Tink, he told him why. For a Christian, this was a time of change and forgiveness and reaffirmation of faith. A faith Tink Puddah did not share. Why couldn't the preacher accept this?

"Didn't you read the Bible I left you, Mr. Puddah? Weren't you able to receive its message?"

Of course the man knew the answer to this question. He'd asked it before. He simply did not like Tink Puddah's answer. "I remember reading of your Christ's ascension."

"He is not just *my* Christ. He is *everyone's* Christ."

Again an uncomfortable pause. Tink hoped the preacher would not ask for the return of his Bible. Tink had burned it by accident when he was cooking and stoking his fire this winter. Tink had pulled the book out of the flames, but it was charred beyond repair. The remaining pages flaked at his touch. He kept what was left of it only because it was a sacred text to men, and he was afraid that throwing it away, even in its unreadable state, might insult the man's religion even more.

"Have you no soul, Mr. Puddah? Is that why you cannot heed the Lord's call?"

No soul? Ah, the mist. Perhaps Tink's answer to Jacob Piersol lay in the mist. Would it be possible to show him that the mist was indeed a part of human nature, like any other limb or organ, except that humans simply did not have the capacity to perceive it? Would this help the preacher understand? It might. Yes, it might at that.

"Jacob Piersol," he said, "perhaps you would allow me to show you something. A demonstration."

"Anything, if it will help open your eyes to the Lord."

"I think it might help open your eyes. We shall see."

Tink Puddah rose from his chair and sat cross-legged on the hearth. "Join me."

The preacher stood and walked to the hearth, where he hesitated before asking, "What's this all about?"

"We are going to meditate together. I will try to show you something of my insight. I do not know if we will succeed, but we can try, if you are willing. It may lead to a greater understanding between us."

"I'm willing to try," the preacher said, "as long as it's not one of your pagan rituals paying homage to false gods."

"No, of course not. I have no false gods. It just might be a way for you to—how can I say this?—see something inside yourself through my eyes."

Tink did not know any other way to explain it, although the process of *seeing* the mist had nothing to do with eyesight.

The preacher nodded. "What do I do?"

"Please, sit down in front of me."

Jacob sat on the floor opposite Tink.

"Now, allow me to touch your chest," Tink said.

The preacher looked uncertain. Tink had expected this reaction. He sensed that the man did not like touching Tink by the way he avoided shaking hands with him, and so would be equally leery of Tink touching him. But it would be necessary if Tink were to search for his mist. He had never tried to show the mist to anyone before, but he had a feeling it might work. It was not the eyes that saw the mist, after all; it was the mind, and Tink might be able to open a man's mind for him so that he could see what Tink saw. It would be an interesting experiment, if nothing else. "This will not injure."

"All right," said the preacher quickly, as if embarrassed that Tink had sensed his misgivings.

Tink quickly reached out and touched Jacob's chest before the man had a chance to change his mind. "Close your eyes," he said, "and you will concentrate better."

Jacob closed his eyes, and in a moment Tink was inside the man. He searched for the preacher's mind. Men had large, simple minds that were easy to locate, easy to draw in. He linked Jacob Piersol's mind to his own.

The preacher, sitting opposite Tink, gasped suddenly. "What is this?" he asked.

"What do you see?"

"Nothing. It's more of a feeling, as if I'm looking for something without trying to look."

"Good, a feeling, very good. Don't try to control the feeling. Allow it to guide you."

"What are we looking for?"

Tink began to peel back the internal layers of the man's soft mind. He would let the man touch his own mist, let him hold it in the fingers of his mind, as Tink had touched and held others, and then he would explain to the man what this mist was, a force of human life.

"What's that?" said the preacher?

What? Tink had not shown him anything yet. "What do you see?"

"That pool. What is it? That dark pool." There was fear in the man's voice.

Tink saw no dark pool. Interesting. Tink heard the man's heart pounding, echoing in his brain. "Try to relax. There is nothing to be afraid of. You are only looking inside yourself."

The man whispered, "Dear Lord, protect me from the devil, from sin, from evil, from sin, from evil . . ."

The man was praying. Why was he praying? "Perhaps I should stop," Tink said.

"No!" Sweat gathered on the preacher's forehead.

Tink still could not see any dark pool. What was Jacob seeing? He tried to move the man's mind back to where they had begun—a clear, colorless, peaceful space where the mind could rest comfortably—but Jacob stopped him.

Tink was surprised at Jacob's mental strength. Perhaps he was looking elsewhere in Tink's mind. Tink had not considered that the man might be able to look or see things without Tink's assistance, to explore on his own. If he did, what would he see? Something much different from human mist, certainly. Perhaps he had glimpsed Wetspace. The dark pool, he had said. Something not meant for the minds of men, minds accustomed to one's own thoughts, not billions of patterns and endless circular memories of the living and the dead from a world that never dies.

Tink started to withdraw his hand from Jacob's chest in order to break their connection, but as soon as his fingers drew back, the man grabbed him by the wrist and held Tink's hand in place over his heart.

"Let go of my wrist," Tink ordered. "I was wrong. This is too dangerous for you."

The man's face became a mask of pain, teeth clenched, eyes shut tight. What was he looking at? He continued to mutter his words of prayer, too fast now for Tink to follow. Tink tried to yank his hand free. Failing this, he slapped the man hard across the face, hoping to break his trance.

"Satan!" screeched the preacher, shaking all over now, his grip bearing down on Tink's wrist.

Tink winced in pain. He fought to wrench free, fought to get control of the preacher's mind, fought everything, but nothing worked. Nothing.

The preacher's eyes snapped open. He stood up, jerked Tink off the ground, nearly popping his arm out of socket. "Satan!" He stared directly into Tink's eyes, but he was not seeing Tink. The preacher's eyes were bloodshot and glazed. What was he seeing? What? "You've burned the Holy Bible!"

Burned the Bible? How did the man know this? How could he have found it in Tink's mind? "No! It was an accident."

"Lucifer!"

"No, please, calm yourself. I will help you regain control of your mind if you—"

"Thou hast killed! Thou hast killed!"

The man dragged Tink over to the hearth. There, beside the fireplace, with his free hand, he seized Tink Puddah's shotgun, the gun that had slain Tink's father, the gun that had been merciful to the bear hunter, Darryl.

Jacob said, "You, Tink Puddah, are that old serpent named the Devil that deceived the whole world!"

He thrust his foot down on Tink's chest, pinning him to the floor. There physical connection was broken, but the madness was still in Jacob Piersol's mind.

Tink could barely breathe. He clutched at the preacher's ankle. Jacob aimed the gun at Tink's head.

"Listen to Revelations!" Jacob Piersol screeched. "'And the beast which I saw was like unto a leopard, and his feet were as the feet of a bear, and his mouth as the mouth of a lion: and the dragon gave him his power, and his seat, and great authority. And I saw one of his heads as it were wounded to death; and his deadly wound was healed: and all the world wondered after the beast—'"

Suddenly Tink saw his father's death. He had glimpsed it before—the dogs, the blood, the gun—but never like this, never so real, so vivid. *A gun, a device that ignites a mixture of potassium nitrate, charcoal, and sulfur, and propels a projectile at high velocity. What has this to do with mercy or with prayer?* Tink's father, Nif Puddah, had begged to know. *What?*

And only Tink could answer him now, now and forever.

Nothing, dear father. Nothing. This is Man. We have misunderstood him for the last time, you and I.

"'If any man have an ear, let him hear. He that leadeth into captivity shall go into captivity: he that killeth with the sword must be killed with the sword. Here is the patience and the faith of the saints!'"

And then Jacob Piersol put the barrel of the shotgun to Tink Puddah's head.

"Think about it! Think!" Bill Oberton insisted. "Where did you get the gun, Jacob?"

A crowd had gathered along Main Street, Palmyra, at the village square to watch Jacob argue with Marshal Braddock and Doctor Bill Oberton. Why was everyone so interested now, Jacob thought, when he'd been trying to get them to listen for months with no success?

The marshal spat a wad of his tobacco onto the muddy street. "Where was the gun before it was in your sack? Do you remember that?"

Before the sack? Jacob didn't know. There was no gun before the sack, was there? He thought about it. No. There was the sack and the gun, both at the same time. The Lord had provided. That was all that mattered. Jacob noticed he was sweating. The rain from the recent downpour was still dripping off his weathered clothing, but he could feel the sweat, too. His heart pounded. His heart was trying to run away. Where could his heart possibly want to go? He decided he should preach again, so he held his Bible up in front of him.

"Damn it, Jacob!" Bill cried, stepping forward. "You've killed a man down at the docks, and it was *you* who killed Tink Puddah, wasn't it? Wasn't it, Jacob? Answer me! It was you who killed Tink Puddah!"

Jacob pointed the shotgun at the doctor. "Who are you to judge? You have no idea what I've seen, or why I've done what I've done. The Lord has pardoned me. He came to me. He came to me and he said, 'I pardon you, Jacob Piersol! I give you the power of God to preach the Word of the Lord! I make you my disciple!' Don't you see? It was written that in the Messiah's name the message of repentance and forgiveness must be preached. It was written that the power from Heaven would come down upon the disciples. I am Tink Puddah's disciple!"

"The gun," Marshal Braddock said. "I think you should put it down now. It's very dangerous to be waving it around like that. Some innocent person might get hurt. You wouldn't want that, would you? Besides, you don't want to preach with a gun in your hand. What kind of message is that?"

Jacob leveled the gun at the marshal. "This is no ordinary gun, Marshal Braddock. This is the weapon of mercy and redemption. I know. I've seen what it has done. I've seen it deliver mercy to the Savior's father. I've felt it take justice upon the evil Larry Skiles. This is the Holy Gun. This is the foundation of my new church."

The marshal removed his hat and brushed the rain off its brim; he didn't put it back on his head, though; he kept it at his side, hiding his revolver. "What else have you seen the gun do, Preacher?"

"I won't listen to your clever snake's tongue, Marshal Braddock. I know what you're trying to do. You're trying to get me to admit to killing Tink Puddah. But Tink Puddah was not killed. That's what you don't understand. His fate was prophesied. It was written that the Savior must suffer and die and rise from the dead. The gun was merely the instrument used to fulfill the Scriptures and to plant the seed of His resurrection."

"But it was you who used the gun, wasn't it?" said his old friend Bill, pointing at him, accusing him.

Why was Jacob arguing? He did not need to defend himself. "There is no higher authority than God. I was acting out the will of God. I didn't realize it at the time—no, I couldn't have realized it then because I wasn't enlightened. But now that I've seen the truth, I know it was divine intervention—"

"Jacob, Jacob, please, listen." Bill moved closer to the buckboard. "Give me the gun and step down. I don't know exactly what happened, what made you do it, but it's time now to put an end to it. Don't you understand what you've done? You've taken two lives. It's time to end this."

Jacob was having trouble breathing. What was wrong with the air . . . the air that was so precious to him . . . God's true gift to mankind . . . why was he gasping for it, sucking at it like a landed trout? Why? He wondered if Beelzebub might be working some evil magic. Perhaps it truly was time to put an end to this, all of this. Oh, his father surely would have known what to do.

*Stupid Jacob Piersol!* That was his father's unspoken slur, always underlying his superiority, his condescension, his infinite and infuriating patience and wisdom. Jacob had studied, had learned, had been a crusader of the Word for so many years, hard, lean years of faith with no feeling, darkness with no light, questions with no answers . . .

"The gun, Jacob," Bill said. "Hand it to me."

Where was this dizziness coming from? Jacob shook his head. The Lord had called him to be a disciple and now . . . now . . . here he was again, dizzy, sweating, heart racing, just as when he was a boy trying to interpret the signs and the mysteries of God and Christ, with his father glaring at him, and Jacob so hopelessly flustered and perplexed. Why was he so dumb?

*"Think, boy. Why can't you think straight?"*

"The marshal mentioned a place especially for men like you," Bill said. "A place where a man of God can work things out when he's confused. You can go there and talk to other men of God."

Tink Puddah was a heathen, then Tink Puddah was Satan, then Tink Puddah was the Savior Lord Jesus Christ. How was he going to work all that out? Which Tink Puddah had risen from the dead? The Messiah? Had he really killed the Messiah with his own hands? How? How could he have been such an idiot? Was God counting on that? Had God deceived him into fulfilling the Scriptures, or had the devil beguiled him into sin?

Confusion, confusion. What was happening to his mind, to his heart? Jacob looked at his hands, the gun in one hand, the Bible in the other. What was wrong with him? Had he truly used one in defense of the other? Which hand held the truth? the justice? the way? the wisdom? the glory? the promise?

"The shotgun, Jacob, hand it to me." Bill Oberton, his dear old friend, took another step forward and held out his hand for the Holy Gun.

"The Holy Gun," Jacob said.

"*Foolish, foolish Jacob Piersol,*" his father chastised. "*You will never learn.*"

Jacob blinked at the tears welling in his eyes. "Bill, I'm sorry, but I must try my best to interpret the Word of God, to understand His message. I must *try.*"

"Drop the gun, Preacher!" Marshal Braddock drew his revolver and trained it on him. "Don't force me to use this."

Jacob shook his head. "Forgive me, but at least if I am wrong this time, it will be the last."

In one swift motion, Jacob jerked the short-barreled shotgun to his chin.

"No!" Bill cried.

"Yes," Jacob whispered. He closed his eyes and pulled the trigger.

The hammer fell.

And then there was nothing.

Was the gun out of ammunition? Jacob was sure he'd fired only one shot at Larry Skiles. That should have left one more shot in the chamber. Had he failed even at killing himself?

No . . . wait . . . something was happening to the sky . . .

Slowly, slowly, the sky began to rip apart—a clear and perfect tear in the fabric of the precious, precious air that kept God's creatures alive. Out of this sudden breach came a scratch of vermilion and a light so raw and hot that Jacob could feel it cut clean through the skin that held him together, penetrate to the marrow of his bones, and touch something buried so deep inside him he did not even know it existed, something that was the essence of his being, the mist that made up his imperfect human soul.

And then this Holy Light spread out to swallow the sky, and a figure stepped out of it, bathed in the clean white glow of the Kingdom of Heaven, a figure he'd seen before. Many times before.

It was the Lord, Tink Puddah.

The Savior smiled down at Jacob and reached out to him. "You are a prophet of the one true God, but things have not worked out for you here on Earth, Jacob Piersol. Come. Come with me to Heaven."

Jacob let go of the gun, reached out, and touched the Lord's hand. He stepped up into the Holy Light, one step, two steps, three, rising into the blue sky toward the white Heaven. He smiled down at Bill Oberton and Marshal Braddock, who had dropped to their knees beside his fallen body, his broken body, his shattered human form.

"Messiah," Jacob said. "How can I leave behind my calling, my mission? I could have led your people into the Promised Land. I had the faith, Lord, the unfaltering faith. I could have done it."

The Lord Tink Puddah took Jacob firmly in His grasp. "They are not ready," the Lord stated simply, and the rightness of His words soothed Jacob's mist and drew him one step closer to Heaven.

Jacob glanced down one last time, but now he could see only distant lines fading to blue and white, the Earth he had once known becoming smaller . . . smaller . . . and suddenly, as suddenly as it had appeared, the breach in the sky closed beneath his soaring spirit, leaving no trace of the world that had once seemed so important to him, and Jacob Piersol was free. Free at last.

At dawn, General Lee's Confederate army attacked the regiment to which Tink Puddah belonged. The crack and hiss of musketry announced the rebels' advance, along with the sound of mini-balls whacking tree trunks and snipping leaves, and bayonets glinting in the morning sun, marching forward among the dense trees and tangled heaps of thickets and brushwood.

Tink Puddah knew that this was a time for men to pray. He felt their hope, desperation, and fear. He saw their lips asking God for guidance and protection. He knew, also, that thousands of those prayers would go unanswered this day.

"We're pulling back!" barked the surgeon, with the same hysterical edge in his voice that always precluded battle. He was a sweaty, red-eyed man whom Tink had never seen sleep. "Let's get these patients moved out!"

Tink immediately started packing up medical supplies—chloroform, bone saws, bandages, sutures, morphine, quinine—while the rear privates broke down tents and cots, covered patients with blankets, and lifted the wounded onto stretchers and decrepit wagons.

Tink was an assistant to the surgeon. He'd joined the Union army after passing the medical student's examination. Tink's small stature and blue skin had not interfered with the Federals granting him a commission. The army had been desperate for qualified medical volunteers and would have taken him, Tink was certain, even if he had shown up in a wheelchair.

Already, in between the explosions of gunfire, Tink heard men screaming in the wilderness. He'd been at war for two years and still hadn't gotten used to the death cries of soldiers. Their pain had a way of fixing him in the sudden reality of men's struggles, shocking him into the immediacy of their brief and urgent lives. Sometimes Tink thought he could distinguish the voices of dying Union soldiers from those of dying Confederates. The Confederates often expired in an elevated pitch, as if they were reaching for something even in their deaths that they knew would be forever unattainable. In the cries of the Union men, Tink thought he could hear an uncivilized anger, directed specifically at the superior principles for which they fought, as if their high ideals had let them down, lied to them, killed them.

The Union troops answered the Confederates with a mournful roar of guns. There would be more gunfire, Tink knew, but most of the fighting from now on in this battle would be of the hand-to-hand variety, brutal and deadly. In this teeming forest, enemy soldiers would fall over each other before they knew they were engaged. The front line of battle might at any moment be as close as twenty yards from the medical bivouac where the surgeon and his small staff struggled to preserve lives.

"Let's move!" the surgeon cried.

Tink quickly checked the packs for which he was responsible. He was about to pull out with the others when he noticed one of his patients, arguing with the two privates trying to move him onto a stretcher. Tink went over to see if he could help.

"Captain Maxwell," Tink said. "What's wrong? We don't have time for delays."

The two soldiers stepped aside. There was a tall one and a short one, and their uniforms were so filthy and ill-fitted that the men looked comically impoverished.

"What's wrong? I'll tell you what's wrong. These privates are trying to tell me what to do." His throat sounded parched and coarse, partly from lack of water, and partly from the injury he'd sustained to his neck and jaw. He had hair the color of butter and a thin mustache that looked like a milk stain on his upper lip.

"They're just following orders, sir," Tink said. "We must move all patients from the front line back to—"

"I'm not a patient, Mr. Puddah. I am a captain, and as long as I can fire a rifle, and the lives of my men are at stake, I will *not* be forced to retreat."

"Captain Maxwell, you cannot even hold a gun. What could you possibly do to help them?" Although this was true, Tink knew he should not have said it. He had not intended to anger or insult Captain Maxwell. Tink truly cared for him, had in fact saved his life and helped him heal. He did not want to see the captain sacrifice his life.

"I can't hold a gun? Is that what you think, Puddah?"

The exchange of gunfire momentarily subsided. The captain put on his cap and ordered the tall private to sit him on the ground and bring him his gun. Captain Maxwell had only one arm, the other having already been amputated. He told the short private to load his rifle. Then he lifted the gun and perched it on his knee, testing his aim. One shot. The captain would only be able to fire once, for it would be impossible for him to reload. Then there would be nothing left for him to do but die.

Tink said, "Please, Captain Maxwell, fall back with us. It's unfair to your men to put yourself in jeopardy before you are fully able to fight. They need you, sir."

"Damn right they need me, and they're going to know I'm here for them."

Tink tried to think of something to say to the captain that might persuade him to retreat, but nothing came to mind. It was a wonder Captain Maxwell was alive at all, after the hits he'd taken. Tink had been advancing behind the lines to assist the wounded when he'd seen the captain shot in the neck and shoulder and ribs. Tink ran to him. The captain's subclavian artery had been lacerated. Tink was able to tie off the artery, but the captain lay unconscious and dying nonetheless. Tink dragged him back to the surgeon's tent, over the rocks and through the broken trees, all without losing the man's mist.

Tink could not pardon everyone, nor, it seemed, even make a perceptible difference during this terrible war. Such an effort would have exhausted him beyond hope. But he found that he could often secure a mist for a few precious moments before it fled the body, giving the surgeon time to attempt his own miracle, and he discovered that he could almost always soothe the pain and fear of men and still maintain enough strength to carry out his duties.

Most of the medical attention these soldiers received was atrocious, through no fault of the over-burdened physicians. Tink had seen hundreds of amputations after gangrene had set into wounds that might have been, under normal circumstances, easily treated. There were deaths from erysipelas, pneumonia, malaria, and typhoid fever. There were deaths from loss of blood and loss of spirit. Tink did all he could. It was never enough.

The doctor had removed Captain Maxwell's scapula and clavicle, his entire arm, and two of his ribs. He'd cut the man open from neck to hip and then stitched him up again. The poor captain had looked like a torn and discarded rag doll, horribly pale and lifeless, drained of more blood than it would have seemed possible to replace in a lifetime. He remained unconscious for days. And yet with Tink's attention, Captain Maxwell rallied. Eventually he regained consciousness.

All of the men who had survived that day's battle came to visit him and offer him words of encouragement. He was an inspiration to them even in his state of utter helplessness. During this time, Tink found that the captain was more than just a fighting man. He had an incredible will to live, a stronger mist than any other man Tink had ever seen. And here he was, now, this remarkable Captain Maxwell, so willing to throw it all away.

"It will be impossible for you to defend yourself," Tink said. "How will this help your men? They will see you killed, and it will discourage them."

"I know you're trying to do what's best for me, Puddah, but there's a lot about fighting men you don't understand. Fighting men need to know their leader is willing to die for them. If they don't know that, why should they be willing to die for him?"

"But—"

"I appreciate all you've done for me. You saved my life. You're a credit to the Medical Corp. But now I have my duty to perform, and you have yours. You'd best pull out with the others."

Tink heard the battle moving closer. The Confederates were pushing back the front line. This was bad. It would mean the captain would have to sit down here on the hard earth and face the enemy, with his one arm and missing ribs and lone musket ball. It would mean, also, that many of the wounded would be abandoned to suffer and die in the woods, with no way for their fellows to retrieve them.

Tink removed the haversack from his shoulder and handed it to the tall private. "Go, both of you. The medics and patients need you. I'll stay behind with Captain Maxwell."

"What?" Maxwell said.

The privates did not wait for the captain to countermand Tink's instructions. They ran off before Tink could change his mind.

Captain Maxwell glared at him. "What do you think you're doing, Mister? This unit needs your skills in the hospital tent. I order you to pull out."

"I'm sorry, but if you insist upon staying behind to fight, I refuse to leave you alone with one round to defend yourself. You can pull your trigger, and I will reload the rifle for you."

"Absolutely not! I'll have your sorry blue hide court-martialed if you don't obey—"

"Not likely," Tink said, "because you are almost certainly going to die here today."

A tremendous fusillade of mini-balls cut through the woods, snapping tree branches, cracking bark, chipping stone, blasting dirt into the air. Tink squatted in the underbrush and covered his head.

"Son of a bitch!" the captain cried. "I don't have time to argue with you, boy." He pulled his trigger and fired into the smoke. "Damn those rebs. Quick, reload me."

Tink took the captain's gun and loaded powder, patch, and ball. The captain propped the gun up on his knee again, and prepared to fire another shot. But suddenly everything went quiet. Not a single gun could be heard. Nobody even moved in the woods. This often happened during war, in the middle of raging battles. Men did not want to give away their positions, so there would be long, horrible moments of wholly unnatural calm.

Finally, shooting and troop movements came from the east. Tink smiled to himself, hiding his relief. If the battle moved away from Captain Maxwell, there would be no way for him to chase it. The man could barely sit up straight.

"Damn it," the captain said, noticing the shift as well.

The two of them waited quietly for a while. Sounds of the battle continued to come from the east. Eventually, Captain Maxwell let his musket slip off his knee. He expelled a great sigh and lay down flat on his back to rest in the dirt.

Tink helped him drink some water from his canteen. Trapped inside the teeming forest, grit and sulfurous gunpowder lingered in the air, along with the rotten decay of horses and mules, hundreds of them, killed by labor and starvation and battle wounds. Some of the animals had died still hitched to the ammunition or supply wagons they'd been forced to pull beyond their limits.

Captain Maxwell drank the water gratefully. "Thank you, Mr. Puddah. You've taken care of me for a long time, and I really don't know anything about you. Where are you from?"

Tink took the canteen and swallowed a bit of water. "I grew up in Pennsylvania. I've spent quite a bit of time in different areas of New York."

"Traveling man, are you? What brought you into the war?"

"I thought I could help relieve suffering in the army. I don't believe in fighting, not at all, but I thought there would be a great need for compassion here."

"Yes, well, you were certainly right about that. You're a brave little man. Got more guts than most soldiers I've seen twice your size. Took real courage to stand beside me like that in the face of a full frontal attack. If we live through this, I'm going to make sure you get a commendation."

Tink knew there would be no commendation, nor would there be any living through this for Captain Maxwell. Tink felt the enemy soldiers closing in around them. There was no perceptual evidence of this, only Tink's instincts and unique inner vision. He could see the Confederates like ghosts in his mind, slowly converging, circling, some loading their rifles, others feeling their way forward with their bayonets like blind men. There were quite a number of them. Most of the Federals had moved off to the east, following a feint, Tink saw now, that had left him and Captain Maxwell directly in the path of the advancing rebels.

"How did you get that blue skin?" the captain asked. "Childhood disease, was it?"

It was odd that not many men in the army had asked him about the color of his skin. They seemed not to care about that, especially when Tink was making them feel better. Wouldn't it be interesting, Tink thought, to tell this man the truth, now that it was all but over for him? He had never told any man the truth about who or what he was.

"I inherited the blue skin from my parents. They were born on another planet, a liquid planet called Wetspace, where all the people live like large, blue pearls in a vast, milky sea of nutriment."

The captain just looked at him for a moment, and then a smile creased his lips, and he began to chuckle. "Owwh. Don't make me laugh, Puddah. It hurts like hell."

Tink smiled and gave him more water. The rebels now were very close. Tink could smell them. He could see, in his mind's eye, the grapeshot being loaded into the small cannon that would be aimed, in calculated ignorance, at their position in the woods. There was no sense in trying to escape. One way or another, it would only be a matter of moments before they were dead. Death by grapeshot would be quicker and easier. A ball or a bayonet promised a slower death with greater suffering.

"How did you get that wound to your head, Puddah?" asked the captain. "And how in God's name did you ever survive it?"

Tink reached up and touched the side of his head. The wound was not yet fully concealed, although his body had been working on it for quite some time.

"I was shot in the head by a crazy preacher because I didn't believe in God," Tink said. "And I did not survive the wound. Not at first, anyway. I was dead for a while, a long time actually, then I came back to life. My body healed itself slowly while I was buried. I did not want to come back. It just happened."

Captain Maxwell laughed. He laughed so hard he held his side, where his ribs had been removed, and a wheezing sound escaped his lips. Tears came to his eyes. "Puddah, Puddah," he pleaded. "Stop. I can't remember the last time I laughed so hard."

Tink laughed along with him. He was happy that he had stayed behind to see the captain through his death. He was a good man, Captain Maxwell, with a vigorous mist that Tink did not expect to see again soon, a mist unique among men, exquisitely, shamelessly beautiful. But Tink was sad as well for he knew that only one of them would ever laugh again.

They reached for each other's hands then, grasped them firmly as if sealing their friendship and their fates, and Tink wondered how many of his own deaths he would have to live through, over and over and over again, before he did not wake, before he slept forever. He wondered if all of his deaths would be this difficult, filling his heart with such a mixture of helplessness and surrender, sadness and grief, exhilaration and fear.

From somewhere out beyond the trees, Tink saw in his mind the murky-gray rebel soldiers fire their grapeshot, and for a moment Tink thought that the captain must have seen it too, must have recognized death rushing forward on the wings of his God, for the captain gasped, and his eyes became fixed on some point far removed from the battle-field—a vision, Tink could only guess—a whisper that revealed the secret of his death, because then, with a sudden, urgent turn of his head, the captain looked at Tink and said—

"Goodbye."

# B O O K  C L U B  G U I D E

1. Early in *A Small and Remarkable Life*, Darryl kills Tink Puddah's parents to free them from their pain and suffering. Later in the book, Tink is faced with the same decision when Darryl is injured. Do you agree that these characters made the right choices? What would you do if you were faced with a similar situation? How do you feel about mercy killing, or what might be described today as euthanasia?

2. Tink and Jacob Piersol are diametrically opposed when it comes to belief in God and the importance of religion. Because Tink is a non-believer, Jacob sees him as nothing more than a savage. Tink, on the other hand, sees no rational or practical purpose for believing in God. Where do you stand on this issue? Do you think there is a definitive right or wrong answer? Is there any common ground that Tink and Jacob might have found together?

3. Are you surpised at Claudia's reaction to Tink when he returns home from the bear hunt? Did you feel Claudia was happy in her marriage? What expectations for marriage might a woman in the middle 1800s have had versus a woman today?

4. Prejudice is a problem that Tink must deal with throughout the novel. First Darryl's friends want to kill Tink because he is a "blue boy." Then Chet, the young man Tink meets on the ball field, instantly hates Tink because of his skin color. In America, in the middle 1800s, racial prejudice was a controversial topic that eventually led to the Civil War. Does racial prejudice still exist in the world today? Have you seen evidence of it? There are many more prejudices than skin color, e.g., obesity, gender, and religion. What are some of the reasons for prejudice? How does discrimination affect people's lives? Can anything be done to eradicate it?

5. How does the children's baseball game in *A Small and Remarkable Life* serve as a metaphor for adulthood?

6. Why is the gunmaker, Mr. Emery, so afraid of Tink? Why does he treat him like a slave? Why is Tink so accepting of this treatment?

7. Why is Papa Bear Goodlowe so upset to find his daughter alone with Tink at the Rochesterville County Fair? Why does he feel his daughter's reputation will be harmed? Do you agree with Papa Bear's ultimatum that Tink must never again be seen alone with Anna?

8. What is the significance of the boar war at the fair, and what does it symbolize to Tink?

9. Do you believe in an afterlife? Do you think the author was trying to suggest the existence of an afterlife when he wrote on page 222 that Jacob "stepped up into the Holy Light, one step, two steps, three, rising into the blue sky toward the white Heaven . . . ."?

10. Do you think that Tink will ever truly die? Or is he fated to live forever, to come back to life over and over again, as the author seems to suggest in the final scene of *A Small and Remarkable Life?*

11. The author has stated that Tink Puddah (rhymes with Buddha) might be described as an "existentialist." If existentialism, broadly defined, reflects a non-reliance on the divine, a belief in self-determination, and an understanding that man stands alone in the universe and must accept responsibility for his own condition, would you agree with the author? Or do you see Tink as a victim in this story, someone who is never in control of his life or circumstances and is, in effect, sentenced to never-ending tragedy?

# ONLINE RESOURCES

NickDiChario.com (Nick's personal Web site).

WriteBookandGifts.com (Nick's independent bookstore, The Write Book and Gift Shop).

Fictionwise.com (Some of Nick's short fiction may be found here).

HMLR.org (*HazMat Literary Review*, for which Nick is fiction editor).

WAB.org (Writers & Books, Rochester's non-profit literary center.)

SFwriter.com (Nick's brilliant and insightful editor, Robert J. Sawyer).

RobertJSawyerBooks.com (for more about *A Small And Remarkable Life* and other books in this publishing line).

ReddeerPress.com (Nick's shrewd and innovative publisher, Red Deer Press).

# ABOUT THE AUTHOR

Nick DiChario's short fiction has appeared in science fiction, fantasy, mystery, and mainstream publications in the United States and abroad. His work has been reprinted in *The Year's Best Science Fiction*, *The Year's Best Fantasy and Horror*, and *The Best Alternate History Stories of the 20th Century*, among others. He has been nominated for a John W. Campbell Award, two Hugo Awards, and a World Fantasy Award, and his plays have been presented in Geva Theatre's Regional Playwrights Festival in upstate NY.

Nick was born on Halloween, and he noticed early on that his friends and family allowed him a certain measure of strangeness because of this. Although they may have always thought he was a little crazy, they never actually said so until, in the summer of 2005, he bought a bookstore: The Write Book and Gift Shop, in Honeoye Falls, New York. Owning a small, neighborhood bookshop has always been a dream of Nick's, and even now, in an age of giant chain stores and online booksellers, when the deck is stacked against independent stores in every conceivable way, he has found it one of the most rewarding and extraordinary experiences of his life.

In addition to writing and selling books, Nick is the fiction editor of *HazMat Literary Review*, a magazine dedicated to publishing new voices and politically aware poetry and prose. He is currently pursuing his Masters degree at Empire State College. *A Small and Remarkable Life* is his first novel.

OTHER TITLES UNDER THE
ROBERT J. SAWYER BOOKS IMPRINT:


*Letters from the Flesh* by Marcos Donnelly
*Getting Near the End* by Andrew Weiner
*The Engine of Recall* by Karl Schroeder
*Rogue Harvest* by Danita Maslan
*A Small and Remarkable Life* by Nick DiChario